BEN
and the
BOOK OF
PROPHECIES

To Henna

KRiddFord

KIRSTY RIDDIFORD

THE PROPHECIES OF BALLITOR

Book One
BEN AND THE BOOK OF PROPHECIES

Book Two
RACE FOR THE HEIR

Book Three
MERIDIAN OBSIDIAN

Published by Arrowbright Publishing 2014
ISBN 978-0-9931408-0-8
A CIP catalogue record for this book is available from
The British Library

Copyright © Kirsty Riddiford 2009
Inner Illustrations by Nina Cadman
Edited by Kayleigh Hart and Natalie-Jane Revell

Printed CPI Group (UK) Ltd, Croydon, CR0 4YY

www.kirstyriddifordbooks.com
www.arrowbrightpublishing.com

For

Matt and Toby

Arrowbright Publishing

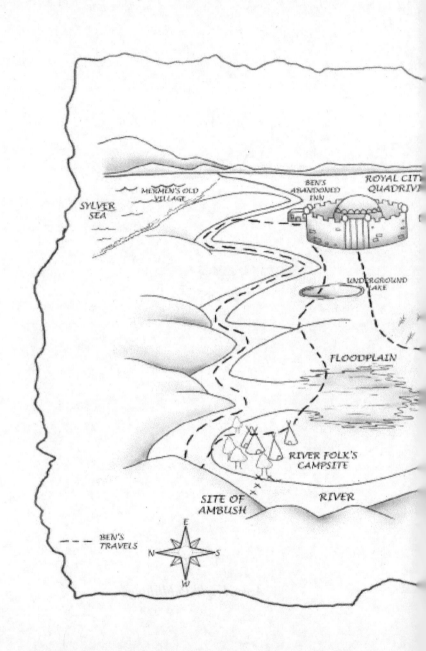

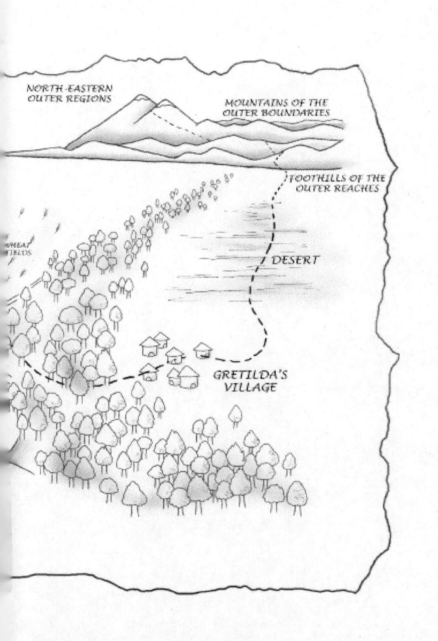

1

From a bird's eye view, the Royal City of Quadrivium looked a bit like a fried egg. The huge, golden dome of the palace was the yolk, while the whitewashed houses encircling it formed the white of the egg. Drawing closer, the city took on the appearance of a danish pastry, with dark raisins of slow-moving carriages dotted along the narrow roads which spiralled up the hill towards the palace. Today this pastry was crawling with busy ants dashing this way and that. These were, in fact, thousands of loyal subjects who had come from all four corners of the Kingdom of Ballitor to see the new heir.

The mighty eagle soaring high above the city was not interested in fried eggs or pastries. He had more important things on his mind: the royal procession was about to start. A sudden thermal caught the bird and flung him heavenwards. Decisively, he pulled his wings close to his body and pointed his beak downwards, dropping like a stone towards the city below.

* * *

The city streets were festooned with brightly coloured bunting. A brisk breeze made the little flags snap and dance above the crowds; it seemed as though the whole kingdom had turned out to cheer the newborn heir. In the distance, a deep, steady drumbeat signalled the approach of the band. Then a faint trumpet blast sounded, getting steadily louder as the procession wound its way through the narrow, cobbled streets.

A boy darted across the rooftops, unseen by the crowds below. In one hand he carried a stick which was curved at one end like a shepherd's crook. He wore an expression of intense concentration which made him seem older than his years. At twelve, Ben was the youngest and most successful thief in Quadrivium. He knew every rooftop, alleyway and rat-run like the back of his hand.

He scrambled across the shiny, red roof tiles of a particularly large villa and finally came to a stop. Peering over the edge of the parapet at the family gathered on the balcony below, his eyes widened at the sight of the jewels adorning both the ladies and the gentlemen below. He cast his expert eye over the gathering and spotted a bulging money pouch hanging from the belt of a boy about his own age. He quickly identified its distinctive spotted yellow fur as that of the rare sun leopard – even empty, the pouch would pay for a week's worth of hot suppers. With difficulty, he dragged his gaze away and turned his attention to the man holding court in the centre of the balcony.

He wasn't a tall man, but he compensated for his lack of height with a large belly and a luxurious purple velvet cloak lined with the silver fur of a snow fox. The cloak was far too warm for the time of year and Ben could see perspiration glistening on top of the man's balding head. He was speaking in a loud voice, commanding the others' attention.

"Of course, the king invited me to be part of the procession, but – being a family occasion – I felt it more appropriate to be with my own family, and so I told the king . . ." As he spoke, the portly man rocked back on his heels and Ben caught his first glimpse of the big prize: the mayoral chain of office, its solid gold links studded with brilliant jewels.

A ripple of excitement ran through the crowd as the drumbeats grew louder. Ben tightened his grasp on the stick and took a deep breath, watching as the mayor rested his hands on the balcony and leaned forward, the heavy chain swinging away from his body. Seizing the moment, Ben reached down with his stick and hooked the curved end under the chain at the nape of the mayor's neck, then hauled with all his might to lift it free of the man's numerous chins.

"Papa!" cried the mayor's son, pointing up at Ben.

The crowd's cheering increased to a roar as the procession entered the square, masking the mayor's howl of rage as he looked up to see his gold chain swinging just out of reach from the end of Ben's stick. Ben braced his feet against the parapet and leaned backwards, but the stick was starting to bend under the weight and he was struggling to hold it. Suddenly, inevitably, and with a sharp crack, it broke, dropping the chain into the crowd below.

Instinctively, Ben sprang off the roof after it, landing like a cat on the edge of the balcony. With a flick of his knife, he severed the strings of the leopard-fur money pouch, catching it in his open palm and stuffing it quickly inside his shirt. The mayor's son stared at him, too surprised to react, but the mayor pushed his son out of the way and reached for Ben.

At this moment, the mounted guards at the head of the procession passed under the balcony. Ducking beneath the mayor's arm, Ben leapt out to land behind the rider of the nearest horse. The horse reared, spooked by the sudden extra weight and by the crowd of people who were scrabbling in the dust around its hooves for the mayor's gold chain. In one fluid movement, Ben slid down its back and onto the ground, intent only on escape.

Unfortunately for Ben, some of the guards had witnessed the theft and shouted at him to halt, wheeling their prancing horses round in circles as they tried to corner him. Ben dived between the horses' legs, curling his body into a tight ball to execute a neat forward roll. He came up onto his hands and knees and crawled quickly between the legs of the onlookers.

"Stop, thief!" cried one of the mounted guards. Desperately, Ben pushed and shoved his way deeper into the crowd, but the forest of legs was thinning as people stepped away from him, leaving him exposed in a circle of curious faces. He jumped to his feet and caught sight of the guards, now on foot, pushing through the crowd towards him. Thinking quickly, he reached into his shirt and drew out the money pouch, taking a few precious seconds to pull apart the severed strings. He looked up to see the guards almost upon him. Grasping the bottom of the pouch, he spun around, showering the crowd with gold and silver coins. The people around him fell to their knees with cries of excitement, blocking the path of the guards who watched in frustration as Ben vaulted over the backs of the crowd and ran in the opposite direction.

The noise and confusion mounted as the marching band entered the square. The trumpeters continued onwards, unable to see over the tops of their sheet music. Stumbling over those on the ground, they fell like dominoes. The steady beat of the drums collapsed into disarray as the drummers in turn fell over the fallen trumpet players. Then a short, fat man with a tuba wrapped over his shoulder tripped over a french horn player and ended up upside down with his head buried deep inside his instrument, his little legs kicking the air.

Unable to hear the commotion over the cheers of the crowds behind them, the royal carriage rolled on into the mayhem.

"What in Tritan's name is going on?" cried the king, surveying the scene before him as the carriage came to a sudden halt. He leaned out and summoned the nearest guardsman.

"Mayor Ponsonby has lost his chain of office, Your Majesty, sir," the guardsman told the king, grinning nervously. "Everyone is helping him look for it."

The king snorted in disbelief and took his hunting horn from the cushion beside him.

"Please don't make a fuss, dear," the queen touched his arm gently. She looked down at the newborn heir who was sleeping peacefully in her arms. "I've only just got him settled."

"Katrina, my darling, we'll be here all day if I don't get this sorted out right now. It would appear that Mayor Ponsonby is at the centre of this mess . . ."

With that, the king leapt down from the carriage, raised the horn to his lips and blew a long, mournful note. Before the sound had ceased, he had the attention of every man, woman and child.

"Right," growled the king, "someone bring me

Ponsonby!"

* * *

A thrill of fear ran through Ben at the sound of the king's horn. As the chaos gradually died down, he raised his head cautiously to see what was going on. A sea of faces stared back at him. Immediately he ducked back down again, his heart pounding. There was a creaking sound beneath him as he lay quivering in anticipation of the punishment which awaited him. He ignored it, and wriggled further into his hiding place, expecting at any moment to be dragged down to face the waiting mayor.

A few minutes passed, and then a few more. Ben was just about to risk another look when, with a sharp tearing sound, the fabric beneath him gave way and he fell into the carriage, landing in a heap at the feet of the queen.

For a second they both froze, each as shocked as the other. Outside the carriage, Ben could clearly hear Mayor Ponsonby babbling to the king, "There were at least five of them, all over six feet tall and armed to the teeth. My poor wife and I . . ."

Ben was brought back to his immediate surroundings by a sudden movement out of the corner of his eye. He leapt up to defend himself, but there was no one else in the carriage except for the queen who was staring at him with wide eyes. He looked down at the blanket in her arms and took a quick step back as it moved, slipping to one side to reveal a chubby fist waving in the air.

Before either could say a word, the carriage door on the side furthest from the square was flung open, and up climbed the tiniest, most wrinkled old lady that Ben had ever seen. She looked down at him calmly.

"I've been expecting you," she said.

* * *

Once the king had intervened, the mayor's chain of office was soon recovered and returned to him in a jumble of broken links. The crowds fell back to line the streets once more, cheering the royal procession as it wound its way towards the palace.

The watching eagle drifted on the warm evening thermals as the king's subjects finally made their way back to their homes, leaving the city deserted. Deserted, that is, except for two figures standing on the balcony which encircled the golden dome of the palace. There was a bright flash as the setting sun caught the tilt of a highly polished surface. The flash came again, and then a third time. Responding instantly, the bird folded back its wings and dived earthwards.

2

On the dome's balcony, the old lady laid the sheet of polished silver carefully at her feet and turned to face Ben.

"You had a very lucky escape today," she began, fixing Ben with her piercing gaze.

Ben looked at the ground and shrugged, as though his close shave with the soldiers was something that happened to him every day, but inwardly he cringed as he relived the moment when his stick had snapped and the mayor's chain had been lost. He finally raised his eyes to find her smiling at him.

"Everything happened exactly as it was foretold," she continued. "Even the clothes on your back match the description I was given . . ."

She broke off as, with a sudden rush of air and a great fluttering of wings, an enormous eagle appeared from the sky and came to rest beside them. Ben stumbled back, away from the huge talons which gripped the gilded balustrade.

To his astonishment, the old lady opened her arms and addressed the bird. "Murgatroyd! Welcome!"

It bowed its head in reply and then turned towards Ben. "Is this the child?"

She nodded.

"Ma'am," came the drawl from its sharply curved beak, "you simply can't be serious."

Ben's jaw dropped as he heard the bird speak. His wide-eyed gaze flicked from the lady to the bird and back again as she continued the conversation as though there was nothing out of the ordinary. "There's no mistake, Murgatroyd. He is the one."

The eagle dipped his beak towards Ben, carefully examining the boy. At first glance, he was not impressed. The child was thin and dirty. His matted, blonde hair stuck up in all directions as though he'd hacked at it with a blunt knife (which, Murgatroyd reflected, may well have been the case). He had a bruise on one cheek and his bottom lip was swollen and scabbed. He appeared no different from any of the other homeless urchins who roamed Quadrivium's streets.

Then Ben raised his eyes to meet Murgatroyd's scrutiny and the bird caught his breath. The child's irises were huge and very dark, almost black. Murgatroyd had the sensation of peering into a bottomless pool.

Ben gazed back at the huge bird, fascinated now that he was over his initial shock of hearing it talk. He stared at the sharp beak and the strong wings which were slightly outstretched for balance on the narrow balustrade. The bird's beady black eyes reflected tiny images of Ben back at himself.

Finally, Murgatroyd shook his tail feathers and looked away. "Perhaps you're right," he conceded, "he just seems so young."

"And that suits our purpose," said the old lady. "He's fit, flexible, and small enough to squeeze through the tiniest of openings . . ."

Ben didn't like being spoken about as if he wasn't there. He cleared his throat noisily and they both looked round at him in surprise. The lady recovered first, laying her hand firmly on his arm in a gesture which he felt was more to stop him running away than to reassure him.

"Forgive me, Ben," she said, "I'm forgetting my manners. Allow me to introduce you to Murgatroyd. As you have no doubt noticed, he can talk. In fact, Murgatroyd is one of the very few beasts left in Quadrivium who can, so he makes the most of it."

Ben wiped his hand on his shorts and was about to offer it to Murgatroyd when he remembered the bird's razor sharp claws. Instead, he let it drop limply back down to his side.

The lady suppressed a smile and turned to Murgatroyd. "Murgatroyd, this is Ben, a very talented and resourceful young man. He's the one I was told to look out for and

he's going to help us – for a suitable payment, of course."
As she spoke she drew a small leather bag from a pocket in
her skirt. Something within chinked enticingly.

She handed the bag to Ben. He pulled it open and
stared down at the gold coins nestled inside. He was about
to reach in and take one when she took the bag back off
him. "Payment comes later. You know you can trust me,
don't you?"

Ben thought back to his narrow escape that afternoon.
If she hadn't intervened he would have been in serious
trouble. She had persuaded the queen that he was a new
page who had been shooing pigeons off the roof of her
carriage when it had given way. Surprisingly, given his
appearance, the queen had accepted this version of events,
allowing the old lady to whisk him out of the carriage just
as the king had clambered back in, muttering dark things
about overpaid civil servants. She had quickly ushered him
into her own carriage, where he was safe from Ponsonby's
household guards who were searching the square for him.
He had discovered that she was the queen's mother and was
known as the Dowager Bella.

He took a deep breath and looked at their expectant
faces. "So, what exactly is it that you want me to do?"

* * *

Murgatroyd had mixed feelings. On the one wing, he

knew Bella had her own reasons for wanting to rush ahead while his instincts urged caution. On the other, he sensed something special about this boy. Despite Ben's youth and questionable background, he felt excitement welling up inside him. Perhaps Bella's fortune teller had been right after all.

Choosing his words carefully, he began to speak. "We need you to steal a book –"

"A book?" interrupted Ben, his forehead scrunching up into a frown. "Don't tell me this is all about a book?"

"This is no ordinary book," said Murgatroyd, picturing it in his mind's eye as he paced up and down the balustrade. "This is a book of prophecies, some of which have already come to pass, many of which are as yet unfulfilled. It also contains the only unabridged, unbiased and veridical history of our world."

Ben frowned.

"He means it's all true," whispered Bella.

Murgatroyd had stopped pacing and was standing with one claw raised as he stared misty-eyed into the past. "As a young bird," he began, "I was privileged to see the precious book with my own eyes."

He pictured its heavy wooden spine inlaid with bronze which was tarnished to a dull, dark sheen. The series of events that had led to its discovery ran through his mind. He had been barely more than a chick when he had encountered a boy exploring the derelict tower where he lived. His new friend was the only son of Bella, who had brought him and his sister to live within the safety of the palace while her husband commanded a platoon in the faraway borderland wars. The boy had the run of the palace and together they had explored every nook and cranny.

Murgatroyd's favourite place had been the palace library with its soaring buttresses and row upon row of books. The ceiling was so high and he loved to stretch his wings, circling upwards to the topmost shelves, but it wasn't quite as much fun for the boy clambering up and down the rickety library ladders after him.

He and the boy had drifted apart, but his fascination with the library never waned and it was here on a remote shelf that he had one day discovered the Book of Prophecies.

He quickly became obsessed with the book. The more he read, the more he yearned to know, and he returned each day for weeks, reading voraciously until he began to recognise certain events which had only recently come to pass. Enthralled, he continued reading until finally, about half way through, he came to the first prophecy.

Murgatroyd shook himself out of his reverie and looked up to see Ben and Bella waiting patiently for him to continue.

"Ah yes, the Book," he began, gathering his thoughts. "As I was saying, I was privileged to read it for myself, but when I came to the first prophecy that privilege became a curse, for the Book predicted the Great Fire of Barbearland in which many would perish."

He had been so alarmed by the destruction and loss of life foretold in the book that he had sought out Bella's son to share his discovery with. It had been a long time since they had last spoken – they were no longer the childish playmates they had once been – but he hadn't known who else to turn to. Bella happened to overhear them talking and persuaded him to tell her of the prophecy. He recalled the look of horror on her face as she realised that her own husband, who was fighting the rebels in the borderland wars, may be caught up in the tragedy.

Realising that Murgatroyd had once again drifted back into his thoughts, Bella took up the story. "Once Murgatroyd had recounted the prophecy to me, I sent Damien, my son, to fetch the book so I could read it with my own eyes. But as fate would have it, in the short space of time between Murgatroyd leaving the book in the library and Damien going back there to fetch it, it had disappeared. The monks who worked in the library had begun a complete reorganisation and it seems the book had been archived."

"Why didn't you just ask the monks if you could have it back?" asked Ben.

"It wasn't that simple," said Bella. "Of course, at the time I made immediate enquiries, but it was firmly denied that such a book had ever existed. You have to understand that I had no influence back then, this was long before my daughter grew up and married the king."

"Hang on," interrupted Ben, "when did all this happen?"

"Fifteen years ago."

"But that's ancient history!" cried Ben. "When is this great big fire supposed to happen?"

"It has already happened," said Murgatroyd, raising a feathery eyebrow at Bella. "It took place fifteen years ago, only a few weeks after I first read the prophecy. Don't they teach you anything in school?"

"I don't go to school," retorted Ben.

Bella shot a warning glance at Murgatroyd.

"The Great Fire was the turning point in the war against the rebels, Ben," she explained. "Many of those fighting for the king were missing, presumed killed – sadly, my dear husband among them – but the rebels also incurred heavy losses and since that time there has been peace and stability in the borderlands."

"So why do you need the book now, after all these years?" asked Ben

"There are signs that the years of peace are drawing to a close. The truce which was put in place with the rebels soon after the Great Fire is crumbling, threatening not only the trading routes but also our settlements in the borderlands and possibly Quadrivium. If we can just read the prophecies, we may be able to prevent another catastrophe as terrible as the Great Fire itself."

Ben looked at Bella, his head on one side, thinking

about what she had told him. "So where is this book and why do you need me to steal it for you?"

She looked him straight in the eye. "I was told to expect you. The circumstances of our meeting were described to me in great detail, exactly as they happened today."

"By who?" asked Ben, wondering who could have known of his plan to steal the mayor's chain.

"Someone I have known and trusted for many years," said Bella. "She also told me that the book is being hidden in the archives beneath the palace. You're small enough to navigate the old tunnel network which is the best way to access the archives without being spotted."

Ben wondered what she wasn't telling him, but he was distracted by Murgatroyd's next words.

"Then all you have to do," concluded the eagle, "is locate the book, climb back into the tunnel and meet us back here to collect your reward."

Ben thought for a few moments. They made it sound so easy.

"I've got one last question," he said. "This book sounds really useful and interesting – if you can read, that is. Why haven't you tried to get it back before now?"

Bella turned to look out over the battlements while Murgatroyd bent his head and fluffed up his feathers. Neither of them would meet his eye.

"Actually, there was a previous attempt – it was made shortly after the book first disappeared," said Murgatroyd finally. "We believe it was unsuccessful."

Bella spoke, her back still turned to Ben.

"It was my son, Damien," she said in a soft voice. "He never returned."

3

The king slumped on his throne, his features set in a deep frown.

"Enough, Ponsonby!" he cried finally in exasperation. "First it was a band of eight foot Heathenites stealing your chain, now you're telling me it was one small boy. What am I supposed to believe?"

The mayor stared at his feet. His chins wobbled as he shook his head gently. "I do apologise, Your Majesty. I got caught up in the excitement and in my befuddled state I believed the butcher's wife and Mrs Smythe from the infirmary to be part of the band of robbers. I now remember the events much more clearly, and it was all started by a singularly scruffy urchin. He must be found and punished! Not only did he make a mockery of the royal procession, he also stole Ponsonby Junior's purse!"

The king stood up with a sigh and stretched his aching back. He really should get a more comfortable throne, he thought to himself, even though this one had been in his family for generations. Audiences with men like Ponsonby seemed to last forever. He felt much more at home with fighting men – politicians always made him uneasy – but he was well aware of the mayor's role in negotiating with the rebels: he was a man of importance, a man with influential contacts in the outlying states, control of the most important trading routes, friends in high places . . . The king didn't know how much higher you could go than himself, but he had taken the advice of his councillors and agreed to see the mayor.

He sighed again and turned back to Ponsonby.

"I would prefer to let things lie," he began, "but I understand that this is important to you, and as a gesture of my esteem I will set out a decree that the boy be found and brought to you for suitable punishment."

Ponsonby's reaction was immediate. His round, shiny face beamed at the king, who wondered briefly why this boy was so important to him.

* * *

Bella led Ben through a heavy wooden door set into the side of the golden dome. By the remains of daylight leaking through a small skylight set into the curved roof, he saw a narrow flight of stone steps which wound higher up into the dome as well as down into the gloom below. They were worn in the middle as though many feet had passed this way over the years.

"We don't have much time," whispered Bella, already a few steps below him, "the moon will soon be rising."

Ben ran to keep up with her. They passed the small door through which they'd entered the dome's staircase earlier that afternoon which led to the stable yard where the horses had been unharnessed from the royal carriages. He paused briefly to catch his breath, recalling how the old lady had slipped each of the carriage drivers a piece of gold, bribing them not to mention her extra passenger. It reminded him of the bag of gold coins in her pocket and he hurried after her.

She was waiting by an open door which was studded with the king's crest. Ben took the last few steps at a jump and looked past her down a long corridor lined with suits of armour. Narrow, arched windows were set deep into the high stone walls and the last rays of the setting sun streamed through the coloured glass, staining the floor and walls with streaks of red, green and blue. Bella put her finger to her lips and led the way into the corridor.

Ben gazed in awe as they passed the suits of armour. They were all different shapes and sizes: some were at least eight feet tall, with tail-like appendages curled round their shining bodies, while others were more human in shape, but tiny in size, too small even for Ben. They had one thing in common: they were all so highly polished that he could clearly see his reflection in them.

Overcome by curiosity, he edged closer to a suit of armour which was low to the ground and propped up on four short but sturdy metal legs. It was topped off with a sharp ridge which ran from the top of its head all the way down to the end of its highly polished tail. Something caught his eye and he looked more closely. The armour was so shiny that Ben assumed that the metal was acting like a mirror, but on closer inspection he realised that the backdrop against which he could see his own face peering back was flickering with an orange glow, and much brighter than the gloomy corridor in which he stood. Suddenly a strange figure loomed into view, behind and slightly to one side of his reflection. He gasped, and looked over his shoulder, but there was no one there except Bella.

"Keep quiet and follow me," she said in a hushed voice. "We're about to enter the throne room."

Ben frowned and looked back at the suit of armour, but all he could see was his own shadowy reflection. He hesitated for a moment, and then raced after Bella who had almost reached the imposing set of gold-studded doors at the end of the corridor.

Suddenly the doors were flung open and a cordon of guards stepped through. Bella shoved Ben behind the nearest suit of armour just as Mayor Ponsonby appeared in the doorway. As soon as he saw Bella, he swept off his feathered hat and gave a sweeping bow, as low as his protruding belly would allow.

"Your Highness," he wheezed, "what a great honour."

Bella looked at the top of his balding head with distaste. "Mayor Ponsonby," she said haughtily, unimpressed by his elaborate greeting, "what brings you to the palace?"

The mayor hurriedly straightened up, his red face glistening with perspiration, unaware in his exertion that two diamond studded buttons had popped off his waistcoat. Ben's eyes followed the buttons as they rolled towards his hiding place.

"Just helping the king instil a little discipline amongst his subjects," he said with false cheeriness. Encouraged by Bella's raised eyebrow, he continued in a more serious tone. "The attempted theft of the Mayor of Quadrivium's chain of office cannot be taken lightly. The king has ordered me to find the thief and exact a strict punishment."

Ben snatched back his hand which had crept out to grab the buttons and pressed his back against the wall.

"It is always so reassuring to know we can rely on men like you, Mayor Ponsonby," said the Dowager Bella through gritted teeth, "to take care of the little things while the king gets on with the important business of running the kingdom."

Ponsonby paused, not quite sure whether her words were meant as a compliment or an insult.

"Yes, ah, yes exactly," he flustered. "A great lady like yourself recognises such things. Perhaps I shall have the pleasure of toasting your health at the banquet tonight?"

Bella looked up at him and raised her eyebrows. Realising he had overstepped the mark, Ponsonby stuttered something about seeing to his wife and ordered his guards forward.

Luckily, Ben's snort of laughter was lost amongst the jingle of ceremonial swords and the stomp of the guards' feet.

"That told him!" he said as he got to his feet and then stopped, surprised by the serious expression on Bella's face.

"That man bothers me," she said softly, half to Ben, half to herself. "He's become far too confident of his position with the king and he's risen too quickly. Where did he come from? I really don't trust him at all."

Still shaking her head, she moved towards a plain wooden door, unnoticeable next to the grand doorway through which the mayor had just left. Looking around quickly to make sure they were alone, Bella drew a small bunch of keys from a pocket in her robes, unlocked the door and motioned Ben through.

He found himself in a narrow passageway bordered on one side by rough brickwork and on the other by what looked to Ben like the back of a huge carpet. The door swung silently shut behind him, blocking off the light from the corridor, and he felt Bella brush past him. He ran his hand along the thick knots of wool until his eyes adjusted to the gloom and he could make out her tiny figure not far ahead. She was peering around the edge of one of the tapestries, so Ben got down on his knees and pushed his face between her robes and the thick, dusty fabric to see what she was looking at.

At first he thought the throne room was empty, but then he followed the direction of Bella's gaze to the far end of the room where a large wooden throne sat atop a raised platform. There sat the king, his head in his hands. As they watched, he leant back with a sigh and got slowly to his feet, leaving the room through the large double doors.

Bella pushed the tapestry aside and entered the large hall. Ben followed slowly, looking around with wide eyes. At every few steps a torch burned brightly, illuminating the enormous tapestries which covered the walls on both sides of the grand hall. He gazed up at lifelike scenes beautifully picked out in many different shades of wool. The first depicted a bubbling stream meandering through a peaceful, green valley. In the distance was a city on a hill, with many spires and a golden dome. He wandered past it to the next tapestry. This one showed a thick forest overlooked by a range of snow-capped mountains with two particularly prominent peaks outlined against a red background, as though backlit by the setting sun. Or the glow of a raging fire.

He leapt backwards suddenly, his heart pounding: there were eyes peering out at him from between the trees in the foreground! After a few moments, once he was quite certain that they weren't moving, he leaned in to look more closely. The eyes had been cleverly woven into the tapestry's intricate design.

Feeling a little foolish, he crossed the hall to look at the tapestries on the other side. The one which had caught his eye showed a party in full swing taking place in a village square. Lanterns had been strung up amongst the trees and tables set out on the cobbles. Life-size figures leaned out of the windows of nearby houses, calling to those below who were eating, drinking and laughing. It took Ben a while before he noticed that not all the figures were human. Mingling amongst the ordinary folk, so naturally that at first glance they hadn't appeared out of place, were birds, animals and a few unfamiliar beasts which resembled nothing Ben had ever seen before in his life.

He looked around to ask Bella about the scenes in the tapestries, but she was nowhere to be seen. The first thought to run through his head was to find something small enough to steal; the second, to run over and sit on the throne.

He was halfway to the throne when he heard her slightly muffled voice. "Ben! Over here!"

It took him a moment to realise that she was behind the heavy velvet curtain which was draped across the wall behind the throne. It twitched to one side and her face appeared, looking impatient. "Hurry up! We haven't got all night!"

Behind the curtain was a wooden door barely as high as his waist. Bella held out a small, dark key which looked valuable and very, very old. Ben took it, startled by its weight.

"This is a skeleton key," said Bella. "It is one of a pair which was made when the original palace was built many, many years before I was born. It will open any door in the old part of the palace, including this one."

She folded Ben's fingers over the key. "Follow the tunnel until you come to the monk's quarters, the archives will be nearby. Once you've found them, locate the Book of Prophecies and get out as quickly as you can. You should be able to make your way back to the dome without being seen as most people will be at the banquet. Either Murgatroyd or I will be waiting for you. And remember, this key will open any door, but do be careful – you never know what may be on the other side."

She paused, taking one last look at him. He suddenly reminded her of her own son who had disappeared all those years ago, taking with him an identical key. She felt a twinge of conscience which she quickly suppressed. The Book would give her the best chance of finding her son. It was her last and only hope.

"Just remember, Ben," she said, "the bag of gold is yours just as soon as you bring me the Book."

With that, she turned on her heel and left Ben standing alone.

4

Ben wasn't used to handling keys, most of his entrances were through windows, or doors which had been left unlocked. He examined this small and infinitely useful object. It fit snugly into the palm of his hand and was heavy for its size, made from some sort of dense, black metal which was very smooth but not at all shiny. There was a ring at one end, which he could squeeze his little finger through, and at the other was a square shape with a 'V' cut out of it.

He closed his fist around the key and crouched down to take a look at the door. It had no doorknob or handle, just a small keyhole. He put his eye up against it, but it was too dark on the other side to see anything so he sat back on his heels, wondering which end of the key to put in the hole.

Suddenly it twitched in his grasp and his hand started to move of its own accord. He had the peculiar sensation that the key was dragging itself towards the keyhole. It wriggled and squirmed until the end with the missing 'V' poked out from between his clenched fingers. He watched in disbelief as his hand was drawn closer to the door, then, smoothly and without hesitation, the key slid into the keyhole and the door opened.

Instantly, his arm dropped down to hang by his side, the key still clasped between his fingers. He peered through the doorway. It was very dark. He looked down at the key in his hand, then, thinking quickly, reached under his shirt and drew out a small silver locket suspended on a worn leather cord. He drew it over his head and picked at the knot. Once it was undone, he threaded the key onto the leather cord, re-tied the knot and slipped it back over his head.

With the key safely secured, he crawled on hands and knees through the low doorway and into the dark tunnel beyond, feeling the stone floor cold and rough against his knees. He felt a moment of panic as the door bumped shut behind him, but, strangely reassured by the weight of the key around his neck, he continued to move forward.

His eyes slowly became accustomed to the dark. A faint gloom penetrated a latticed panel set into the tunnel near the floor, enough to make out the ancient stones and mortar forming the walls around him. He froze as he heard footsteps heading directly for him. The light became steadily brighter and the latticework created dancing patterns on the sides of the tunnel. Finally, a shadow passed by and the footsteps receded, taking the light with them. Ben shuffled forward once more, pausing each time he heard footsteps. He wondered what the owners of the footsteps would say if they knew he was only inches away, on the other side of the wall.

He was starting to feel a bit cramped when he came to a fork in the tunnel. In one direction he could hear the faint sound of music and voices, so he decided to take the other passage, which was darker and quiet. He hadn't gone very far when he noticed a warm breeze blowing towards him. He hurried onwards, eager to get out of the narrow tunnel.

Gradually, he noticed the smell wafting towards him. He paused, sniffing the air. It was a delicious, warm and comforting smell. His mouth began to water and he shuffled forward more quickly now, guided by his sense of smell. His stomach gurgled loudly, reminding him that he hadn't eaten since that morning and even that had only been the stale end of a loaf which someone had thrown out for the birds.

He was brought back to his senses by a sudden, sharp blow to his head. Muffling a cry of pain, he sat back on his heels and looked up to see a solid wall blocking his path. He closed his eyes and rested his forehead against the rough bricks, wondering what to do next. The shaft was too narrow for him to turn around and he was starting to feel claustrophobic.

Opening his eyes once more, he looked down to see the

key swinging gently backwards and forwards from around his neck, emitting a faint light of its own. He took hold of it and waved it in front of him like a torch, hoping to find another keyhole, but instead of opening a door in the wall his arm was yanked suddenly downwards. His hand hit the ground with a hollow thud, the floor beneath him instantly gave way and he dropped like a stone into the room below.

He landed instinctively on his feet like a cat, staring wildly around. The room appeared to be deserted. Taking a deep breath, he noticed that the tantalising smell of food was stronger here. Running down the centre of the room, taking up much of the floor space, was a large, wooden trestle table covered with flour. He looked past the empty table to a row of huge ovens on the far side. He sidled over to the nearest one and wrestled open its heavy door. It was still warm, but empty. He tried the next one, but it, too, was empty. He almost groaned out loud with disappointment.

Ravenous, he licked his finger and swept some of the flour off the wooden table and into his mouth. Sucking the flour from his finger, he scanned the room. At one end was a pair of large white doors with porthole windows, at the other was a smaller door standing slightly ajar. He was deciding which of the doors to investigate first when one of the double doors unexpectedly swung open and a large figure entered the room backwards, pushing the door open with an enormous behind. Ben dived beneath the table, his heart pounding.

"More grog, more fowl, more bread," sang the man, swaying beneath a large tray which he held aloft. "The ale's gone to my head!"

He chortled with delight at his little rhyme, dropping the tray with a thunk onto the table directly over Ben's head. Ben drew himself up into a little ball, staring at the man's large feet and the hem of his filthy robe. The man wriggled his horny toes as he noisily unloaded the contents of the tray. Ben peered out from his hiding place as the man strode over to the smaller door and emerged holding a cooked chicken by the leg, which he dropped with a juicy thud onto the tray. After more visits to the pantry, and three more chickens, four loaves of bread and four sloshing jugs of ale later, the man left, staggering under the weight of the loaded tray and leaving splashes of ale in his wake.

Ben raised his head warily. Once he was certain the man had gone, he crawled out from under the table and began tearing at the remnants of food which he had left behind. Fat ran down his chin as he sucked on chicken bones, crunched on crispy wings and poked his tongue into neglected crevices. Having mopped up all the juices with a discarded crust of bread, he was finally satisfied. He wiped his mouth on the back of his hand and crossed over to the big white doors. Raising himself up onto his tiptoes, he peered cautiously through one of the porthole windows into the room beyond.

Four monks were gathered around a roaring log fire. One was slumped in his armchair, snoring softly, ale dripping slowly from a jug hooked loosely around his finger. The other three, including the one who had almost discovered Ben, were taking it in turns to throw a handful of dice onto the low table between them.

Ben jumped as one farted loudly, and then wafted his habit at the others, sniggering. "I must apologise, dear brothers! I do believe the Abbot's fine ale has put the wind up me!"

"Brother Bernard!" cried another. "Your unholy stink is going to get us into trouble! Go and check on the Book before you gas us all!"

Ben pricked up his ears.

The monk who had spoken fished a key from his habit and threw it to Brother Bernard. It sailed past the other monk's outstretched hand and skidded across the stone-flagged floor towards the double doors where Ben was hiding. He watched in horror as it slid towards him, as though responding to the magnetism of his own key which he felt twitch against his chest.

Brother Bernard waddled over to pick up the key, tripping over the edge of his habit as it slid from his grasp. Grunting with irritation, he stamped his foot on it and reached down to pick it up.

"Don't know why we bother," he grumbled as he made

his way back across the room to a heavy wooden door on the far side. "It's perfectly safe down there. No one can get into the lower archives without the key, even if they did manage to get past the . . ." His voice died away as he left the room. The other monks went back to their dice, chuckling to themselves.

Holding his breath, Ben inched open one of the double doors and slipped into the room. He edged carefully round the outside, keeping to the shadows until he reached the door through which Brother Bernard had left. At that moment, the sleeping monk gave a massive snore. The jug slipped from his grasp and hit the floor with a crash, breaking into pieces. Startled from his doze, he sat up and looked straight at Ben.

"Who are you?" he said, his voice thick with sleep.

The other monks looked up from their game and followed the direction of his gaze. They all stared at Ben in astonishment as he pushed desperately at the door. When he glanced back over his shoulder, the monks were all on their feet. They rushed towards him, but each of them managed to step in the spreading puddle of ale from the broken jug and they skidded, arms flailing, across the floor, landing at Ben's feet in a heap of arms, legs and tangled robes.

With no time to lose, Ben suddenly remembered the key. He didn't pause to remove it from around his neck, but simply grasped hold of it and shoved it towards the door. It found its own way to the lock and slid straight in. The door instantly burst open and Ben slipped quickly through, slamming it behind him.

He felt their fists pound furiously against the door, but it held fast. Ben looked down at the key which now hung serenely from the cord around his neck. He closed his hand around it, grinning to himself, then tucked it beneath his shirt and looked around.

He found himself in a narrow passageway with no doors or windows in either direction, that he could see. Flaming torches fixed to brackets on either side of the door cast flickering shadows on the dull stone walls. After the warmth of the monk's den, he immediately noticed a damp chill in the air and shivered, wondering which way to go. The passageway sloped gently downhill in one direction so, as the monks had referred to the lower archives, he decided to go that way. Ignoring the muffled sounds of fists beating against the door behind him, he set off down the passageway.

The noise from the monks' den was soon swallowed up by the thick, stone walls. Now the only sounds were the slap of his feet on the cobbled floor and the occasional hiss and splutter from the burning torches.

As he turned the corner, he caught sight of a long shadow disappearing around the next bend. He hurried to catch up, slipping on the cobbles which were damp with moss. The ground became steadily steeper as the passageway curved round and round in an endless downwards spiral. Just as it seemed that he would have to resort to sliding down on his bottom, he came to some steps which had been crudely fashioned by removing one or two cobbles every few paces, leaving just dirt and gravel for better grip.

He froze as he heard the monk's voice up ahead, closer than he had expected. "Why does it always have to be me what goes out into the cold? Why me? The others never do their share ... it's not fair ..."

Ben could now hear the monk's laboured breathing as he followed him down the steps, taking care to remain out of sight. The torches were spaced further apart here and he had to feel his way carefully from one step to the next. It was noticeably colder and there was a dank smell in the air. He felt dizzy from going round in circles and dragged his hand along the wall for balance as he continued to follow the monk ever downward.

Concentrating on his footing, it was a moment before he realised he could no longer hear the monk. He peered cautiously around the next bend. The passageway had finally come to an end and, just a few feet away, the monk was facing a moss-covered wooden door set deep into a stone archway. Ben watched as the monk drew his key from his habit and placed it carefully in the lock.

The door creaked slowly open.

5

By the time Bella had changed her clothes, put on her best jewels and hurried in to the banquet, the hall was almost full. She noticed with relief that the king and queen had not yet made their entrance and looked around to find her seat. Then she groaned inwardly as Mayor Ponsonby jumped up from his place beside her empty chair, and held it out for her with a small bow.

"This is such an honour, your Highness," he simpered, "to meet again so soon."

Bella sat quickly. Turning her head to hide her grimace, she recognised the person on her other side and exclaimed with joyful surprise, "Penthesilean, I didn't know you were back!"

A giant of a man grinned down at her. Blue eyes twinkled from beneath bushy, white eyebrows in a deeply tanned and weather-beaten face. A row of colourful medals were prominently displayed on the pocket of his smart velvet dress coat which strained across his broad chest. He reached down and enfolded her tiny hands in his.

"Bella, Bella, Bella!" he murmured, ignoring Ponsonby who was peering over her shoulder. "It is so good to see you! We have so much to discuss . . ." The end of his sentence was drowned out by a loud fanfare. Conversation immediately stopped and chairs were scraped back as Quadrivium's courtiers rose to greet the king and queen.

Penthesilean took the opportunity to lean down and speak softly into Bella's ear. "I need to speak to the king – urgently. Can you get me an audience?"

Bella looked at him in surprise. He was seated at the king's table – that alone would guarantee him an audience.

"In private," added Penthesilean.

Suddenly Bella's pleasure at seeing her old friend evaporated as she noticed the lines of exhaustion on his face. She opened her mouth to speak, but he shook his head slightly, his eyes focussing on something over her shoulder. She understood and, moving as though to rearrange her robes, swiftly drove her elbow backwards. It sank into the mayor's fleshy stomach.

"Forgive me, Your Highness," he gasped, winded by her blow, "I dropped my napkin! So clumsy of me . . ."

Bella eyed him thoughtfully as he fumbled around, knocking over a full goblet of wine in the process. As waiters rushed to mop up the rich red liquid soaking rapidly into the white tablecloth, she pondered the situation. Ponsonby wasn't as foolish as he appeared; he was not a man to be trusted. She would have to make every effort to divert his attention.

* * *

Ben drew back into the shadows, watching the monk who stood motionless in the open doorway just a few feet away, seemingly reluctant to enter into whatever lay beyond. Finally, with an agonised sigh, he hitched up his habit and stepped over the threshold. Almost immediately, the door started to swing shut. Without stopping to think, Ben ran forward and sprang through the narrowing gap. A moment later the door closed behind him with a solid thud.

It was pitch black on the other side. The air was cool and, although he couldn't see a thing, Ben sensed that he was standing in a large, open space. He took a step back until he could feel the reassuringly solid door behind him. The ground beneath his feet scrunched and shifted like pebbles on a beach. He wondered for a moment whether he was outside, but immediately dismissed this idea as it was simply too dark and too quiet for the outdoors.

After a moment of indecision, he took a few small steps into the darkness, gasping involuntarily as the ground suddenly shelved downwards and his feet sank into something cold and wet. He leant down and dipped his fingers tentatively into the liquid before tasting it: it was salt water. As he moved his hand away, he realised that he could see its pale shape in front of his face and wiggled his fingers just to be sure. Imperceptibly, his range of vision grew until he could see the rest of his body down to his ankles disappearing into water which was as dark as mud. Crouching down, he ran his hand across the surface. Ripples emanated from his fingertips, chasing each other into the darkness.

As the light grew steadily brighter, he found that he was standing in an underground chamber at the edge of what appeared to be an enormous lake. Once the ripples had died down the water returned to a still, inky blackness. It gave no reflection of the growing light, which he noticed was coming from lanterns suspended from long chains which snaked up into the gloom. He couldn't see the ceiling, only the rough stone walls which continued interrupted into the dark as far as his eyes could see.

He gradually became aware that the silence had been replaced by a gentle hum. He listened intently, noticing how it grew steadily louder before subsiding and then swelling in volume once more. It was made up of many different harmonious notes which echoed around the cavern so that he was not quite sure from what direction it came.

A sudden movement at the very edge of the darkness caught his attention. It was the monk, illuminated by the growing light from the lanterns. He was shuffling sideways around the edge of the lake like an ungainly crab, his robes hitched up around his knees.

As Ben watched, the surface of the lake stirred, creating small waves which splashed against his ankles. The monk stopped dead, his back pressed against the wall. A stream of ripples appeared, moving rapidly towards the trembling man like a giant arrow. He started to whimper. Even from this distance, Ben could sense the monk's fear.

The ripples grew into a larger swell. It was as though the lake was being whipped up by a furious wind, but the air was as still as before. Suddenly, a great wave appeared from nowhere, rearing straight up like a wall of water and heading directly for the quivering monk. Ben saw the whites of the man's eyes as he looked frantically around for an escape route, but he was too late and, with a crash, the wave broke over his head. The monk toppled face first into the lake with a faint cry.

The humming, which had been growing steadily louder, disintegrated into loud peals of laughter. It was warm and infectious and Ben couldn't help smiling. The monk reappeared, coughing and spluttering, trying desperately to keep his head above the water while his heavy robes threatened to drag him under. Then, to Ben's amazement, he began to rise up, his legs kicking feebly at the air.

Emerging majestically out of the water beneath him was the most extraordinary creature Ben had ever seen.

* * *

Bella sat motionless in the midst of the bustling ballroom, her mind racing. Why had Ponsonby been trying to eavesdrop on her conversation with Penthesilean? Could he possibly suspect her of helping Ben escape? Did he know about the Book of Prophecies?

She was so distracted that she barely noticed the delicious food which the waiters laid before her. There were paper-thin slices of salty angel-fish from the mountain lakes of Upper Pemble, delicately crunchy antelope ribs from the forests of Outer Veridian, and the unexpectedly fiery chilli and chocolate puddings with the molten centres – usually her favourite – to finish. All of these passed her lips without her tasting a single morsel.

Penthesilean covered up her silence with frivolous chat, requesting a full account of the day's events from those around them and feigning interest in every last detail. Mayor Ponsonby's wife, a rather large lady who was seated to his left, was in the middle of an interminable description of what she and her extended family had worn that day, when Princess Madeleine, the king's niece who was sitting opposite, leaned forward and interrupted.

"Great Aunt Bella!" she cried, her face flushed from her first glass of sparkling wine and the excitement of attending her first banquet. "Tell Penthesilean about the boy who tried to steal Mayor Ponsonby's chain!"

Bella felt the colour drain from her face, but fortunately no one noticed as, at that moment, Ponsonby, who had just taken an enormous mouthful of the chilli and chocolate pudding, turned scarlet and began to cough. Penthesilean immediately leapt to his feet and pounded the mayor's back with great enthusiasm as several waiters hurried over with glasses of water.

Undeterred, Madeleine continued. "It was so entertaining! There were all these grown men chasing one small boy – Mayor Ponsonby's entire household guard and some of the king's men too – but the boy managed to outwit them all and escaped without a trace! Fortunately for the mayor he didn't manage to get away with the chain as it was far too heavy, but he came pretty close! I haven't laughed so much in years! And then . . ."

Wiping tears of laughter from her eyes, she continued to tell how three matronly housewives had fought over the gold chain before it was finally rescued and restored to the mayor. By now, her lively voice had attracted the attention of those around them and soon the whole table was laughing and joining in. Red-faced and still coughing, Ponsonby pushed back his chair and hurried from the ballroom.

* * *

Ben watched, spellbound, as the creature from the lake lifted the monk out of the water. It appeared human in shape, with muscular shoulders and a large head with long, flowing hair. But what struck him more than anything else was the grey-green hue of its skin, and the way the water pooled on the skin's surface rather than running straight off, giving the impression that the creature was made of water itself.

Moving smoothly forward, it deposited the monk on the ledge which ran round the edge of the lake. The monk struggled to stand up, weighed down by his sodden robes. He grasped at stones that jutted from the wall, but the ledge was narrow and slippery from the water which streamed from his habit and instead he stumbled and fell back into the lake with a great splash.

The infectious laughter rang out once more. It echoed around the chamber, wrapping itself around Ben like a warm cloak. The monk, however, did not appear to be comforted by the sound. He shrieked as the creature lifted him out of the water for the second time.

"Get your hands off me!" he spluttered. "Or flippers, or whatever you call them!"

"Brother Bernard," sang the deep voice of the watery creature, "why won't you swim with us? We get so few visitors! Perhaps your friend is a bit more adventurous?"

Still holding the monk in its arms, the creature turned to face Ben. The monk immediately stopped thrashing and stared at Ben in shock.

"Who are you?" he cried. "Where did you come from? Did you follow me? Who are you working for?"

Ben ignored the torrent of questions; his attention was entirely focussed on the strange creature. He felt no fear as it glided towards him and deposited the monk in the shallows at his feet. The sodden monk scrambled frantically towards the door, his eyes darting from the boy to the creature in the lake.

Ben took a step closer to the creature which now lolled in the water before him. Close up, he could see that it was covered in tiny scales which cast dappled reflections upon the surface of the lake. Its human-like torso ended in an enormous tail which swept lazily through the water.

"I am Prince Trestan," it said in its deep, soft voice, "Holder of the Trident and Leader of the Mer-people. Welcome to our prison."

* * *

In the ballroom, the empty platters were being cleared and the dancing was about to begin. The moment the musicians struck up the first few notes, Penthesilean took Bella's arm and led her out onto the floor. They danced a couple of steps in silence, until he could bear it no longer.

"What's going on, Bella?" he murmured as he spun her round. "I'm finding it impossible to see the king without going through that ridiculous fool, Ponsonby – something which I refuse to do! And now I find the very same bumbling bureaucrat hovering around you like a fat wasp on a picnic, and you a bundle of nerves."

She began to voice a denial.

"Bella, I know you too well," he interrupted. "We go back a long way – you should know by now that you can trust me. So tell me, what is going on?"

Bella looked up at him thoughtfully. It would be a relief to share the burden with an old friend. Making up her mind, she continued the story from where Princess Madeleine had left off, describing how she had saved the young thief from being discovered by Ponsonby's men and then smuggled him into the palace.

She hesitated a moment before saying, "I've sent him to steal the Book of Prophecies."

"The Book of Prophecies?" cried Penthesilean, louder than he had intended. He quickly lowered his voice. "I thought you'd given that up after what happened all those years ago . . ."

He broke off as a couple danced close to them. They both smiled a polite greeting at the large, overdressed and bejewelled duchess who glided past clutching an elderly military gentleman to her bosom, his feet barely skimming the floor.

"I never gave up!" hissed Bella fiercely, once they were out of earshot. "And I never will, especially now. It's more important than ever that we find the Book. The rebels are restless, and, to those of us who remember, this echoes the time of the Great Fire of –"

"Of Barbearland," said Penthesilean, completing her sentence.

"You sense it too," said Bella, once more noticing the lines of weariness on his face. "But that's not all. Since the wall went up around Quadrivium it has become a different place, full of fear and suspicion. People are starting to lose faith in the king with each new law which is passed by the council. They've even banned those who claim to be able to read the future, including traditional fortune tellers: all branded as cheats and con men by Mayor Ponsonby."

"Can't you stop it?" asked Penthesilean, surprised. "You're a senior member of the king's council, aren't you?"

"Not anymore," answered Bella. "I was forced into retirement after I was the only member to speak out against the building of the wall. I was accused of being uninformed and out of touch! Can you believe it? But at least it gave me more time to spend on locating the Book . . ."

She stopped as she caught sight of Ponsonby re-entering the ballroom. He stood just inside the grand entrance, scanning the room with intent. His expression changed as he caught sight of them on the dance floor and he headed quickly in their direction, threading his way through the dancers. In a loud voice, she said, "Oh Penthesilean, I suddenly feel a bit faint! Would you be so kind as to escort me to the terrace?"

A flicker of annoyance crossed the mayor's face as he watched them depart. It was instantly replaced by an ingratiating smile as the plump duchess greeted him loudly. "Mayor Ponsonby, just the person I wanted to see! Allow me to introduce my dear friend, the General . . ."

The duchess's voice faded into the general babble of conversation as Bella and Penthesilean stepped through the glass doors and onto the terrace. It looked out over beautifully manicured lawns where tiny coloured lights had been strung up in the branches of the trees, creating a festive atmosphere. Couples strolled arm in arm through the gardens, enjoying the cool night air. He ushered her to a quiet spot close to the french windows which stretched the length of the terrace. Through the windows they had a good view of the ballroom where the dancers twirled and spun like many coloured butterflies.

Bella sank down onto a stone bench while Penthesilean paced up and down before her.

"I can understand why you want to find the Book," he began, "but was it really a good idea to send a boy to do a man's job, especially after what happened last time? Damien was barely more than a boy himself when he disappeared!"

He turned on his heel and stared down at Bella, who had the grace to look a little shamefaced.

"This is going to sound desperate," she began, "but hear me out. I went to see a woman I know in the old part of the city, she sees things and has been useful to me in the past – although, strictly speaking, what she is doing is now against the law. She told me that the Book was being kept under guard right here in the palace, and that there was only one who would be able to retrieve it."

She took a deep breath. "Penthesilean, she described the boy to me in great detail – and not just that, but the exact time and place where I would meet him, which is exactly as it happened and as I have just described to you. And the boy is ideally suited to the task: he's small enough to fit into the old tunnels and nondescript enough to be mistaken for a servant if he's discovered. Perhaps that's where we failed before . . ."

Tears welled up in her eyes and she paused, unable to go on. Penthesilean stopped pacing and knelt at her feet, instantly full of remorse. "Forgive me, Bella. I was insensitive. Your son was a very brave young man."

She looked deep into his honest blue eyes. "You do realise that this could be my chance to find out what happened to him?"

"I hope you're right," said Penthesilean, "but please be careful. Something strange is afoot in the corridors of power, which is one of the reasons I'm here to see the king. I've had a number of battalions recalled to Quadrivium in recent months at a time when I need more men, not less, to control the increasing rebel threat. A wall around the city is not going to be of any use unless we can keep these savages at bay!"

They suddenly realised that the musicians in the ballroom had stopped playing. Bella rose from her seat, peering through the french windows. Between the bemused dancers they caught a glimpse of the spectacle unfolding on the dance floor. In the middle of the room, surrounded by a curious knot of onlookers, stood a very wet, very bedraggled-looking monk gesticulating wildly at a very angry looking Mayor Ponsonby.

6

Ben wondered if he should bow to the strange creature of the lake which had introduced itself to him as a prince. He had just begun to dip his head when he noticed a host of similar creatures emerging from the water and stopped, staring in wonder at the magical sight. The light from the lanterns reflected off their shimmering torsos like dappled sunlight playing on the surface of the underground lake.

The strange rhythmic hum he had noticed earlier had grown louder, and it suddenly occurred to Ben that the creatures were singing. The sound filled him with a deep sense of contentment mixed with an undefinable feeling of sadness. When one of them reached out to him, he did not hesitate. He waded out into the water, which was noticeably warmer than before, and took the welcoming hand of the creature.

* * *

His mother was brushing her hair, singing a lullaby he did not recognise, the notes rising and falling in time with her brush strokes. Starting at the top of her head, she ran the silver brush through her long hair, and he watched each strand fall from the brush as she reached the ends. Then she started over again.

Ben was content to rest his head on the soft pillow and listen to her sing as she brushed her hair, the candlelight casting a warm glow on the smooth skin of her shoulders. Mesmerised, he watched the hair fall from her brush, strands of long, greeny-blue hair, as beautiful as woven water . . .

He gradually became fully awake. The beautiful mermaid put down her brush and smiled at him. Then, without a word, she flipped backwards and disappeared with a splash.

He propped himself up on his elbow, blinking the sleep from his eyes. He was in a small wooden boat which rocked gently as he moved. Tiny candles had been placed along the sides, their flickering light illuminating the bed on which he lay, which took up almost the whole of the boat. The dream of his mother lingered and he struggled to recall her features. His memories of her were vague and elusive. He recalled soft, sweet-smelling skin, long, fair hair which tickled his face when she leant down to kiss him, and a sense of security and happiness, much the same as he felt right now. Unbidden, recollections from his earlier childhood came flooding back.

His mother had disappeared one day when he was very young, when he could barely walk, and his father had remarried. His stepmother was a dark-haired, slovenly woman who had produced three children in quick succession, swarthy children whose appearance contrasted sharply with his own fair colouring. She found fault in everything he did, and he began to spend more and more time away from his father's house, making friends with the street children who sheltered by night in an abandoned inn. One day he had returned to find his father and step-family gone. A neighbour, seeing him standing by the gate, told him that they had disappeared suddenly overnight, and had hinted at his stepmother's gambling debts. Then she had taken a locket from her apron pocket and handed it to him.

"Your father gave me this a few days before they disappeared," she had told him kindly. "It was your mother's – he told me it was the only thing he wouldn't sell to settle your stepmother's debts. He asked me to give it to you if you ever returned."

He recalled how she had hesitated before adding, "He loved you and your mother very much, you know. It wasn't easy for him to take you in, you being another man's child and all, but he loved you like his own. And then when your mother just upped and left, well . . ."

After the revelation that the man who had brought him up was not his real father, Ben had not waited to hear any more. He had grabbed the locket from her hand, then turned and fled. Ever since that day he had worn it on a leather cord around his neck, hidden beneath his clothing. The locket was his only link to his mother and he had never told anyone about it.

Reaching up, Ben felt for the locket. With a jolt, he realised it was gone.

* * *

The roof of the cavern rippled with light as the mer-people gathered beneath the central stalactite. One by one, more faces appeared above the waters of the lake as Prince Trestan's summons spread. Those who had not yet seen the boy were curious to know why this stranger had been admitted to the Inner Depths rather than being turned back at the Shallows. Their purpose was to guard the chamber from intruders; only the monks were meant to have access, although even they rarely ventured beyond the Shallows.

Prince Trestan looked out over the sea of faces gathered before him. Holding the locket above his head for all to see, he prised open the twin ovals of silver. On one side was a miniature portrait of a young woman with long, fair hair. Gasps echoed round the chamber.

"Teah!"

"He is her child!"

"She has sent him to us!"

Prince Trestan waited for the joyful cries to die down.

Finally he spoke. "If any among us still doubt that the Deliverer is in our midst, let them speak."

There was silence. Prince Trestan continued, "So there is complete agreement that he be taken to the Book of Prophecies?"

There was some muttering from the back. Prince Trestan turned towards the sound. "Trenor? Do you have something to say?"

With muted splashing, the crowd parted and a slightly-built merman made his way to the front. His skin was pale compared to the rich green-grey hues of Prince Trestan's colouring. He bowed his head briefly in the prince's direction before turning to face the gathering, holding up one hand to silence their anxious murmuring.

"I agree that this boy may be the Deliverer," he said, "but we are duty-bound to protect the Book."

"Duty?" snorted Prince Trestan in disgust. "Do not speak to me of duty! We were tricked into this underground cavern and blackmailed into serving the one who imprisoned us! This child is Teah's son; she has sent him to us as was foretold by our ancestors. Surely our duty is to him, the Deliverer, the one prophesied by our forefathers to save our race and others like us?"

Many of the mer-people splashed their tails on the water in a chorus of agreement. A high, female voice rang out, "The Deliverer may be our only chance to see our children again, Trenor!"

Trenor bowed his head at these words. "I too want to

see our young ones, and feel the open water on my tail!
But can we risk everything on this boy?"

Prince Trestan looked deep into Trenor's eyes. "I would
put my trust in the Deliverer a thousand times over rather
than trust the one who trapped us in this cavern! Do I
have to remind you, Trenor, of how our children and our
freedom were taken from us? Now we have a chance to
regain our dignity, if nothing else!"

Drowning out Trenor's response, the mer-people called
out in unison, "Let us take the Deliverer to the Book of
Prophecies!"

* * *

Ben was jolted fully awake with the realisation that his
locket was missing. He soon discovered that all his clothes
were gone too – beneath the soft furs he was as naked as
the day he was born. He scrambled to the side of the boat
and leaned out. Staring back up at him was the face of a
young, blonde-haired boy. It took Ben a moment to realise
he was looking at a reflection of himself. He reached up
to touch his hair; it felt strangely soft and unusually free of
tangles. He looked down at his hand; even his fingernails
had been scrubbed clean, and he felt as refreshed as if he'd
enjoyed a full night's sleep. He wondered how long he had
been asleep.

The last thing he remembered was a pretty girl with long,
blue-green hair which cascaded over her shoulders like a

waterfall handing him a deliciously creamy concoction which he had wolfed down without hesitation. He groaned out loud as he realised he had fallen for the oldest trick in the book: she must have slipped him a sleeping draught.

He had a vivid recollection of the look in Bella's eyes as she'd handed him the skeleton key. He'd seen that look many times before; he knew that she expected him to steal it and he'd looked forward to proving her wrong. But now the key, along with his clothes and his precious locket, was also gone.

He looked down into the water again, trying to see through his reflection to gauge how deep the lake was. He wished that he had learnt to swim, but it had never seemed important in his line of work. With another groan, he flung himself back onto the bed of furs.

Consumed with frustration, Ben did not notice the boat begin to rock. Suddenly Prince Trestan appeared, his elbows resting gently on the side of the boat.

"Your belongings are in a chest under the bed," he said in his soft, deep voice. "You have rested well and now it is time for you to leave us."

Ben was scrambling through the furs before Prince Trestan had finished speaking. He found the chest and flung it open to reveal his clothes, clean and neatly folded. But, more importantly, lying on top of them were his locket and Bella's key. He snatched them up and pressed them to his bare chest.

After a moment, Prince Trestan reached forward and

gently eased the two objects from Ben's hand. He carefully unthreaded them from the worn leather cord which he dropped into the water, then, reaching up, he pulled a single strand of greeny-blue hair from his head. He threaded first the locket and then the key onto the strand of hair and secured it with an intricate knot before placing it around Ben's neck. Ben felt the familiar weight of the key and locket against his chest and touched the hair, doubtful whether it would hold. He looked down in surprise. The hair had vanished and in its place was a fine silver chain.

"My gift to you," said Prince Trestan. "It will keep your treasures safe."

Ben hesitated, not wanting to seem ungrateful. "Thank you," he began, "but . . . there's something else I came here for."

"I know," replied Prince Trestan. "You are here for the Book of Prophecies."

Ben opened his mouth in surprise, but before he could speak, the merman continued. "And now you are here it is my duty to take you to it." Dropping back down into the water, he added with a chortle, "Although it may be a good idea if you got dressed first . . ."

Ben quickly pulled on his clothes, enjoying the unfamiliar sensation of clean fabric against his skin. He lost his balance as the boat began to move and collapsed back onto the bed. Quickly pulling himself up, he saw that Prince Trestan had been joined by a large group of mermen, each of whom was pulling a rope which was attached to the boat. Ben gazed into the water, fascinated by the powerful sweep of the creatures' tails as they pulled him and the boat swiftly onwards.

* * *

It became steadily colder and darker as they made their way deeper into the cavern. One by one, the candles on the boat sputtered and died. The boat moved silently between the pools of light cast by the overhead lanterns like stepping stones on the water.

Ben peered forward, his eyes straining to penetrate the darkness. Suddenly he saw a flicker of light up ahead, smaller but much brighter than the lanterns. At first he thought it was his imagination, but no matter how many times he blinked it was still there. He kept his eyes fixed on it.

As they drew closer, a cage appeared out of the gloom, suspended a few feet above the water. The light shone out from within, casting striped shadows across the calm surface of the lake. Ben held up an arm to shield his eyes. The light was so bright after the darkness of the cavern that he found it hurt his eyes to look directly at it. One by one the mermen released the ropes and the boat's momentum carried it gently forwards.

Ben was almost directly beneath the cage when a strong current caught the boat side on, nearly throwing him into the water. He grabbed the side of the boat with both hands and clung on as it rocked violently. Then the current caught it again, dragging it round in a huge circle beneath the cage, slowly at first, and then faster and faster. The boat listed heavily to one side and he found himself looking down into a giant whirlpool as it continued to spin madly round and round. He looked frantically for help, but the mermen were watching from a safe distance, steadying themselves against the pull of the current with their powerful tails.

"We can come no closer, the power of the cage weakens us," called Prince Trestan over the sound of the water. "Therein you will find what you seek. Don't be afraid, you possess more power than you know."

Ben watched in dismay as the mermen disappeared beneath the waters of the lake. Feeling utterly helpless and alone, he clung to the side of the boat as it was sucked inevitably towards the centre of the vortex.

Then suddenly, with a loud crack, the boat began to break apart. Water rushed in between the boards until the furs on the bed were swamped. Ben jumped up into a crouch, balancing unsteadily on the bed as the boat continued to spin. The water inched steadily above his ankles. He rose into a standing position, then ducked as the cage loomed suddenly overhead.

Thinking quickly, he timed the next rotation and took a flying leap. He got one hand around the bars at the bottom of the cage and clung on. The water below him churned and bubbled as the boat disappeared into the whirlpool.

And suddenly the waters calmed and were still once more, as though nothing had ever happened. Ben was alone in the silence, hanging by one hand from the bottom of a cage in the middle of an enormous, dark and very deep lake.

* * *

Back in the ballroom, the dripping monk had been hurried away by Mayor Ponsonby, and the dancing resumed. Bella had rushed from the terrace into the ballroom at the sight of the monk, followed closely by Penthesilean. Now she sank down into the nearest chair.

"That was one of the monks who guard the Palace Archives," she whispered, white-faced with shock. "They must have discovered Ben . . ."

"We don't know that," said Penthesilean, grabbing a glass of sparkling wine from a passing waiter and pressing it into her hands. "Drink this, it'll make you feel better."

"And Ponsonby," continued Bella, "I knew there was something suspicious about that man. He must have been involved all along . . ."

"Bella!" said Penthesilean firmly, finally getting her attention. "Listen to me: there's no use speculating. I'm going to follow Ponsonby and see what I can find out."

"I'm coming with you," said Bella, getting to her feet.

"No, it's too dangerous," replied Penthesilean. "If they do have the boy it won't be long before they find out who sent him."

"Well, I can't stay here!" she cried, standing firm before him, even though the top of her head was just about level with his chest. "And I'm sure I'd be much safer with you."

Penthesilean frowned as he looked down at her. He'd commanded thousands of men in his time, but they were nothing compared to this tiny, determined woman.

"Come on, we're wasting valuable time," she said, turning on her heel and colliding with the person behind her.

"Mother!" cried the elegant lady, raising a hand to straighten her tiara which had been knocked askew. "Are you all right?"

"Your most excellent majesty," said Penthesilean, dropping into a low bow.

Queen Katrina smiled at him as she extended her hand. "Penthesilean," she said in her soft, sweet voice. "It is lovely to see you back at court. Is Mother giving you a hard time?"

Penthesilean glanced at Bella, who was hiding her impatience with difficulty.

"Not at all, your majesty," he said, seizing his opportunity. "In fact, she was just telling me how pleased she was to be a grandmother. Now, with your permission, ma'am, I will leave you ladies to talk in peace."

Bella shot him a dark look as he backed away.

"Is everything really all right, Mother?" asked the queen. "You don't look quite yourself tonight."

Bella forced a smile as she watched Penthesilean slip out of the ballroom without her.

"Everything is fine, my dear," she replied. "How could it not be? I am finally a grandmother!"

The queen's lovely face lit up as she thought about her baby boy.

"Yes, we have a lot to be thankful for," she said, softly. "An heir at last! I think it calls for another toast, don't you? To Prince Alexander, may he reign long and in peace, just like his father!"

As they raised their glasses, a nurse dressed in the pale blue uniform of the Royal Nursery entered the ballroom, crying hysterically.

"Your Majesty," she sobbed, as she stumbled towards the queen, "Prince Alexander has vanished! The baby! The baby is gone!"

7

Ben clung to the cage with nothing between him and the still, deep waters of the lake. He tried not to panic, thinking of the many tight spots he'd been in before – but none had been anywhere near as bad as this. His arms felt as though they were being pulled from their sockets and there was no sign of the mermen or the boat, both of which had vanished without a trace beneath the surface of the lake.

He craned his neck to examine the cage, squinting against the bright light which came from somewhere within. The tubular bar which he was clinging to was one of many which interlocked to form the floor of the cage, but he could tell from a glance that the bars were too close together for him to squeeze through.

He considered his options: if he let go of the bars he would drown, and if he held onto the bars eventually he'd become so tired that he'd have to let go and he would drown. He felt the hopelessness of the situation begin to press in on him. His heart began to pound and his breathing suddenly seemed very loud in the silence of the cavernous chamber. An involuntary groan escaped from his lips. Even to his own ears it sounded suspiciously like a whimper, but it felt good to have broken the silence, so, feeling slightly ridiculous, he took a deep breath and began to hum.

A musical note immediately rang out from above his head, continuous, like the sound of someone running their finger round the rim of a crystal goblet. The cage started to vibrate, gently at first but with increasing force. Ben clung tightly to the bars, almost losing his grip as they began to move apart. Soon a large gap had opened up.

He swung his body backwards and forwards, gathering momentum until he was able to hoist his legs up and into the cage. The rest of his body quickly followed with practiced ease and he lay on his back until his pounding heart had slowed to a more normal speed, his eyes screwed shut against the bright light above. He barely noticed the bars rearranging themselves beneath him. Eventually the vibrations stopped and the silence resumed. Ben lay still, waiting for the ringing in his ears to stop.

A small, hard object landed on his face and he brushed it away. It was quickly followed by another which struck him sharply on the nose.

"Ouch!" he cried, opening his eyes and sitting up.

A shower of small missiles struck his head and shoulders. He looked down at his lap which was covered in small, brown seeds.

"What are you doing in my cage?" asked a shrill voice, making him jump. He looked around but there was no one there.

"Up here," sighed the voice.

Ben shielded his eyes with his hand and looked up. Perched on a swing a foot or so above him sat a brightly coloured bird. The emerald crest on its head bobbed up and down as it examined him, its long tail feathers of scarlet, turquoise and yellow sweeping down to almost touch his face.

"What do you want? Who are you? Who sent you?"

Ben stood up slowly, coming eye to eye with the strange bird. It hopped back and forth on its perch in agitation.

"I'm Ben," he said. "Murgatroyd sent me."

The reaction was not what he had hoped for.

"Murgatroyd!" spat the bird, showering him with more birdseed. "What's he doing sending human chicks into my domain?"

"He sent me for the Book of Prophecies," replied Ben, deciding that honesty might be his best policy.

The bird snorted loudly and a burst of steam appeared from its bright orange beak. "The Book? The Book of Prophecies? Murgatroyd really thought that I would give it to you?"

Ben laid his hands on the swing and leaned towards the bird. "Listen, birdie, I have a big reward riding on this, so why don't you just tell me where it is?"

The bird fluttered off its swing and onto a higher perch, squawking loudly. "You can't threaten me! Anyway, you're too late! Ha! Too late! The Book isn't here! And even if it was, I wouldn't give it to you!"

"So what's that then?" asked Ben, pointing at the light. Either the glare had faded or his eyes had grown accustomed to it, for he found that he was now able to look straight into the ball of light and see – suspended in the centre as if floating within the brilliance – a roll of parchment tied with a red ribbon.

"Ha! That's nothing of importance," scoffed the bird. "He had to leave part of the Book here so those fish-folk would still be bound by the enchantment. But it's only a blank page . . ."

It snapped its beak shut, suddenly aware that it had said too much, but Ben had heard enough. If this was a page from the Book of Prophecies, it might be enough to ensure at least some of the reward, he thought to himself. He stood on his tiptoes and stretched his arm out, but he couldn't quite reach it.

"What are you doing?" shrieked the bird, jumping up and down.

Ben looked around the cage thoughtfully, then, taking hold of the swing, he wedged one foot on its crossbar and pulled himself up, balancing precariously with all his weight on that foot. He brushed the bird away with one swift motion of his hand and placed the other foot on its perch.

The bird's shrill protests reached a crescendo as Ben reached out to take the roll of parchment. "No, don't do it! The enchantment will be broken! We'll all be doomed!"

Ben felt a slight resistance, like plucking a grape from a vine, as he pulled the parchment from the centre of the light. With a slight plop, it came away in his hand. Two things immediately followed. The light vanished, plunging the cage into darkness. At the same time, the cage itself began to shudder and shake. Ben lost his balance and lunged for the bars, but instead, grabbed a handful of feathers. As he hit the floor of the cage, the bars moved swiftly apart with a noise like swords clashing and he fell straight through, into the dark lake below.

He gasped in shock as he entered the icy water, instinctively screwing his eyes tightly shut. The cold seemed to penetrate to his bones. He bobbed back up to the surface just long enough to take a deep breath of air before the weight of the key around his neck pulled him headfirst down through the water. He opened his eyes in panic; to his astonishment, he found that he could see perfectly well. The underwater world was lit by a milky glow, as though moonlight were shining up through the water from the bottom of the lake.

He wasn't sure how much longer he could hold his breath. In desperation, he was about to wrench the silver chain from around his neck – along with the key and his precious locket – and kick his way back to the surface when he spied a large door looming up towards him. Before he had time to react, the key smoothly entered the lock and the door fell outwards, tumbling Ben and gallons of water in a gushing waterfall through the open doorway at the bottom of the lake.

* * *

Ponsonby narrowed his eyes, which were already pushed into slits by the mounds of flesh on his cheeks. His bodyguards' flaring torches laid bare the scene before him. The empty lake looked like the surface of some uninhabitable planet, covered with a thick, slimy mud and pockmarked with craters the size of a carriage. There was not a single drop of water to be seen.

Without a word, the mayor reached out a hand towards the group of trembling monks standing behind him. One of them quickly passed him a small telescope which he raised to one of his small, piggy eyes. He sighed as the sight only confirmed what he already suspected: there was no sign of the mermen, no Guardian and, most importantly, no Book of Prophecies.

Carefully scanning the bottom of the empty lake, he

found a single, bedraggled red feather lying next to the Guardian's battered cage. He lowered the telescope.

"You imbeciles!" he erupted. "The door was to be kept locked at all times! This location was supposed to be a secret! What happened?"

The other monks hurriedly pushed Brother Bernard, still in his wet robes, to the front of the group and shuffled backwards into the shadows.

"It's like I said, sir, the boy had a key of his own!" protested Brother Bernard, pausing for a loud sniff. "I made sure the door was locked behind me, but the boy had a key! I saw it around his neck after the mermen attacked me!"

Ponsonby turned his back on the snivelling monk, grinding his teeth in frustration. Twice in one day he had been made to look a fool by a mere boy! He didn't believe in coincidences.

"Get me the captain of my household guards!" he yelled, furiously. "I don't care if he is busy helping to look for the prince; I want to see him in my chambers immediately!"

Growling an unprintable curse, he turned on his heel. But the wet mud lay thickly underfoot and his shoe stuck fast, leaving his stockinged foot to pop free. He teetered on the other foot, arms flailing.

"Help me, you fools!" he cried as he lost his balance and slowly, inevitably, keeled headfirst into the mud.

*   *   *

Ben opened his eyes and looked up at the night sky. He smiled dreamily to himself as a shooting star blazed a trail through the darkness, but before he had time to make a wish, he saw another one. And then another. He slowly came to his senses as it dawned on him that something was not quite right: in his experience, shooting stars were not usually red.

He sat up and looked around, rubbing his elbow. His immediate surroundings were lit by the reddish-pink glow of the bright lights overhead which flared and then ebbed as they burnt up and fell to earth. Tall reeds surrounded the little patch of wet mud on which he sat surrounded by puddles of water. His clothes were soaking wet. Shivering, he got to his feet and pushed the reeds aside to find that he was surrounded by more water.

Something caught his eye and he looked down to see a limp red feather caught amongst the reeds. He reached over and fished it out, images of the argumentative, jewel-coloured bird flashing before his eyes. He suddenly remembered falling through the bars of the cage and into the underground lake, and the awful sensation of being pulled under the water by the weight of the key. That was the last thing he remembered. He felt like he had swallowed gallons of water.

He reached instinctively for his locket and relaxed slightly when he found that it was still there along with the key, both secure on Prince Trestan's chain. Then he remembered the page from the Book of Prophecies and his heart gave a sickening lurch. He clearly recalled grasping it tightly in his hand as he plunged into the water, but he guessed that he must have dropped it somewhere between the lake and this muddy island. It had probably been destroyed by the water anyway, he thought to himself; it would be nothing more than a soggy mess. He could say goodbye to Bella's reward. He felt dizzy and sat back down in the mud. He was too busy pondering his streak of bad luck to notice a rustling in the reeds behind him.

"Thought I saw something!" said a cheerful voice, making him jump. "Hang on a sec' and I'll be right with you."

The prow of a boat nosed its way between the reeds and came to rest in front of him. A short, stocky man dressed in loose trousers and a tunic made of coarse brown cloth jumped out and hauled the boat up onto the mud. He looked down at Ben.

"That's a lucky escape you've just had, friend," he said. "Flash floods like that can take a man out in seconds, never mind a scrap of a lad like you!"

"What's going on, Monty?"

The head of a second man appeared above the reeds, gliding smoothly towards them.

"It's just a wee boy, Jared," called Monty. "Why don't you carry on with the patrol while I take this young 'un back to the camp for some dry clothes."

The other man peered at Ben suspiciously, a frown creasing his forehead. Then his expression suddenly changed.

"What in Tritan's name is that?" he cried, pointing at something behind them.

Ben turned to look and jumped to his feet with a cry. Shining out from amongst the spindly branches of a nearby tree was a bright, twinkling light. Before either of the two men could react, he had raced over, reached one hand into the centre of the light and pulled out the page from the Book of Prophecies. As soon as he touched the parchment, the light went out.

"What is it?" asked Monty, his eyes wide.

"Witchcraft!" growled Jared. "It's his kind that brought us to the attention of the palace in the first place. He's trouble, Monty! We should just leave him here for the soldiers to find. I'm willing to bet that he's the reason for those flares."

"If that's the case, then all the more reason to help him," said Monty reasonably. "We common folk need to stick together in these troubled times." He held out his hand to Ben. "Come on, lad, let's get you back to camp. You look like you could use some of my Minny's hot soup."

Jared scowled and pulled on his oars to back his boat

out into the river.

"He's trouble, I tell you," he called over his shoulder as he disappeared behind the reeds. "Take him back to camp if you must and then get back on patrol! Our priority is to keep our families safe from the soldiers and I need every available man out on the water!"

Monty smiled apologetically at Ben as Jared disappeared.

"You've got to excuse him," he said. "We've had a lot of trouble from the soldiers lately. It seems some laws have been passed to stop us moving about so much, but that's what we do, we river folk, we go with the tides like Tritan intended. But someone up there in Quadrivium doesn't like it . . ."

Ben took hold of Monty's outstretched hand and stepped into his boat, clutching the page from the Book of Prophecies to his chest.

"Now, I don't know what you've got there," continued Monty, "and to be perfectly honest, I think I'd prefer it if you didn't tell me. One of our elders dabbles in the ancient arts and I've no doubt she will be very interested in what you've found, but the only thing I'm interested in is getting you off the floodplain and safely back to camp."

Once Ben was settled in the bottom of the boat, Monty pushed off and with a few expert strokes had soon reached a deeper channel. Ben watched the muddy water flow by. Eventually the excitement of the last few hours, helped by the gentle rocking of the boat, caught up with him and he fell asleep.

* * *

Ben woke the instant the boat stopped moving. He lay still with his eyes closed, warm and content under the blanket which Monty had thrown over him. He felt the boat rock as Monty stood up, then heard a splash followed by the rasp of the flat-bottomed boat on sand.

Hearing voices, he reluctantly opened his eyes and lifted his head. A group of people were converging on Monty from a nearby thicket of trees.

"What are you doing back so soon?"

"Where's Jared? What's happened?"

"Who's that in the boat?"

Suddenly, a commanding voice cut through the voices. "Silence!"

The knot of people surrounding Monty parted, revealing a hunched-back old woman carrying a large staff which was taller than she was. A long, grey plait hung down over one shoulder, almost touching the ground. She glared at the others who fell back to give her room.

"Where is he?" she asked Monty, poking him in the shoulder with her staff. "Where is the boy?"

Monty glanced back towards the boat. Ben quickly lowered his head.

"He's asleep in the boat," said Monty. "But Dolora,

how could you have possibly known about him?"

She was already hurrying past him to the water's edge, but turned suddenly and flung both arms in the air.

"The bird knows all," she cackled dementedly, pointing the staff into the night sky.

Peeping over the edge of the boat, Ben's eyes followed the direction of her stick. He caught a fleeting glimpse of the silhouette passing overhead, before it disappeared into the shadows of the trees.

8

The celebrations in the ballroom had come to an abrupt end with the news of the young prince's disappearance. The musicians stopped playing and guests gathered in small groups, shocked that such a thing could have happened. On hearing the news, the queen had rushed sobbing into the king's arms and now they stood clasped in a tight embrace in the centre of the dance floor. Finally the king gently broke away to address the head of the Royal Household Guards who was waiting for his instructions.

"Seal all exits!" he commanded, his voice steady despite the worry on his face. "No one goes in or out of this room or the palace until I say so. The search begins immediately! We must find Alexander!"

He strode from the room followed by the queen supported on all sides by her ladies-in-waiting. Bella tagged onto the back of the little procession and the doors closed behind her, locking all the other guests inside the ballroom with a posting of guards to ensure that no one entered or left according to the king's orders. She followed the cluster of weeping ladies along the hallway towards the queen's private chambers, falling behind until she could slip away unnoticed.

She made her way swiftly back to the entrance hall with the wide staircase which led to the corridor of armour and the throne room. Kicking off her dancing shoes, she hid them in a nearby potted palm, then, silent in her silk-stockinged feet, she ran up the stairs. At the top, she paused to check that the coast was clear. She heard footsteps and men's voices approaching and raced in the opposite direction, not wanting to have to explain why she wasn't comforting her daughter. As she rounded the corner she skidded to a halt. The corridor ahead was lit by a fierce glow, so sudden and bright that it dazzled her eyes. Instinctively, she raised an arm to protect her face. The suits of armour which lined the walls were engulfed in flames leaping up the high stone walls towards the wooden ceiling.

Slowly she lowered her arm as she realised she could feel no heat from the flames, nor were they doing any visible damage. The corridor was not on fire, instead the flames appeared to be projected onto the walls by the suits of armour. She walked slowly towards them, gazing in wonder at the silent inferno raging within. She had never before witnessed anything like this.

Abruptly, the flames vanished and the armour reflected nothing more than a dull gleam in the dim, unlit corridor. If it hadn't been for the image of the flames dancing on the insides of her eyelids, she would have thought that she had imagined the whole thing.

A sudden footstep behind her broke the silence. She spun round, going weak with relief as she saw Penthesilean's unmistakeable figure at the far end of the corridor, silhouetted against the lamplight from the staircase behind him. She rushed forwards and then stopped. He was holding himself very still, tense and upright. Something was wrong.

Then out of the shadows behind him stepped Mayor Ponsonby, holding a needle-like dagger against Penthesilean's side. He was accompanied by a group of rough-looking bodyguards and the same damp monk she had seen in the ballroom.

* * *

Ben lay in the bottom of the boat with his eyes tightly closed. He heard footsteps approach.

"Open your eyes, boy," said a voice. "I know you're not asleep."

He slowly opened one eye and looked up into the face of the old woman hovering over him.

"That's better," she said, not unkindly. "So, you're

Ben. Murgatroyd told me to expect you. He had some urgent business to deal with, but he'll be back soon. In the meantime, we'll try and make you comfortable."

She beckoned Monty over and instructed him to take Ben back to the camp and make sure he was given food and drink.

"Don't worry," he whispered as he led Ben towards the trees. "Dolora can seem a bit scary, but she's not dangerous. I just think she's a bit mad. She says the animals talk to her . . ."

When they reached the camp, a silent, dark-haired woman took Ben's arm and led him to a deerskin tent filled with soft, warm furs and candlelight. Laid out neatly on top of the furs was a set of clothes just like Monty's. Another woman entered the tent and wordlessly handed him a steaming mug of broth, and then both women left, pulling the tent flap closed behind them.

He sniffed the mug suspiciously, then took a cautious sip. It was delicious. Before he knew it, he had finished the whole lot. Still standing, he drew the rolled parchment from beneath his shirt where he had tucked it for safekeeping. He was surprised to find that it wasn't the slightest bit damp, unlike his clothes. Instead it smelt old and musty and the yellowed paper crackled drily in his hands. He threw it down onto the furs and quickly changed into the warm, dry clothes. The trousers were too large for him, but once he had rolled up the bottoms and tightened the rope belt about his waist, they fit well enough. Then, unrolling the parchment, he gazed for the first time at the page from the Book of Prophecies.

Despite what the bird had told him in the underground chamber, the sheet was not blank. It was completely covered on both sides with tiny scribbles and diagrams, scratched so deeply that they had left indentations in the thick paper. He brought the parchment closer to his eyes, trying to decipher its meaning.

A large yawn took him by surprise. The warm soup was starting to take effect and his eyelids were growing heavy. He blinked a few times and stared once more at the diagrams, but they swam before his eyes, merging into one another. Reluctantly he released the parchment, allowing it to spring back into a roll, and tucked it carefully under his dry shirt, next to his locket and the key which were still securely attached to Prince Trestan's silver chain. Then, curling up amongst the furs, he fell into a deep sleep.

* * *

Bella stared down the corridor at Ponsonby and his henchmen. She darted towards the nearest suit of armour and tugged at the axe held tightly in its grasp, but it would not come free.

A moment later she felt herself grabbed roughly from behind.

"Unhand me at once!" she cried, trying to shake off the two burly men who had taken hold of her.

"I'm afraid they can't do that," said Ponsonby with an arrogant sneer, showing none of his earlier deference. "You see, they take orders from me and me alone. Now, I think you have some information I need rather badly, so if you'll just come this way. We don't want the king to find us in this awkward predicament, now do we?"

Without waiting for her reply, he set off at a surprisingly quick pace down the corridor. The two guards lifted her clear off the ground and followed, with the grim-faced monk following silently behind.

But the guards holding Penthesilean were struggling to restrain him. Despite the fact that he was older by far and outnumbered four to one, he was taller and stronger than any of them and refused to go quietly. He twisted in their grip, wrenching his arms free and kicking out. One of the guards fell to the ground, clutching his shin. Another covered his face with his hands, blood pouring from his nose.

Ponsonby stopped and sighed. Drawing the dagger from his robes, he turned and walked slowly back to where the old soldier stood, chest heaving, finally restrained by the two uninjured bodyguards. Tapping the blade against the palm of his hand, he thrust his jowly face up towards him.

"I only need one of you," he said in a low voice, "and

now that I have the Dowager Bella – who, I suspect, knows a great deal more about the boy than you –" he placed the end of the blade against Penthesilean's chest for emphasis, "I believe you are now surplus to requirements!"

Turning on his heel, he said over his shoulder to the guards, "Shackle him and throw him in the dungeons!"

* * *

Ben was woken by a high-pitched scream. He opened his eyes and stared at the canvas above him, his heart beating loudly against his ribs. It took a moment before he remembered that he was in a tent in the camp of the river people. He sat up as another scream came from just outside his tent.

Strange shadows danced on the canvas all around him, silhouetted against a fierce orange glow. He quickly threw aside his fur covers and pushed back the tent flap, then froze in horror at the sight which met his eyes.

The camp had been engulfed by a fire which raged in all directions. Through the flames he could see shadowy figures running back and forth. He flinched as a four-legged creature leapt out of the flames towards him. Its tail was on fire, spitting sparks in every direction as the beast flicked it from side to side, desperately trying to shake off the flames. Without thinking, he snatched up one of the furs from the tent and grabbed the beast's tail. With a loud scream, it reared up on its hind legs. Ben fell to the ground and rolled into a ball, covering his head with his arms.

With a thud, the animal came back down onto all fours. It had stopped screaming. Cautiously, Ben lifted his head. The beast was standing over him, its hooves inches from his face. His eyes travelled slowly up the strong hairy legs to the broad chest of the animal, and then into the face of a bearded man who was staring back at him with a mixture of relief and surprise.

"You put out the flames!" it said in a deep baritone, its voice trembling with emotion. "You saved my life!"

Ben sat up slowly, staring at the beast before him. For the second time in only a few hours he was looking at the strangest creature he had ever seen in his life. It had the muscular body and strong legs of a horse, but from the chest upwards its appearance was that of a man. From the top of its head, all the way down its human neck to its more equine parts, ran a ridge of hair very much like a mane.

The creature got to its knees before him. "If you saved me, you can save the others. Please, climb up onto my back. We must hurry!"

Ben stood and gathered up all the furs from the tent, which was now starting to smoulder as the flames drew closer. Throwing the furs across the creature's back, he took hold of its mane and clambered on top of them. The creature rose in one smooth motion, crying over its shoulder as it first began to trot and then broke into a canter, "Hold on!"

With these words, it took off and with one flying leap was over the wall of flames and into the heart of the blaze.

* * *

Bella opened her eyes. She had guessed where Ponsonby and his men were taking her as soon as they had begun climbing the interminable circular flight of steps. Now that she had been left alone, she had time to look around and found that her guess had been correct. The turret room was small and perfectly round. The only light came from the pale, milky glow of the moon which seeped in through narrow slits set deep into the curved stone walls. Apart from the heavy wooden chair to which she was tied, the room was completely bare. The only way in or out was through the trapdoor set into the wooden floor.

As she stared longingly at the trapdoor, it was suddenly flung open. Two filthy hands appeared, followed by the greasy, grey hair and leering grin of her gaoler as he clambered up the ladder and into the room.

"Hello, milady," he said, rubbing his hands. "Bit nippy up here, isn't it? Can I tuck you in for the night?"

Taking a thin, dirty blanket from over his shoulder, he tucked it carefully around her. Bella strained against the ropes binding her to the chair as he wheezed his disgusting breath into her face.

"We're going to get along just fine, you and me," he said, walking behind her chair and placing his hands on her shoulders. "Mayor Ponsonby promised to find me a new wife after poor Ermintrude's untimely accident with the pigs. And he's a man who always keeps his promises. . ."

She repressed a shudder as the old man ran a bony finger down her cheek.

"Jobsworth! You're wanted in the kitchens."

The old man jumped as if he had been shot. Ponsonby climbed up into the room and stood before them.

"Yes, yes, immediately Mayor Ponsonby, sir!"

The mayor's eyes didn't leave Bella's face as his servant bowed and scraped before him and finally disappeared down the ladder.

"Don't think you can charm your way out of here," he sneered. "Jobsworth may think he's found himself a pretty prize, but before he has you for his wife, you're going to tell me everything I want to know."

"How dare you?" whispered Bella furiously. "My daughter will be looking for me! The king will have you beheaded for treating me in this appalling way!"

Ponsonby strolled around the small room, examining his fingernails.

"Oh, I really don't think so," he said, nonchalantly. "It's very late, you see, and His Royal Highness has other things on his mind, what with the disappearance of his son and heir. Oh, and don't think Penthesilean will come to get you either. He's a bit . . . ah, shall we say *tied up* at the moment."

After snorting through his nose at his own little joke, Ponsonby suddenly grew serious. He thrust his face down towards her. "Where is the boy?"

"I don't know who you mean," replied Bella firmly, turning her head away.

"Oh, I think you do," said the mayor menacingly, circling her chair. "Who else would send a boy to steal the Book of Prophecies, except the mother of the one who went before?"

She flinched, surprised by how much he knew.

"And I don't believe it was a coincidence that a boy vanished without trace this afternoon after trying to steal my chain of office," he continued. "Do you know that the only place my men didn't search was in the two royal carriages? And I certainly don't suspect the king of concealing the thief!"

"I don't know what you're talking about!" said Bella, thrusting her chin in the air.

"Then you had better start thinking quickly!" Ponsonby turned on her angrily. "Where is he?"

She stared up at him defiantly. "Even if I did know where he was, I'd never tell you! I don't know what your game is, but I've never trusted you and believe me, once I get out of here, you won't be swanning around as mayor for very much longer!"

"Oh, my dear Bella," laughed Ponsonby humourlessly. "No one is going to be looking for you while the young prince is still missing, are they? And he can remain missing for just as long as it takes to get the Book of Prophecies back!"

Bella managed to conceal her look of shock, but her brain was analysing the mayor's words. If the Book was missing, it meant that Ben had been successful. But what was more important now: reading from the Book of Prophecies in order to prevent a war with the rebels, or getting back the heir to the throne?

She was brought back to the present as Ponsonby placed his hands on his knees and bent over to look her straight in the eye.

"Now, I'm not an unreasonable man – trust me, I'm not. What I'm proposing is a simple swap . . ." He licked his lips and brought his head so close to hers she could see crusted remnants of the chilli and chocolate pudding at the corners of his mouth. "You tell me where I can find the boy, and once I have him, I will release Prince Alexander. If you refuse, then the only way you'll get out of this tower will be as Jobsworth's new wife – and no one is going to take much notice of the wife of a latrine cleaner!"

With a snort of grim laughter, he turned away and, huffing and puffing, made his way down the ladder, pulling the trapdoor closed behind him.

Bella let her head fall down onto her chest and considered her situation. Her disappearance could go unnoticed for days while everyone searched for the young prince! But she had no idea where Ben was right now. She needed to get out of here and find Murgatroyd.

She was so deep in thought that she didn't notice the scratching above her head until a small heap of dust landed in her lap. Startled, she looked up to see an extraordinary face peering through a newly made gap in the turret roof. Bulging eyes stared out from a face of such startling ugliness that Jobsworth would have appeared almost handsome in comparison. A wrinkled, pig-like snout protruded above a mouth filled with too many teeth and a long, curling tongue with which the creature licked its fat lips. Bella frowned. She had seen a face like this before, many times.

"You're a gargoyle!" she blurted out in disbelief. As a little girl she had been fascinated by these grotesque stone figures which adorned nearly every wall of the palace. Her nanny had told her they were placed there to ward evil away from the palace and its occupants. Clearly, she thought wryly to herself, they hadn't done a very good job.

The creature stretched its mouth into a wide, dog-like grin.

"But you're not real," she said softly, more to herself than to the creature. "How can you be moving about on the roof of the palace?"

As though in response, the gargoyle continued to tear at the hole until it was big enough for it to squeeze through. A pair of short, stubby wings protruded from its shoulders which it used to lower itself gently down, landing with a thud as its stone feet hit the wooden floor.

Bella stared at the creature as it stood before her, twisting its mouth into many different shapes until it finally emitted a low grunt. "Mugggghhh!"

She frowned. "Are you trying to tell me something?" she asked gently.

The creature's goggle eyes looked as though they would pop out from the strain of trying to speak.

"Take a deep breath," she suggested, wondering as she did whether statues needed to breathe. "Slow down and think about what you want to say."

The creature tried again. "Murrgghhh . . . troyd."

"Murgatroyd? Murgatroyd sent you?"

The gargoyle nodded its stone head so energetically that it knocked a chip out of its chin. "With me. C . . . cc . . . . come."

"You'll have to untie me first."

Half jumping, half flying, the gargoyle tripped round to where her hands were tied to the chair behind her back. Bella tried hard not to flinch as she felt the stone tongue rasp against her wrists. Seconds later, the rope fell to the floor.

She stood up, rubbing her wrists. "Now how do I get

out of here?" she wondered out loud.

The gargoyle had been standing patiently before her like an eager dog awaiting its master's command. Now it began to frantically flap its stubby wings, rising slowly off the floor until it reached the hole in the roof. Bella watched it clamber out, leaving only its stone tail dangling back into the room. The pointed tip hung in front of her nose, seeming to beckon her to grab hold of it. This she did, with both hands, and slowly, inch by inch, the gargoyle pulled her out of the room and onto the roof of the turret.

9

Penthesilean awoke to darkness.   He found himself
lying on a cold, hard floor covered with sharp stones which
dug painfully into his back.   He had no idea how he had
got there; the last thing he remembered was Bella being led
away by Mayor Ponsonby and his henchmen.

He raised a hand to his aching head and groaned
out loud.   Instantly he heard a movement to one side: a
scattering of stones which rattled across the floor.   He sat
up quickly and stared into the impenetrable blackness.
All was still once more, but he could sense someone, or
something, staring back at him.

Slowly and carefully, he placed his hands on the ground
and edged away.   As he moved, a curious slithering noise
followed him.   He shuffled backwards more quickly,
but there was a sudden jerk on his leg and he could go
no further.   His mouth filled with a bitter taste and his
heart began to pound as he realised he was defenceless.   He

strained his ears for any sound which would give away the location of whatever was stalking him, but there was only silence.

Tentatively, he felt down his leg until his fingertips came into contact with an iron shackle clamped round his ankle. Attached to it he could feel a chain pulled taut and he exhaled with relief as he realised that it must have been this which had made the sound. Then he froze as a sigh, slightly hoarser and more like a pant, came through the darkness.

"Who's there?" he cried, his voice sounding very loud and high-pitched.

As though in reply there was another burst of scattered stones and something brushed against his foot. Jumping up into a crouch, Penthesilean waved his arms in front of him. He flinched as he touched something scaly and warm and very much alive. There was a loud hiss and the chain attached to his foot was tugged sharply, causing him to lose his balance. In a flash, the creature was on him, knocking the breath out of him as it bowled him over onto his back. Its weight pressed so deeply onto his chest that he struggled to draw breath. He thrashed from side to side in a desperate attempt to dislodge the creature, but its sharp claws simply dug deeper as it clung on. With one hand he tried to push the creature away, while the other groped in the darkness for a weapon. His fumbling hand touched one of the jagged stones he'd been lying on and he closed his fingers tightly around it. Unable to see a thing in the pitch darkness, he knew that he would only get one chance. He felt the creature's vile breath in his face, its saliva dripping onto his cheek, and aimed carefully for where he guessed its head must be. Then he drew back his arm.

Suddenly he was blinded by a brilliant light. The creature leapt off him and was gone before he could get a good look at it. He lay still for a second, stunned.

Gradually, his eyes became accustomed to the light. Looking up, he saw the figure of a man silhouetted in a doorway. He sat up slowly, brushing the grit from his shoulders. The man watched him, silent and motionless. Penthesilean took longer than necessary to get his breath back, all the while keeping his eyes fixed firmly on the man in the doorway. There was something familiar about his stance which he could not put his finger on. Finally, when he could delay no longer, he stood up and approached the doorway, the chain dragging on the ground behind him.

As he drew closer, the man turned to one side and indicated that he should pass through into the room beyond. He was very tall and wore a white suit so clean and bright that it hurt Penthesilean's eyes to look directly at him. His hair was blonde, almost the same shade as his pale skin. As Penthesilean stepped over the threshold, the chain dropped from his ankle and slithered back into the darkness with a life of its own. He looked up, startled, straight into the pale eyes of the man.

"You?" he cried in recognition, stepping hurriedly away from the man and into the room. He whirled round as he heard the sound of the door close behind him.

"What happened to you?" he began, trying to hide his shock. "Does anyone know you're here?"

Ponsonby rose from where he had been sitting unnoticed in a corner.

"I do," he said, handing a folded sheet of thick, creamy parchment to Penthesilean.

"What's this?"

"Just read it," said the mayor.

Penthesilean unfolded it slowly, glancing at the pale man who had still not said a word. After a moment, he looked down. It took a moment for the words on the page to sink in.

ARREST WARRANT FOR ARAMATTIUS PENTHESILEAN ON SUSPICION OF THE KIDNAPPING AND UNLAWFUL IMPRISONMENT OF PRINCE ALEXANDER THE FIRST

He gasped with shock, unable to read any further.

"No one will believe this," he said furiously. "I was in the ballroom with the Dowager Bella when the prince was kidnapped, surrounded by hundreds of witnesses, including the king himself."

"No one has to believe it," said Ponsonby, "but it will explain to the guards why you are to be kept in the dungeons while the claim is being investigated, at least until the Book of Prophecies is returned to us."

"And you," said Penthesilean to the man in the white suit, "you're involved in this? You're working for this. . . this . . . worm?" He waved one hand furiously at the mayor, but the pale man simply gave a thin-lipped smile. Then, without having said a word, he gestured to Ponsonby to follow him and turned and left the room without a backward glance. Ponsonby scurried after him, locking the door behind them.

Penthesilean stared at the locked door as it dawned on him that, of the two men, it was not the mayor who was in charge.

* * *

Ben stood in the clearing, surrounded by the wall of flames. The creature that was half horse, half man had entreated him to wait for its return. He felt that he didn't have much of a choice: he had no idea where he was, and he certainly couldn't leap the flames like the strange beast had done.

The roll of parchment beneath his shirt had slipped down and he drew it out, intending to tuck it more securely into his waistband. He noticed that one corner was curling up and smoothed his hand over it, but still it curled up.

He raised the document to his face and studied it more closely. The thick parchment appeared to have split. The diagrams on the top sheet were just as indecipherable as before, but his glimpse of the hidden sheet below revealed some clear triangular shapes. Inserting one finger into the flap, he carefully peeled back the top layer of paper.

In the blink of an eye, the wall of flames disappeared to be replaced by the shadowy outlines of bushes and trees. He took a step back in surprise. Turning slowly around, he saw the comforting glow of a campfire through the trees. Blinking to rid his eyes of the memory of the flames, he started to walk towards the light.

"Ben! Ben! Where are you?"

He broke into a run as he heard his name being called. Stepping out of the trees and into the clearing he stopped in surprise. Where just a moment ago there had been fierce flames, burnt tree stumps and barren ground, there was now a thriving campsite.

"Ben! Where have you been?"

His friend Monty stood before him surrounded by men who appeared distinctly less friendly.

"The campsite was on fire . . . there were animals screaming. Didn't you hear them?"

"What are you talking about, boy?" said Jared, pushing Monty aside. "Why don't you tell us what you were really doing out here at this time of night? You were spying, weren't you? You're working for them up at the palace."

The other men began to grumble and mutter amongst themselves as Monty tried unsuccessfully to calm them down.

"I wasn't spying!" cried Ben, still bewildered at finding himself back in the camp. "I was trying to help the animals . . ."

"What's this?" growled Jared, snatching the parchment out of Ben's hands. He unrolled it, glaring at him all the while in an extremely hostile manner.

Without warning, a streak of feathers suddenly appeared from above and knocked Jared off his feet. The manuscript went flying and Ben leapt forward to grab it as the other men hurriedly took a few steps back. Jared rolled on the ground, clutching his bleeding hands between his knees.

"What is going on here?" cried a shrill voice.

Murgatroyd picked himself up and shook out his feathers as Dolora strode past him towards the group of men.

"Jared Montrose, are you bullying that young boy?" she screeched, prodding him in the chest with her staff.

He backed away.

"No, Dolora," he said, looking from her to the large eagle, who was now preening his feathers. "We found him wandering around the edge of the camp . . . I thought he must have been up to no good."

"Well he wasn't!" she snapped. "Now get back on patrol before I turn you into something nasty!"

She dismissed him with a wave of her stick. Jared cast a surly backward glance at Ben as he trudged off, followed by the other men. Monty gave Ben a quick wave before hurrying after them.

Once they had gone, Murgatroyd finally spoke.

"I was right!" he said, triumphantly. "There hasn't been rain for weeks, so when I heard of this flash flood I knew it had to have something to do with you and the Book of Prophecies! Now, where is it?"

Before Ben had time to explain that he didn't have the Book, Monty reappeared at the edge of the clearing.

"Soldiers approaching," he gasped, breathlessly. "We need to move . . . fast!"

* * *

Bella shivered in the chill night breeze, gripping the ledge around the turret roof very tightly with both hands. After a long moment, she risked a quick glance over the edge at the city which lay spread out below her. She could see torchlight moving through the lanes and alleyways, and guessed that it must be the king's men searching for the missing prince. Now that she knew who was responsible for his disappearance, she feared that they were searching in vain.

She shivered again, feeling cold in her ball gown. She had no idea how long she had been in the tower, but judging from the position of the moon it was more than a few hours. She turned to the gargoyle which was crouched on the roof beside her.

"Now what?" she asked, trying hard not to remember how high the turrets actually were.

But she received no response from the gargoyle which had frozen into position, one claw raised and its dog-like grin replaced by a fierce-looking snarl. She prodded it with one finger and felt only cold, hard stone. Trying to stay calm, she took another tiny peep over the edge.

"I wouldn't go that way if I were you," came a sleepy voice from behind her.

Bella slowly turned her head to find an enormous owl perched on the roof next to her.

"I'd never get a moment's rest if anything happened to you," continued the owl, "Murgatroyd can be very vocal when he's upset!"

She stared at the owl in surprise. "Did Murgatroyd send you too?"

"Not exactly," said the owl, "he just asked me to keep an eye on you. So I have – both eyes in fact." As though to contradict its words, it then closed both of its large, round eyes in a long, deliberate blink.

"So what now?" prompted Bella.

The owl opened its eyes sleepily and looked at her.

"Well," it said, raising its feathery eyebrows, "that depends on you, I suppose. What would you like to do now?"

Bella considered her options. She couldn't go to the king about Ponsonby's plot: it appeared that the man had spies everywhere and she couldn't risk placing Prince Alexander's life in further danger. But while she knew it would be best for her own safety if she left Quadrivium, she couldn't bring herself to go until she knew that her grandson had been found. She would have to stay within Quadrivium's walls until that happened, and there was only one place where she knew she'd be safe.

"I have to get to the dome," she said.

The owl swivelled its neck completely round, leaving Bella staring at the back of its feathery head. Finally it swept back round to face her.

"Wait here," it said, and flew off into the darkness.

Just when she thought it wasn't going to return, the owl reappeared carrying something in its beak. As it landed on the ledge beside her, Bella realised it was one end of a rope. The other end trailed off into the darkness.

The owl stared unblinkingly at her. After a moment, she took the rope from its beak.

"Good," said the owl. "Now, tie it to something secure."

She looked around, unable to find anything at all on the roof to which she could attach the rope. Her eyes finally came to rest on the gargoyle. It was leaning outwards over the dizzying drop, cemented to the wall by its feet. After a brief moment's hesitation, she lashed the rope around its body and secured it with a triple granny knot.

She noticed the owl eyeing her knot with some scepticism.

"It's the only knot I know," she offered.

The owl looked up at her. "It'll do. Now throw your sash over the rope and hang on."

Bella's heart sank as she followed the direction of the rope. "You're not suggesting . . . ?"

"I'll be with you all the way," said the owl, reassuringly, "I'll slow you down when you approach the dome."

Certain that this would be the last thing she ever did, Bella lifted her silk sash over her head and looped it over the rope. She wrapped her hands around each fringed end and then, keeping her eyes fixed firmly on the dull gleam of the dome far below, she launched herself into the open air.

It was unexpectedly exhilarating. Her sash slid smoothly over the rope as she rushed through the cool night air, her long dress billowing out behind her. The owl flew alongside, catching hold of her skirt with its beak every now and then to slow her descent.

Just when she thought she was going to make it, the rope gave a sickening lurch.

"What's happening?" hissed Bella, her heart in her mouth.

The owl did not reply. It was now bumping her from behind to make her go faster. She almost lost her grip on her sash as the rope plunged down once more, dropping by about a foot before holding fast.

She realised with horror that her knots were coming loose. She risked a glance at the ground below. The dome was approaching rapidly, but there was still a long way to fall if the final knot gave.

She suddenly bounced in mid-air as the rope became taut once more. She slid the last few feet and landed safely on the dome's balcony. Shakily, she turned and looked back towards the turret. Silhouetted against the glow of the moon, she saw the gargoyle turn and fix itself back into position.

* * *

There was controlled panic in the camp at the news that soldiers were approaching. Most of the river folk had been fast asleep when the alarm was raised, but they were quick to spring into action. Women ran to and fro, shaking children awake and dousing campfires, while the men packed up the tents and herded the chickens and goats deeper into the forest where they would be safe from the soldiers. Dolora hurried off, muttering to herself and shaking her stick at anyone who got in her way.

"Stay close to Monty," Murgatroyd hissed into Ben's ear before disappearing into the night sky.

Very soon, the river folk were packed and ready to go. Ben hovered uncertainly, aware that he was still viewed with suspicion by some of the men.

"Come on!" said Monty, grabbing his arm and pulling Ben after him. "Let's go!"

Together they followed the crush of river folk all streaming in one direction. They moved quickly and silently, even the children were strangely quiet. They've done this before, thought Ben to himself. He looked briefly over his shoulder and saw a flicker of torchlight through the trees, closer than he expected, and hurried after Monty.

Suddenly they were out of the trees and onto a sandy riverbank. By the faint light of the approaching dawn, he could see two or three of the small, flat-bottomed boats already floating off downstream towards a bend in the river, moving more quickly as they were caught by the current. The remaining boats were filling rapidly with river folk who muttered urgently amongst themselves as headcounts were made and oars taken up.

Soon Ben and Monty were the only ones left on the riverbank as the last boat departed.

* * *

Murgatroyd circled silently over the heads of the approaching soldiers. They had spread out and were wading slowly and carefully through the thigh-deep water of the floodplain, sweeping their flaming torches back and forth.

"Seems a lot of fuss just to find a boy," he heard one of

the soldiers mutter to another. "It's not like he actually managed to steal the mayor's chain."

"Tell me about it," grumbled the other man. "I'd much rather be up at the palace searching for the prince than trawling through swamps in the middle of the night for some street urchin."

"I heard he went on to steal something even more valuable," piped up a third soldier.

"What?"

"Dunno, but it must have been something big . . ."

"You don't think it was him who kidnapped the prince, do you?"

"Surely not, why would a boy that age take a baby? He'd barely be able to carry him . . ."

Their discussion was interrupted by a shout nearby. "Sir! Over here!"

Another soldier was standing on a small island of mud. "I think I've found something!"

The officer in charge hurried over. "What is it, private?"

"Footprints," cried the soldier, thrusting his torch down towards the mud. "They're small enough to be those of a child. And look, my guess is that these marks were made by a boat being dragged up through the reeds, and there are some larger footprints next to it, clearly from an adult."

"Looks like our hunch was right: those river people have got him," said the officer. "It's a good thing we covered all bases by setting up an ambush downstream. They're slippery devils, in my experience."

Having heard enough, Murgatroyd turned sharply on a wingtip and flew swiftly in the direction of the river.

* * *

Ben stood on the riverbank gazing after the last of the departing boats. He heard shouts from the trees behind him and looked back, expecting to see the soldiers appear at any moment.

"Get in!"

He turned to see Jared struggling against the current as he manhandled one of the boats towards the shore. He hesitated, recalling the man's earlier hostility.

"Do as I say," cried Jared. "They'll be here any minute."

Ben turned to Monty, unsure of what to do. His friend nodded, tight-lipped.

"I'll hold them off for as long as I can," he said, unslinging a longbow from his shoulder.

Ben was about to climb into Jared's boat when a piercing scream suddenly ripped through the dawn. It was coming from downstream, from the direction the other boats had taken. He froze, one leg over the side of the boat and the other ankle deep in water.

"Go!" shouted Monty, waving them off. A moment later, a group of soldiers emerged from the trees.

Jared grabbed hold of Ben's shirt and pulled him into

the boat. It rocked dangerously as he pushed off, then steadied as it was caught by the current and swung round to face downstream. The soldiers raced to the water's edge, shouting at them to stop, while Monty slipped unnoticed into the bushes.

One of the men hurled his sword after the departing boat. It fell short, thumping harmlessly against the side and sinking rapidly. Ben stared back at the riverbank as one of the other soldiers knelt on the sand, fixed an arrow to his bow and carefully took aim. Suddenly, his arrow seemed to spring from his bow of its own accord and fell harmlessly to the ground just in front of him. With a little moan, he toppled face first into the sand, a different arrow protruding from his ribs. The other men whirled round and immediately spotted Monty hiding in the bushes. Ben looked on from the boat, helpless, as they converged on his friend and forced him to the ground, before the little boat rounded the bend in the river and the scene was hidden from view.

* * *

Penthesilean examined his surroundings. Harsh light flooded the room from a single globe set into the ceiling. The room was featureless but for the door through which he'd entered, which was now firmly shut, and a tiny grille near the ceiling, which was too small to climb through even if he could have reached it. A table and two sturdy timber chairs were the only furnishings. He kicked one of the chairs in frustration and then gasped in pain. Both the chairs and the table were riveted firmly to the floor.

The door opened unexpectedly and he turned, expecting to see Ponsonby or the pale man returning. Instead, two soldiers entered the room, closing the door firmly behind them. He was relieved to see that they were dressed in the smart green uniforms of the king's Royal Household Guard.

"Thank Titan!" he cried, moving towards them with his arms outstretched.

"Sit down, sir," ordered one of the soldiers, pushing him back into one of the chairs.

"You don't understand," said Penthesilean. "Mayor Ponsonby is a traitor; he had me thrown in here and he's also holding the queen's mother hostage . . ." He broke off as the other soldier grabbed his arms and manacled them to the chair. "What is going on?" he roared in outrage. "I am a senior officer. Release me at once!"

"You are to be held in this secure facility until someone returns to interrogate you," said the soldier. "And you will speak only when spoken to."

"This is utter insubordination!" shouted Penthesilean, straining against the manacles. "I'll have you court-martialled for this!"

The first soldier opened the door and then looked back

at him. "Sir, all the facts are in the arrest warrant." He nodded at the parchment which lay on the table where Penthesilean had thrown it.

"But that's nonsense," protested Penthesilean. "It's a smokescreen! Why would I kidnap the prince?"

The other soldier made to follow his colleague out of the room, but paused in the doorway.

"That's something for the interrogator to find out," he said with a smirk. "I wouldn't try hiding anything from him: he always gets what he wants in the end."

* * *

Jared manoeuvred the boat expertly into deeper water. It jerked suddenly as it caught the fast-running current and began to move faster.

"Stop!" came Murgatroyd's cry as he appeared suddenly overhead. "Go back!"

Jared flinched at the sight of the bird which had attacked him earlier.

"Go back!" cried Murgatroyd insistently.

"We can't!" Ben called back. "The soldiers are on the riverbank!"

He had never seen the eagle look as ruffled as he did now. The boat rocked as he landed heavily on its prow.

"You must turn round! The soldiers have laid an ambush!"

The man stared at the eagle, his words finally penetrating the shock of hearing the bird speak. "An ambush? Where?"

"Downstream! Go back!" said Murgatroyd. "You must go back . . ."

Jared instantly resumed rowing with the current, directly towards the bend in the river beyond which lay the ambush.

"What are you doing?" cried Murgatroyd.

"We can't just leave them!" yelled Jared, pulling hard on the oars.

"It's too late!" Murgatroyd flapped his wings in front of Jared's face as though trying to shoo him back upstream.

The man stood up, trying to push the bird away. "I have to help them!" he cried. "That's my family, my friends –" He broke off suddenly and his eyes widened in surprise. He looked down; an arrow had pierced his leather vest just below the heart. Slowly, without a sound, he toppled forward, landing with a splash in the fast-flowing river.

"Take cover!" cried Murgatroyd, launching himself off the boat towards the archer standing on the shore.

More arrows flew overhead, but Jared had presented an easy target and none struck Ben, who crouched in the bottom of the boat, white-faced with shock. After a few long seconds, the arrows ceased and he raised his head cautiously. The archer had gone, so too had Murgatroyd. Ben was alone in the boat, heading rapidly downstream towards the ambush.

10

The river folk turned the faces of their children away from the man whose pale skin seemed to shimmer in the early dawn light. With drawn faces they watched as he paced the riverbank slowly and thoughtfully, his eyes alight with a fierce glow.

Turning suddenly on one heel, he thrust the tip of his sword into the shoulder of the man kneeling before him.

"Where is the boy?" he said slowly, twisting the sword into the wound.

The man at his feet cried out in agony, "I don't know! I swear it!"

The pale man glanced at the woman kneeling beside him. "Is this your wife?"

"Yes," mumbled the man.

The pale man yanked the sword from the man's shoulder and used the flat of the blade to lift the woman's hair from her face.

"Hmph!" he remarked, unimpressed, then barked a command to the men behind him. "Drown the wench!"

"No! Wait!" cried the man. "Yes, the boy was brought to our camp, but when the soldiers arrived it was every man for himself! I just assumed he was in one of the other boats."

The pale man paused and looked down at the man clinging to his boot. Shaking him off, he summoned one of the soldiers. "How many boats did you catch in your little net?"

"Fifteen, sir!" came the prompt reply.

Turning back to the man slumped at his feet, he lifted his chin with the toe of his boot. "How many boats does the river clan own?"

"Sixteen," whispered the man wearily.

"Aaah," breathed the pale man, suddenly showing all his teeth in a terrible smile. "One boat short! I think we can stop worrying. The boy will be joining us very soon."

* * *

At that very moment, the sixteenth boat was being drawn inexorably downstream towards the ambush. In desperation, Ben grabbed one of the oars and stuck it straight down into the river, trying to pull the boat around. Reaching for the other oar, he put all his strength into fighting the current. Despite the cool dawn air and the splashes of icy river water, he was soon covered in sweat. His arms felt as though they were being pulled from their sockets and blisters were already forming on his hands.

Despite his efforts and determination, the current was too strong for him and the boat's progress was barely checked as it continued downstream towards the ambush. Foam surged against the oars as he pulled hard on them, summoning his last ounce of energy. Unexpectedly the boat came to an abrupt halt. Both oars were jerked out of his hands and fell into the water. Ben watched in dismay as they floated away down the river.

Then slowly, inexplicably, the boat began to move upstream. Water rushed past in a foaming torrent, rocking the boat from side to side, but still it advanced against the current, steadily gaining momentum.

Ben hauled himself up from where he had been thrown by the boat's sudden halt. Stumbling to the prow, he looked down into the water. There was a flash beneath the foam, then a familiar face broke the surface.

"Hello, Ben," said Prince Trestan.

* * *

Penthesilean was surrounded by monks. Their robes were dripping wet, leaving a damp trail as they slowly circled him. They were chanting in a language he didn't recognise, their faces thrown into shadow by the cowls pulled low over their heads. He opened his mouth, but no sound left his lips. As one, the monks suddenly stopped and turned to face him. The identical, masklike face of the pale man stared out from beneath each hood. Penthesilean shrank back as one reached out a skeletal hand towards him. It grabbed his arm and this time he heard himself cry out.

"Shhhh," whispered the monk. Except this monk's face was different from the others and he was not wearing a habit. Instead he wore the king's uniform and looked vaguely familiar. Penthesilean blinked a few times, his nightmare quickly receding.

"Keep quiet and do as I say," said the soldier, taking a bunch of keys from his belt. "My name's Arrowbright. I'm here to get you out, but we have to be quick, before Manson returns."

He had the manacles off in seconds. Penthesilean immediately tried to stand but his legs gave way and he stumbled, sitting heavily back down onto the chair. At that moment, the door opened and the soldier who had manacled him to the chair entered the room. It took him a few seconds to realise what was going on, but Arrowbright reacted instantly. Reaching the door in a few quick strides, he slammed it shut and wrapped his arm round the other man's neck. He struggled and kicked, but Arrowbright was the stronger of the two and, with Penthesilean's help, they had soon wrestled him into one of the chairs.

"What are you doing?" he spat, furiously.

"My duty," replied Arrowbright, fastening the manacles around his wrists. "This man saved my father's life, Manson, he's no traitor!"

He took hold of Penthesilean's arm. "Can you walk, sir?"

Penthesilean nodded as he felt the feeling seep back into his legs.

"This is madness, Arrowbright!" cried Manson. "How far do you expect to get with him?"

Penthesilean looked at Manson speculatively.

"He's right," he said to Arrowbright, "I am a bit conspicuous in this outfit . . ."

Between them, they quickly stripped Manson down to his underclothes, undoing one manacle at a time to remove first his combat trousers and then his tunic. Penthesilean slipped out of his own formal dress uniform and into the more familiar uniform of the working soldier.

"That's more like it," he said. "I never did like velvet!"

He paused to unhook his medals from the front of his ceremonial jacket before draping it over Manson's lap. Shoving them into the pocket of his combat trousers, he followed Arrowbright from the room, leaving Manson sputtering with helpless rage.

* * *

The pale man stood on the riverbank, staring upstream and muttering impatiently. He didn't seem to notice the water lapping around his feet and soaking into the fine leather of his shoes, so intent was he on waiting for the last boat to appear.

He spun round at the sound of someone clearing their throat behind him.

"What is it?" he snapped, displeased at having been caught off guard.

"The archers have returned," replied the soldier staring at the pale man's shoes, afraid to meet his eyes. "They have a prisoner."

"The boy?" cried the pale man, his eyes lighting up.

"No, sir," said one of the archers, stepping into the clearing. He gave his prisoner a shove and Monty stumbled and fell at the feet of the pale man.

"Who is this? Where is the boy?"

The archer swallowed nervously, feeling sweat break out on his forehead despite the cool dawn air.

"The boy escaped in the last boat," he said looking around, expecting to see the boat washed up on the bank. "This man attacked us on the riverbank; he killed Jameson before we could overpower him. The boy got away but Hunter managed to shoot the man with him in the boat."

"I believe I killed him, sir," interjected Hunter. "The boy was no threat by himself. There was no way he could singlehandedly have held that boat against the current."

"And where is this man whom you supposedly killed?"

As though in answer to his question, there were suddenly cries and screams from the river folk huddled further down the bank. A body had become caught in the net which was still strung across the river. Someone had recognised the clothes, the hair.

The pale man pushed his way past the two archers and strode towards the net. He ignored the river folk who shrank from him with fear and loathing on their faces.

"Cut the body loose and bring it to me," he growled. He turned back towards Monty who was lying exhausted on the muddy beach.

"Who else was in the boat?" he asked in a reasonable tone. "Tell me and I may spare your life."

"There was no one else," said Monty, his head bowed.

"Then where is the boy?" roared the pale man, his calm demeanour suddenly replaced by fury. He raised his sword as though to strike Monty.

"Wait!" cried an imposing voice.

The pale man paused. Without lowering his sword, he turned his head and then laughed incredulously. A few paces away stood Dolora, her staff pointing straight at him. A couple of soldiers hovered uncertainly to either side of her, reluctant to grab the smelly, mad old woman who nonetheless had an air of authority about her.

"What do you have to say on the matter, old woman?" he asked, his tone dripping with scorn.

"The bird is with him," cried Dolora. "The bird will protect him! You are powerless against the terror from the skies!"

The pale man stared at her for a few moments before finally lowering his sword.

"Get them both out of my sight," he said, dismissively. "You, archers, head back upstream and find that child. I am holding you personally responsible for bringing him to me before noon today!"

* * *

The sky had been growing steadily lighter until finally a ray of light burst through a gap in the trees. Prince Trestan turned his face towards the sun.

"It's been a long time since I've felt the sun on my face," he sighed happily. "Once more, my people owe your line a debt of gratitude."

"What do you mean?" asked Ben, leaning over the prow of the boat to watch Prince Trestan pull it upstream.

"You broke the enchantment of the lake," said the merman. "You released us from our underground prison."

"But what did you mean by 'my line'?"

Prince Trestan rolled onto his back and looked up at Ben.

"Your mother once did my people a great service," he said, solemnly. "You have followed in her footsteps, as I knew you would."

Ben's mouth went dry. "You knew my mother?"

"Very well," said Prince Trestan. "I painted that portrait which you keep around your neck."

Ben's hand closed protectively around his locket. "But how . . . when?"

The merman turned his face back to the sun. His eyes closed and a wistful expression crept across his face.

"It was a long time ago, when our kind lived peaceably within sight of Quadrivium on the shores of the Sylver Sea. Teah, your mother, approached us requesting sanctuary, and we took her in. All we knew was that she was from the mountains and was running away from someone or something. But she didn't like to talk about it, so we didn't ask questions.

"Shortly after she joined us, a rumour sprang up in the city that some mermen were committing acts of piracy by luring ships onto the rocks in order to steal their cargo. Of course, the rumour was entirely unfounded, and my father – the King of the Mermen – travelled to Quadrivium to reassure the king that all travellers through our waters would be guaranteed safe passage. Teah had been waiting on the rocks for him to return and so was the first to see the men coming for us with nets and chains, creeping over the sand at low tide. She raised the alarm and selflessly offered to act as a decoy. They won't harm me when they see I'm human, she said, and with child.

"It was then that I realised her rounded belly was not due to our nutritious diet of kelp and whelks, but a baby growing within her. That's the last we saw of Teah, sitting on the rocks with her legs disguised by seaweed, combing her long, golden hair and looking for all the world like one of us.

"When we returned at high tide, the men had vanished – but so too had Teah."

Ben's mind reeled. He had learnt more about his mother in the past few minutes than he had in his entire life.

"Do you think the men took her?" he asked finally.

"At first we feared that was so," said the merman, "but later we learned that the men were Conscriptors, whose sole purpose was to forcibly recruit men and beasts as conscripts into the king's army. They wouldn't have taken Teah – a pregnant woman would have been of little value to them – and later something else happened which led us to believe that she had escaped.

"Someone came looking for her, a year or so after she had disappeared. Even if we had known where she had gone we would not have told him, but he refused to take no for an answer. Hoping that one of us would finally break, he took our children from us and used an enchantment to imprison us in the underground lake beneath the palace. We may have perished there if it hadn't had been for you, Deliverer."

A shadow passed over the boat. Ben looked up to see

Murgatroyd circling overhead. The bird descended swiftly, landing on the side of the boat just as the merman sank silently below the surface.

"Thank Tritan you're safe!" cried Murgatroyd. "I thought the worst when I couldn't find the boat. How did you get so far upstream? Where is the Book?"

Before Ben could respond, Prince Trestan exploded from the water, drenching Murgatroyd.

"Leave the boy!" he boomed before crashing back down, the echoes of his voice ricocheting off the surrounding trees.

"It's all right!" called Ben to the merman as he resurfaced for a second attack. "He's one of us!"

Murgatroyd had collapsed in a heap of wet feathers in the bottom of the boat. Ben backed out of range of his flailing claws until the bird finally managed to right himself, while Prince Trestan looked on, slightly shamefaced.

"My feathers!" spluttered Murgatroyd. "Is that a... are you a Merman?"

Murgatroyd's reaction surprised Ben. He had assumed that he and Bella had known about the presence of mermen beneath the palace.

"I thought you were extinct," said Murgatroyd when he had recovered from the shock. "Are there others of your kind?"

"There are many of us," confirmed Prince Trestan, and he proceeded to tell Murgatroyd of the mermen's escape from the underground lake. "We made our way across the flood plain to the river. My people have gone on ahead to search for our children, but I returned to make sure the Deliverer was safe."

"Why do you call me the Deliverer?" asked Ben curiously.

"There is a prophecy passed down through generations of mermen that one day, when the kingdom is wavering on the brink between good and evil, a human child shall be born to another whose selfless deed once protected our kind. When we saw the locket and remembered what your mother had done for us, we knew you were the Deliverer."

Murgatroyd had remained uncharacteristically silent throughout this discussion, but now he spoke up.

"I've heard many different legends which speak of the Deliverer," he said, sceptically. "Each species seems to have its own interpretation. How can you be so sure this is he?"

"Because he has already accomplished the first part of our legend by releasing my people from the enchantment," said Prince Trestan. "The Book of Prophecies is in good hands."

At that, both turned to look at Ben, who shifted uncomfortably under their expectant gaze.

"I don't have it," he said in a small voice. As he watched the look of disbelief spread across Murgatroyd's face, he quickly remembered the roll of parchment and drew it out from under his shirt. "I did find this, though: it's a page from the Book."

Murgatroyd almost snatched the parchment from Ben's hands. He examined it carefully, turning it over to look at both sides before handing it back to him.

"It's completely blank," he said, unable to keep the disappointment from his voice.

"No it's not," said Ben impatiently, taking it from him. He pointed at the scribbles and diagrams covering the parchment. "Can't you see? I think it's some sort of code."

"It will lead you to the Book," said Prince Trestan confidently. "You must follow the signs."

Murgatroyd looked at him sharply. "Is this another part of your legend?"

"No," admitted the merman, "but I have every faith in the Deliverer. Many trials will be sent to test him and this is but the first. Nothing worthwhile is easily won."

Murgatroyd suddenly remembered the soldiers. "We have to get off the river: the soldiers will come looking for the missing boat when it fails to appear."

"First I will take you further upstream," said Prince Trestan. "I can swim faster than the soldiers can march."

Murgatroyd settled himself uncomfortably in the bottom of the boat, many questions about the Book of Prophecies swirling about his head, and the boat surged against the current on a small wave of foam as Prince Trestan effortlessly hauled them upstream.

* * *

Arrowbright led Penthesilean cautiously through the dimly lit dungeons which linked the interrogation room to the rest of the palace. It was unusual for prisoners to be brought to these ancient cells so deep underground, and he tried hard not to think of the stories which circulated around the barracks – particularly amongst the younger officers – stories of bloodsucking monsters which roamed the dungeons leaving only the bones of former prisoners as proof of their existence.

The hairs on the back of his neck were standing on end by the time he spotted the first of the stone steps which led above ground. It was then that he realised the old soldier was no longer beside him. He looked back to see Penthesilean standing a few paces behind, his hand groping at the place where his sword would ordinarily have been.

"Did you hear that?" he whispered, his eyes wide and staring.

"Hear what?" asked Arrowbright, looking nervously over his shoulder.

Penthesilean suddenly leapt at him, knocking him to the ground. In one swift movement, he wrenched Arrowbright's dagger from its sheath and rolled off him. Arrowbright felt a cold draught as a dark shadow passed over his body and landed where Penthesilean had been just a split second before. He froze, his mind struggling to comprehend what he had seen. Before he could react, Penthesilean leapt forward, driving Arrowbright's dagger down onto the head of a monstrous creature the size of a small horse. The beast reared up, throwing the old soldier to the ground but leaving the dagger embedded in its skull.

It thudded back down onto all fours, landing face to face with Arrowbright who was still lying on the ground, winded by Penthesilean's unexpected onslaught. He watched in morbid fascination as it shook its scaly head slowly from side to side, a mixture of blood and drool hanging from its jaws. It took two unsteady steps towards him. He stared into its bloodshot eyes, unable to move a muscle. It took another step and then suddenly sat down heavily on its hindquarters.

Arrowbright finally came to his senses and skittered backwards, but the creature had already lost interest in him. It raised a claw to its head, scratching in vain at the dagger. It looked faintly puzzled as blood poured down into its amber eyes, then raising its head it bayed in agony, a long drawn out sound which sent a shiver down his spine. Finally its eyes lost focus and it slipped onto its side, panting loudly as it rested its head on the stony floor. Arrowbright watched the light gradually fade from its eyes until at last its heaving sides were still.

He dragged his horrified gaze from the dead beast to where Penthesilean was leaning against the wall of the dungeon.

"My father used to tell me you were the bravest warrior he had ever met," he said, slowly getting to his feet. "I now understand what he meant."

He stepped forward and yanked the dagger from the dead creature's skull. Wiping the blood on its scaly back, he handed it hilt first to Penthesilean. "I'd like you to have this."

Penthesilean accepted the dagger gravely, before turning towards the dungeon steps.

"Hadn't we better get moving," he said over his shoulder, "before its mate arrives?"

* * *

Ben shifted uncomfortably under Murgatroyd's gaze as the boat continued upstream.

"Why do you believe this bit of parchment to be from the Book of Prophecies?" the eagle eventually asked.

"The bird told me," said Ben. "It said the page had been left behind to maintain the enchantment which kept the mermen imprisoned…"

"What bird? Describe it to me."

Ben closed his eyes, picturing the bird's brightly coloured plumage and its sharp beak and claws. He still had some of the scratch marks on his arms.

"It had a bright green crest on its head," he began, "with

a yellow breast and a very long tail with feathers of red, blue and . . ." He suddenly remembered the bird's reaction when he had mentioned Murgatroyd's name. "And it knew you!" he finished, triumphantly.

"Oh, no!" sighed Murgatroyd, covering his eyes with his wing.

"But I didn't get the impression it was a friend of yours."

"She was once, I taught her to speak!"

Murgatroyd recalled the day he had first encountered the bird as though it were yesterday. The event had caused the first of his many arguments with Bella's son, his friend Damien. One day, while his mother and sister were out, Damien had taken Murgatroyd to see his family's living quarters where he had heard exquisite singing coming from another room. He had followed the sound only to come face to face with a caged songbird. He had never seen anything so beautiful or so shocking. Damien had followed him into the room in time to catch him opening the door of the birdcage. The boy had been furious with him and chased him away, but Murgatroyd could not forget the sight of the caged bird and had returned that night to release her from captivity.

The little bird hadn't known what to do with her freedom, standing uncertainly at the open door of her cage and resisting his efforts to shoo her towards the window. Eventually, Murgatroyd had taken her under his wing and built a nest for her on a high shelf in the palace library near the Book of Prophecies, where she had caused much consternation amongst the scholars and monks by singing all day and all night.

Murgatroyd had spent hours trying to teach her to speak. When she finally did, instead of a single word she spoke an entire sentence. From that moment on she ceased singing and began to talk non-stop. She also grew considerably. She wasn't accustomed to his rich and varied diet of fish, rat or whatever small mammal he had hunted that day, and soon ballooned beyond all recognition.

"What happened to her?" asked Ben.

"She disappeared at the same time as the Book of Prophecies," said Murgatroyd. "I assumed that the monks had either set her free or put her back in a cage . . ."

He shook his feathers as though clearing the memory from his head, and looked back down at the parchment.

"So you found this with the bird," he said, "but there was no sign of the Book itself?"

"She said that I was too late," said Ben, trying to recall her exact words, "that the Book had already been taken."

"By whom?" asked Murgatroyd sharply.

"She didn't say," replied Ben, remembering the bird's arrogant manner. "She wasn't exactly forthcoming . . ."

As they entered a wider stretch of river the shady trees fell away and the full force of the sun fell on Ben's face. The current was not so strong here and a moment later Prince Trestan's head appeared above the water.

"This is a good place for us to part," he said in his deep, gentle voice. "The soldiers won't expect you to have travelled so far in such a short space of time."

He guided the boat towards the riverbank. Murgatroyd took to the air to check that the coast was clear while Ben clambered out of the boat and onto dry land.

"It's safe to come ashore," reported Murgatroyd on his return. "There's a path through the trees over there."

"I'll take the boat further upstream and tether it to the opposite bank," said Prince Trestan. "That should give you some extra time if the soldiers should find it."

He manoeuvred the boat back out into the river. "It has been an honour serving you, Deliverer. I hope we meet again in happier circumstances."

With that, the merman sank beneath the water and within moments the boat once again began to move upstream, propelled by the force of his powerful tail. Ben and Murgatroyd watched until it had disappeared around a bend in the river.

The peace was suddenly shattered by a racket in the undergrowth behind them as something ricocheted off a tree and fell into the bushes a few yards away.

"Stay here," whispered Murgatroyd, stretching his wings to their full span and moving over to where the object had fallen. He reached forward a claw to draw back the bushes just as a feathery object exploded towards him. It rolled across the ground and came to rest at Ben's feet. He took a few quick steps back before he realised what it was: a very large and confused-looking owl.

* * *

The owl had flown through the night and into the morning searching for Murgatroyd. He wasn't used to travelling by daylight and was utterly exhausted. It took a few false starts before they had all the information, as he kept dozing off in mid-sentence. They eventually pieced together that Bella had been kidnapped by Ponsonby but was now safely hidden in a secret room in the dome. Having imparted all the information, the owl fell fast asleep with his head under his wing.

Murgatroyd looked thoughtful.

"This is all starting to fall into place," he said to Ben, "Bella never trusted Ponsonby, there was just too much about him that didn't add up. He must have panicked when he heard that someone had discovered the underground lake, and a mere boy at that. I wonder if he realised you were the same boy who tried to steal his chain."

He paced back and forth. "If he was bright enough to put two and two together, that would explain why he suspected Bella of being involved. His household guards would have searched everywhere for you after you tried to steal his chain, everywhere but the Royal Carriages . . ."

He suddenly straightened up and looked at Ben.

"I have to go back for her," he said, "she's not safe in Quadrivium, queen's mother or not. Ponsonby is more powerful than we suspected." He looked at the roll of parchment in Ben's hand. "You had better keep hold of that, seeing as you're the only one who can read it. Is there somewhere you can go to lie low until I can get Bella out of the city – somewhere safe?"

Ben thought for a moment. Almost immediately, the solution popped into his head.

"I know just the spot," he said with a grin.

11

The inn looked utterly derelict. Thick planks of wood were nailed across all the windows and weeds as high as Ben's waist blocked the path to the front door, which was also boarded over. Ben paused for a second at the crossroads, staring up at the ramshackle building. Then he grinned in relief. It was exactly as he remembered.

He took a last look over his shoulder. Satisfied that he hadn't been followed, he raced across the road and within seconds had shinned up the rusted drainpipe and squeezed through a gap between the planks covering an upstairs window. He paused for a second to allow his eyes to adjust to the gloom, sensing immediately from the ear-tingling silence that the building was empty.

There were no internal walls on this floor, just one enormous room with spindly wooden pillars holding up the ceiling. Upstairs was the attic, which some of the older boys had turned into a smoking den. Narrow strips of daylight lay across piles of rags which were heaped in neat rows on the floor. Beside each were objects precious to the child who slept there: scraps of paper, an empty bottle filled with wilting wildflowers, a collection of sea shells.

Ben picked his way through the piles of rags to a ladder propped up against the far wall. He had decided the attic was the safest place to wait for Murgatroyd; if anyone entered the inn he would know about it before they spotted him.

He clambered up the ladder and kicked it away behind him, wincing as it fell to the floor with a crash, throwing up a cloud of dust. Then, closing the trapdoor behind him, he turned to find a comfortable spot to wait.

The attic was small with a low, pitched roof. Tucked under the eaves was an upside down crate covered with a piece of faded green baize cloth. He approached it, sniffing the air with a puzzled expression. As he looked down at the makeshift card table, it finally occurred to him what was wrong.

A couple of half-smoked cigars had been stubbed out on the crate beside a small pile of coins and four piles of playing cards, laid face down. The boys he knew would never have left in the middle of a game, and certainly not without scooping up the coins and pocketing the cigar butts. He had the distinct impression they had left in a hurry.

As he slipped the coins into his pocket, he heard a noise

from the room below. He froze, his ears straining against the silence, and then he heard it again: a faint scratching sound. He dropped to his hands and knees and prised a knot of wood from one of the floorboards. He put his eye close to the hole and peered through, but the room appeared just as deserted as it had been a few minutes before.

Telling himself that it was probably just a rat, Ben was about to move away when a shadow flitted across the light from the window. He cursed softly to himself, then watched and waited for the person to reveal themselves.

Nothing happened for a long while. He was beginning to think he had imagined it when the boards across one of the big windows were suddenly and noisily wrenched away and bright daylight flooded the room. A man clambered over the sill and into the room. He was tall and heavily built, dressed in the familiar green uniform of the king's guards. Two smaller men in the same uniform climbed in after him and stood awkwardly by his side.

"Spread out," ordered the first man. "I want every inch of this dump searched until he's found."

Ben felt his stomach lurch. He looked around the attic, but he already knew there was no way out other than the trapdoor. Drawn back to the hole in the floorboards, he watched the soldiers make their way swiftly through the room below, kicking at the piles of rags with their large black boots.

"Owwww!" came a sudden cry.

One of the men reached down and pulled a small boy from under an old blanket. "Got him, sir!"

The boy was dragged by his ear towards the officer in charge. Ben held his breath. The man was standing directly beneath his spy-hole. He reached down with his swagger stick and tilted the boy's chin up to face him.

"Right, you little mole," he barked. "I won't have any more of this nonsense! Men, tie his hands – and make sure you do a better job than last time!"

The boy raised his eyes to look up at him. He must have sensed Ben's presence, for his gaze slid on over the top of the man's head and up towards the hole in the ceiling. Without moving his eyes from the spy-hole, he hawked loudly and then spat a slimy, green blob of mucus onto one of the officer's shiny boots.

For a second everyone, including Ben, stared in horrified fascination at the glistening globule. Then one of the young soldiers ran forward and carefully wiped the offending mess from the officer's boot with his handkerchief.

While the soldiers were distracted, the boy gave a sly wink in the direction of the spy-hole. Ben jumped as a jolt of recognition shot through him. It was Joe, the boy who had found him wandering the streets of Quadrivium and introduced him to the inn, but he looked very different from the last time Ben had seen him. It took a few minutes for him to realise that Joe was clean. His face was pink and shiny, as though it had recently been vigorously scrubbed with a rough flannel, and he was dressed in a pressed white shirt and grey shorts, long white socks – bunched around his ankles – and shiny black shoes.

Ben took his eye from the spy-hole and sat back on his heels, wondering what was going on. As he did so, one of the coins dropped out of his pocket and rolled across the floor before spinning noisily round a few times and finally falling flat. He froze, hardly daring to breathe. The room below had gone quiet.

"La, la, la-di-dah, la, la, la laaaah!"

The silence was broken by the sound of Joe's tuneless singing and stomping feet.

"Will you be quiet!" yelled the officer. "Men, there's something in that attic! Whoever or whatever is up there, I want to know about it, whether it's animal, vegetable or mineral! Get a move on!"

Ben heard the sound of the ladder being dragged back into place. He threw himself behind the crate just as the trapdoor opened. His heart sank even further as he heard another shout from below.

"You men search that attic properly, do you hear me? You need to redeem yourselves after letting this little beggar escape for the fourth time!"

Before the man had finished speaking, Ben felt a hand grab the back of his shirt. "Found him! It's another boy, sir! Mayor Ponsonby is going to be very pleased with us."

* * *

"What's going on?" hissed Ben, after being dragged out of the inn and thrown into the back of a waiting carriage with Joe.

The other boy wiped his nose on the back of his sleeve, leaving a slimy trail on the clean, white cotton.

"School!" he spat in disgust. "It happened late last night. Soldiers turned up at the inn while everyone was asleep and carted us off to this big place in the city. They took away our old clothes and half drowned us in hot water before putting us in these rooms full of desks and blackboards and stuff, with snooty ladies telling us to mind our p's and q's, whatever they are. The only upside is the grub, but you have to sit still for hours and keep quiet otherwise you don't get any."

He looked at Ben with suspicion.

"This hasn't got anything to do with you, has it?" he said. "You didn't come back to the inn last night. We thought you must've been rounded up with one of the other gangs, but you hadn't, had you? How'd you manage to avoid the soldiers?"

Ben looked hard at his companion. "And how'd you escape, Joe? Why'd you lead the soldiers back to the inn? How do I know this isn't something to do with you?"

Joe thought about this for a moment, and then

brightened.

"Fair dos," he said. "Just seemed strange, that's all, the soldiers suddenly bothering with us lot overnight. The king must have got a bee in his bonnet about cleaning up the streets for his precious new son, or something."

But Ben was no longer listening. Through the barred window he could see signs that they were approaching the city. Quadrivium was completely surrounded by a high wall built from huge blocks of creamy-yellow stone with four main gates located at the cardinal points of the compass: north, south, east and west. Ordinary folk had to enter and exit through these gates, which allowed those in charge to keep track of the number of people inside the city walls at any point in time. The secondary gates, one of which they were fast approaching, were used exclusively by the king's men.

The carriage rolled to a stop beside a sentry.

"Anything to declare?" he called out, pressing his face up against the bars to stare in at Ben and Joe.

"Another two boys for the school," said one of the soldiers, flicking the reins to hurry the horses past.

The carriage clattered beneath the stone arch and into the city, and Ben's heart sank as he wondered how he was going to get back to the inn in time to meet up with Murgatroyd.

* * *

Bella woke suddenly, disorientated. Dusty shafts of daylight filtered up through the cracks in the hard wooden floor on which she lay. It took a moment before her memory came flooding back and she relived the heart-stopping slide from the turret to the dome. She closed her eyes again, wondering what had become of Penthesilean.

There was a loud tapping just above her head, which stopped as abruptly as it had started. Bella held her breath and listened. After a moment, the tapping began again, causing old plaster to shower down from a crack in the arched ceiling. She shifted slightly to shake the dust from her face, then froze as one of the floorboards creaked beneath her. The tapping immediately ceased.

"Bella, are you there?"

She gasped with relief.

"Yes, I'm here, Murgatroyd!" she whispered. "Is it safe to come out?"

There was a pause, then, "The battlements are clear, but there's a lot of activity going on down below so keep away from the edge."

Bella opened the trapdoor. The bright light of early morning poured through the small window in the side of the dome, illuminating the circular stone staircase below, which was deserted as far as she could see. She pulled a lever to release the ladder, wincing as the clanking machinery broke the silence. As soon as it was fully extended, she climbed down and groped along the wall for the matching lever which would pull the ladder back up into the secret room.

She was constantly amazed by the clever mechanism which her son Damien had designed and built with his own hands. She wondered what he would think, wherever he was, if he knew that his hiding place was now providing a refuge for his mother. She pushed these thoughts to one side as she located the lever behind a loose stone and the ladder slowly and noisily disappeared back into the ceiling, the trapdoor easing shut behind it with a gentle thud.

She sidled down the stairs, keeping close to the wall and expecting at any moment to hear the sound of footsteps racing up towards her. Reaching the door to the gallery without incident, she opened it a crack and slipped through, heeding Murgatroyd's advice to stay well away from the balustrade which overlooked the main square.

"You must leave Quadrivium at once," said Murgatroyd from behind her, making her jump.

She pressed a hand to her racing heart. "Murgatroyd, I've got so much to tell you! Ponsonby is a traitor: he's kidnapped Prince Alexander; he knows that Ben has stolen the Book of Prophecies and he wants us to give him Ben in exchange for the prince . . ."

Murgatroyd interrupted as soon as she paused for breath. "Ben doesn't have the Book."

Quickly, he gave her a concise update of all that had

happened since she had left Ben in the throne room with the skeleton key the previous evening. Bella looked at him, speechless, as he told her about the mermen and how they believed that Ben was the Deliverer of their legends.

"But when they took Ben to where the Book had been, it was no longer there," explained Murgatroyd. "All he found was a single page, which the mermen believe will lead us to the Book itself."

"It doesn't make sense," said Bella when she finally found her voice. "Who else knew about the Book? Who else could have taken it? Ponsonby thinks it was Ben, and he won't release the prince until –" She paused and looked at Murgatroyd. "Where is he?"

Murgatroyd guessed what she was thinking. "No, Bella, we can't hand Ben over to Ponsonby: he's the only one who can read the signs that will lead us to the Book. And anyway, do you really think that Ponsonby would release Prince Alexander when he realises that Ben doesn't have it? At the moment, Ben's still our best chance of finding the Book and the longer we stay here, the longer that will take."

"Well, I can't leave Quadrivium," said Bella firmly. "Not while Alexander is still in the hands of that devious man. He's got Penthesilean too."

"Penthesilean?" repeated Murgatroyd. "Are you sure?"

"Of course I'm sure," said Bella. "The last time I saw him, he was being dragged off to the dungeons by

Ponsonby's henchmen!"

Murgatroyd peered over the edge of the balustrade into the courtyard below.

"That's strange," he said, "because I've just seen Penthesilean marching across the courtyard dressed in a sergeant's uniform . . ." He turned back to her. "If you must stay, Bella, promise me you'll be careful. You may be the queen's mother but Ponsonby has already proved how ruthless he can be. I'll return just as soon as I can."

And with that, he launched himself from the dome and disappeared after Penthesilean's rapidly retreating figure.

* * *

"The Great War of Barbearland took place one hundred years ago in the Northern Outer Regions of the Kingdom."

The class was in full swing as Ben and Joe entered the schoolroom, their arms grasped firmly by the young soldier who had escorted them from the inn. A very tall, thin woman stood in front of a large chalkboard, her dark hair pulled into a tight bun at the nape of her long neck. Perched on the very end of her nose was a pair of narrow, black-framed spectacles through which she glared down at the open book clasped between her bony hands. Before her were rows of desks with identically dressed children who were all staring at the newcomers. Ben grinned and waved, recognising a few faces from the inn.

"More children, Miss Spark," said the young soldier. "Sergeant Tully said to bring them straight to you."

"What's that?" cried the teacher, flustered, looking everywhere but at the soldier. "More children? No, I'm sorry, I'm afraid this class is already full . . ." She made a weak gesture at the desks full of children.

"Sergeant Tully said to bring them here," insisted the soldier.

Her gaze flickered towards him and then she looked away again.

"Well, I suppose the children can share desks until we get some more brought in," she said finally. She made flapping motions at the children in the front row who shuffled up to make room for the two boys. The soldier pushed them forward and Ben and Joe swaggered over to the empty seats, pulling faces at the rest of the class.

Ben was now dressed in the same uniform as the other boys. He had endured a thorough scrubbing at the hands of a pair of school matrons, one of whom had held him while the other had scrubbed at his skinny body with carbolic soap. She had been particularly thorough with his ears, scrubbing behind them and twisting her fat fingers into his earholes to get every last bit of dirt. With sleight of hand, he had managed to conceal his locket, Bella's key and the page from the Book of Prophecies from the matrons, transferring them deftly from the pile of his discarded clothes into the pocket of his new shorts without catching their attention.

The young soldier folded his arms and leaned against the wall next to the door.

"I'll just make sure they settle in," he said to the bemused teacher.

"Er, right then," she said, looking down at her book and trying to regain her composure. "Who can tell me which tribe was renowned as having the bravest and fiercest fighters in the Great War?"

Ben stopped trying to kick Joe under the desk and pricked up his ears. His hand shot up.

"Was it the bears, ma'am?" he called out before Miss Spark had chance to point to him. "Or perhaps the lizards? They've got some pretty mean-looking spikes on their backs!"

The rest of the class tittered as Miss Spark looked at him in shock. She glanced nervously at the soldier, who had unfolded his arms and was staring at Ben with sudden interest.

"What are you talking about, boy?" she said, her voice quavering slightly. "It was the king's own fusiliers, of course! The same regiment which now guards the gates of Quadrivium."

"But what about the sun leopards?" asked Ben. "Surely they were pretty fierce?"

"Sun leopards?" said Miss Spark. "Fighting in the Great War? Whatever are you on about, boy?"

"My name's Ben," he volunteered, before continuing. "I've seen their armour up at the palace. It's amazing! It's still so clean and shiny after so many years – the king must have an army of servants to polish it every single day!"

He looked around at his classmates, proud at knowing something the teacher didn't.

"There were no fighting lizards or bears or any other animal in the Great War," said Miss Spark firmly, preparing to go back to her reading. "The idea is preposterous! You'll be saying animals can talk next!"

"Well, I've never met a talking bear," conceded Ben, his head on one side. "In fact, I've never even met a bear. But I've met a talking bird: his name's Murgatroyd."

The class erupted with shrieks of laughter. Soon the room was a noisy hive of activity as the children scrambled over the desks to hear more from Ben about fighting bears, lizards, leopards and talking birds.

Not one of them noticed that the soldier had left the room.

* * *

Arrowbright scurried after Penthesilean. No one had recognised the old soldier yet, dressed as he was in Manson's uniform, but Arrowbright was having great difficulty in persuading him to behave more like a lowly sergeant and less like the decorated brigadier that he was.

"I need to find Bella," said Penthesilean, striding past yet another senior officer without saluting. The man glowered at his departing back and Arrowbright apologised, saluting for both of them before hurrying after Penthesilean.

"You need to get out of Quadrivium!" he said in a low, urgent voice. "And who is Bella?"

Penthesilean shot him a look from beneath his bushy white eyebrows. "The Dowager Bella, man, the queen's mother! She was taken hostage by Ponsonby last night, just after the scoundrel laid his hands on me."

Arrowbright frowned. "Mayor Ponsonby was the one who ordered your arrest, and now you're saying he also kidnapped the queen's mother. I wonder if he was behind Prince Alexander's disappearance too?"

"Ponsonby's a fraud," said Penthesilean in a loud voice, causing Arrowbright to cringe and look around. "But he's not the brains of the operation; he's taking orders from someone else and I want to know why! But first, I need to find Bella."

"We don't have time!"

"Why did you release me?" Penthesilean stopped suddenly and wheeled round to face the young soldier. "It was in direct contravention of your orders. I don't expect you'll get a promotion for this!"

Arrowbright looked him steadily in the eye. "You saved my father, sir, at the battle of Pemble. Bartholomew R. Arrowbright, sir. You won't remember him, but he never forgot you. *Arrowbright, my lad*, he would say, *if you turn out to be just a fraction of the soldier that Brigadier Penthesilean is, you'll have done me and your mother proud.*"

Penthesilean looked at him thoughtfully. "I can't say I remember your father, Arrowbright, but I'm sure he's a fine man."

"Was," said Arrowbright sadly. "He disappeared near the Mountains of the Outer Boundaries at the time of the Great Fire, presumed dead along with the rest of his battalion."

Penthesilean was silent for a moment. When he spoke, it wasn't with the words of condolence which Arrowbright expected to hear.

"Men like your father do not just disappear!" he said, barely controlling the fury in his voice. "Something very strange happened back then, and I fear it's happening again. I think perhaps Bella was right in trying to find the Book, but I fear it may have brought a lot of trouble down on all of us . . ."

They had reached the main courtyard which was overshadowed by the great dome. Striding across the open square with Arrowbright hurrying to keep up, Penthesilean was suddenly stopped in his tracks by a loud shout.

"Halt, soldier! Halt, I tell you!"

* * *

Miss Spark felt her already fragile grip on authority slip from her thin fingers. She took off her glasses and pinched the bridge of her nose, feeling another one of her migraines coming on.

She didn't notice the shadowy figures which appeared in the frosted glass of the classroom door until it was suddenly flung open and two soldiers entered the room, their heavy boots clattering loudly on the wooden floor. A screwed up ball of paper, aimed at another child, flew directly towards one of them. The soldier swatted it to one side and stood to attention just inside the classroom door. The other man stepped to the front of the class and glared at the children.

"The boy known as Ben," he barked, "step forward now!"

Miss Spark looked up from behind her desk where she had retreated to sit with her head in her hands, wondering why she had ever wanted to become a teacher. At his words she jumped to her feet, knocking over a pile of books in her haste.

"There he is," she said, pointing at Ben with a trembling finger. "He's the one you want. Take him, please!"

The soldier swung his whole body towards her and stared at her with his piercing blue eyes.

"Been troubling you, has he, miss?" he asked. "Been stirring things up a bit, eh?"

"Er, well," she faltered under his gaze, "he does have some strange ideas . . ." She petered off as the soldier turned back to face Ben.

"Chop chop!" he cried. "No need to bring anything, young man."

Ben stood up slowly.

"But we want to hear more about Murgatroyd!" cried Joe, tugging at Ben's arm.

Ben noticed the soldier stiffen at the mention of Murgatroyd.

"Come along, boy!" he cried, suddenly agitated. Striding forward, he took hold of Ben's arm in an iron grip.

"Good day, ma'am," he nodded to Miss Spark and was out of the door in two long strides, dragging Ben with him. The door slammed behind them and the class was silent once more.

*　*　*

Outside the classroom, the soldiers each took one of Ben's arms and half carried him down the corridor. Beyond the steady clomp of their boots marching in step, he could hear the drone of adult voices from behind closed doors and the occasional sharp squeak of a chair.

Suddenly there was the sound of voices and more boots up ahead. A large group of soldiers appeared at the other end of the corridor, headed directly towards them. The corridor was not wide enough for the two groups to pass and neither showed signs of giving way.

"Stand aside!" barked the soldier who had escorted Ben from the classroom, stepping forward to block the other soldiers' path.

"Fall back for Mayor Ponsonby of Quadrivium!" countered the other soldiers, their green uniforms emblazoned with fancy gold epaulettes.

Ben froze at the sound of the mayor's name. The words also seemed to make an impression on his escorts, for they quickly gave way. Pushing Ben back against the wall, they stood facing him with their backs to the corridor, blocking his view. He heard the sound of boots pass by and then, as soon as they had gone, the two soldiers sprang apart.

"Run!"

Before he knew what was happening, they grabbed his arms, lifted him off the floor and sprinted down the corridor with him. Skidding round a corner, they collided head on with a grey-haired teacher coming the other way. The man screamed and threw up his arms in a gesture of surrender, the pile of papers he was carrying flying up in the air and cascading around them like confetti.

"Don't hurt me!" he cried, backing away fearfully. "I'm only teaching what I'm told, I swear on Tritan's mantle!"

The younger soldier released Ben's arm and began to help the teacher gather his papers. Ben grabbed his opportunity. Taking a deep breath, he wrenched his arm from the other soldier's grasp and dived between the old man's legs. The man immediately lost his balance and fell to the floor, blocking the narrow corridor. Up ahead, Ben could see the double doors which marked the entrance to the school. He scrambled to his feet and made a dash for freedom.

"Ben, wait!"

Ben stretched out his hand to grasp the door handle.

"I'm a friend of Bella's!"

He had the door open before the soldier's words finally registered. He hesitated, looking back. The soldier leapt over the fallen teacher and in a few long strides was by Ben's side. He slammed the door shut with one hand and clasped Ben's shoulder firmly with the other.

"My name is Penthesilean." He paused to catch his breath before continuing. "Ben, Mayor Ponsonby has been looking for you and now he knows you're here. We have to get you out of Quadrivium as soon as possible." He glanced back at the other soldier who was helping the teacher to his feet. "Arrowbright and I are your cover. Without us, you won't stand a chance of escaping."

He released Ben's shoulder and opened one of the double doors, motioning for him to take a look. Directly ahead, beyond a manicured lawn criss-crossed by neat, white gravel paths, was a wrought iron gate with the words 'School' arching above it. When he and Joe had arrived earlier that morning, Ben had noticed only one man standing at the open gate. The gate was now closed and he could see ten or more men guarding it.

At that moment, one of the guards turned and saw the two of them standing in the open doorway.

"Excellent! You've got the boy!" he cried, taking a few paces towards them down one of the gravel paths.

"Stick with me and move quickly," murmured Penthesilean out of the corner of his mouth. "Arrowbright, wait for my signal."

With Ben by his side, he strode down the steps and onto the gravel path towards the approaching guard. When they were no more than a few paces apart, he grabbed Ben's arm and stepped off the path and onto the lawn.

"Off the grass!" ordered the guard automatically. He made a grab for Ben who dodged nimbly out of reach. The man lost his balance and teetered on the very edge of the path, his arms waving wildly. He finally regained his balance and stepped backwards into the centre of the path, letting out a cry of frustration at Ben and Penthesilean standing just out of reach.

"Go!" cried Penthesilean to Arrowbright who was standing on the school steps waiting for his command. The younger soldier set off in the opposite direction, his heavy boots making deep impressions in the grass. There was an audible gasp from the guards by the gate and they immediately took off down the paths towards him, leaving the gate unguarded.

Staying out of their reach, Penthesilean pulled Ben across the grass towards the gate.

"I don't understand," said Ben, "why can't they walk on the grass?"

"School rules," replied Penthesilean. "Even the guards aren't allowed to break them!" He waved distractedly at the grass as he scanned the route ahead. Ben followed the direction of his arm and noticed for the first time that the lawn was dotted with small, white signs, each one reading: 'Keep Off the Grass'.

Suddenly he heard the sound of children's voices. He looked up and was surprised to see Joe climbing out of a window, followed by a swarm of children. They all kicked off their shoes and danced barefoot across the grass, turning cartwheels and laughing and shouting to each other.

"Off the grass! Get off the grass!" cried the guards, running up and down the gravel paths, grasping helplessly at the children who simply skipped away.

With the guards distracted, Ben and Penthesilean headed directly for the gate where Arrowbright was already waiting. With a brief backward glance at his classmates, Ben followed the two soldiers through the gate and away from the school.

12

Bella had retreated back into the safety of her secret attic hideaway tucked inside the roof of the dome, and was trying to decide on her best course of action. She suspected that Mayor Ponsonby would have hidden the prince somewhere within the palace, or at least within the walls of the city, close enough to triumphantly bring forth at a moment's notice once he was no longer required as a secret hostage, once Ben had been captured and the Book of Prophecies was safely back in Ponsonby's possession. Naturally he would take all the credit for finding the prince and some poor innocent would take the blame for the kidnapping. She was going to have to rely on her wits in order to work out where the prince was being held and rescue him without getting caught herself. It was not going to be easy: the palace was crawling with Ponsonby's men.

She was distracted from her thoughts by a loud clattering on the steps below. She pricked up her ears as she recognised the cry of frustration.

"Drat!" said the voice, followed by the sound of footsteps running lightly down the steps.

Bella opened the trapdoor and called out in a loud whisper, "Madeleine!"

A moment later, the figure of a young girl appeared around a curve of the staircase. A wooden easel was tucked awkwardly under one arm and in her other hand she held a bunch of assorted paintbrushes. She stopped in astonishment at the sight of Bella's head poking out from the wooden ceiling.

"Great Aunt Bella, is that you?" she asked in a loud voice.

"Shhh," cautioned Bella. "Are you alone?"

Madeleine looked around and then nodded mutely up at her aunt.

"What are you doing up here?" whispered Bella.

"I often come up to the dome to paint," said Madeleine in the same loud voice as before. She caught the look on Bella's face and winced. "Sorry," she whispered. "I come here to paint: there's the most amazing view of the entire city from up here. What are you doing, Aunt Bella?"

Bella released the ladder and climbed down to join Madeleine, a plan forming rapidly in her mind.

* * *

The two soldiers walked either side of Ben, holding his arms as though he was their prisoner. The school gates opened onto a large square which was bustling with people going about their day-to-day business in the afternoon sunshine. They had resisted the temptation to break into a run once through the gates and had managed to attract only a few curious glances from passersby as they crossed the square. Penthesilean even remembered to respectfully salute the few officers they encountered.

Ben glanced back as they passed a group of workmen erecting a statue and was surprised to recognise Mayor Ponsonby's smug, jowly features atop the tall, slim figure. He was about to point out to the others how much artistic license the sculptor had used, when a cry went up behind them.

"Halt! Stop those men!"

A group of soldiers had appeared at the school gates, the same men who had been accompanying Mayor Ponsonby. They started to make their way across the square towards them.

"Stop in the king's name!"

"I don't think the king has anything to do with this," snorted Penthesilean. "Come on, run!"

Dropping all pretence, he and Arrowbright released Ben's arms and they raced across the square. Small and nimble, Ben was soon out in front, darting in and out of the crowds, heading for a cluster of stalls surrounded by prosperous townsfolk. Lurking on the fringes he could see two or three grubby street children waiting for handouts. He was briefly surprised by how few there were, before he realised that many must have been rounded up like Joe and sent to the school.

As they approached the stalls, he spotted a narrow side street and motioned for the others to carry on, but instead of following he doubled back to the stall selling sweets. Darting forward, he grabbed a handful of sugar mice and threw them up into the air. The children instantly dived for the treats, pushing and jostling each other out of the way. The stallholder lunged towards Ben, but he easily wriggled out of the man's grasp and raced after the others, knocking over buckets of flowers in front of the flowerseller's stall as he passed.

He didn't stop when he reached the others who had paused to catch their breath in the relative calm of the side street. Behind him he could hear the cries of the soldiers as they battled their way through the chaos he had created.

"This way!" he cried, ducking through a stone archway.

It led to a short flight of steps which he took at a single leap, landing in a crouch at the bottom and pausing briefly to get his bearings. He found himself in a shady walled courtyard paved with cracked flagstones. On each wall was an archway identical to the one through which he'd just come. Arrowbright and Penthesilean clattered down the steps after him and waited for him to decide which one to choose, relying on his superior knowledge of the city's backstreets.

Ben looked around, indecisive. The courtyard was unfamiliar. There was an old stone sundial in one corner, partly covered in leaves, and he wondered who had placed it in such a shady spot. At that moment, a dusty ray of sunlight penetrated the trees to fall directly onto the face of the sundial. Ben swept the leaves from its surface, and the shadow cast by the sundial's upright pointer instantly fell in a straight line towards one of the archways.

Without wasting any more time, he dived through the archway, the others following close on his heels. It led into a narrow passage flanked on both sides by high stone walls. They hurried down it, bouncing off the walls in their haste as they navigated the sharp twists and turns.

Suddenly they heard a volley of shouts behind them. Ben took a sharp turn off the main passageway, down a steep flight of steps which brought them unexpectedly into a busy street lined with houses. Bringing up the rear, Penthesilean glanced over his shoulder as he descended the steps and caught sight of a soldier who ran past the steps. The man immediately backed up and shouted at him to stop, but Penthesilean ignored him and ran into the street to join the others.

There were people everywhere. Women bustled to and fro, carrying bundles of washing under their arms or balancing baskets of folded linen on their heads. The houses were tall and narrow, built one against the other with only the occasional gap in between, and toddlers played in the doorways which opened directly onto the busy street. Every few minutes, everyone would be forced up against the houses as a cart rattled past loaded down with washing.

Ben darted down a narrow side street off the main thoroughfare in an attempt to lose the soldiers. Here the afternoon light was subdued, filtered through multi-coloured bed-sheets hanging overhead, suspended from washing lines strung up between the houses. The musty smell of laundry filled the air.

He stopped suddenly and the others piled into the back of him.

"It's a dead end," he whispered. "We'll have to go back."

They began to retrace their steps when a soldier appeared at the entrance to the side street. He was facing the other way, speaking to the man next to him, but he half-turned as they watched, as though sensing their presence.

"In here, quick!"

A door had opened behind them and a woman beckoned them towards her. Gratefully, they piled in and she shut the door quickly behind them. Leaning against it, she shooed at them with her apron. "In the back with you! I'll get rid of them."

A second later there was a sharp knock on the door.

The three of them ducked behind a curtain and into

a small, windowless room which felt warm and humid. A wooden tub filled with soapy water took up much of the floor space, surrounded by wet sheets which hung like tents from clothes horses propped up against the walls. The two soldiers concealed themselves beneath the hanging laundry, while Ben dived beneath a pile of washing which sat in a heap on the floor next to the tub. From this angle he had a clear view under the curtain which separated the two rooms. He watched the washerwoman's fat ankles approach the door. It opened to reveal two pairs of highly polished boots.

"Now then, boys," came the woman's voice, this time high-pitched and girly, "to what do I owe this pleasure? Have you brought me your dirty laundry?"

"Sorry to disturb you, ma'am," came a man's voice over the sound of her giggles.

"OOooooooh!" interrupted the woman in her sing-song voice. "Aren't you polite? I haven't been called ma'am since before the wall went up!"

"We're looking for two men," said the voice.

"So am I, love!"

"They have a young boy with them, about twelve years of age," continued the soldier, ignoring her remark. "Have you seen them?"

"I wish!" said the woman. "Luella across the way might have, you should ask her. But first, why don't you boys come on in and let little old Gertie see if she can't get your grubby uniforms clean?"

Ben could sense the young soldiers' embarrassment as they shuffled their boots. One of them took a tentative step backwards, quickly followed by the other. Their voices faded as they backed away from the doorway.

"No, no! We've disturbed you enough! Luella, you say? And she is . . . ?"

"Just along the way there, dearies," said Gertie, "but you won't get nearly as good a service wash from her . . ."

All went quiet as the washerwoman's voice trailed off. Finally, Ben saw the door close and the curtain was drawn back.

"Now then," she said. "I suppose you three will be wanting some grub?"

* * *

Gertie talked while Ben, Arrowbright and Penthesilean devoured the chicken dumpling stew which she placed before them.

"I just don't know when it will all stop," she cried, ladling out another huge helping of food onto Ben's plate. "The wall was one thing, although Tritan knows why the king felt we needed it! It's caused more trouble than it's worth, I can tell you! My daughter's husband lost his brick-making business when they built the north-east section right through his yard! They had to leave the kiln to go to rack and ruin when they moved inside the wall, and to add insult to injury, the king's builders didn't even use his bricks! No, everything had to go through the mayor's own contractors. Backhanders, I tell you. It's a case of corruption in the first degree!"

Penthesilean swallowed a large dumpling and drew a breath to speak, but didn't get the chance as the washerwoman continued.

"And now with this ban on fortune telling, well, it's just turning people's lives upside down! Horoscopy, astrology: you name it, it's banned! How are we supposed to know whether or not it's a good washing day without reading the weather first, I ask you? I really don't know what has got into the king's head!"

Penthesilean was reminded of what Bella had told him only the night before. It had been a fortune teller who had told her to expect Ben, and he wondered whether Mayor Ponsonby's ban on fortune telling had something to do with Ben and the Book of Prophecies.

"How did you know we were right outside your door?" asked Ben through a mouth full of food.

Gertie waved her large, mottled arm in the direction of the washtub.

"Well, I know it's not strictly allowed under the latest decree," she said, only slightly abashed, "but if I'm going to be laundering the king's own bed-sheets, I may as well make use of the auguries coming from them. There's powerful aura in royal linen, you know . . . Anyway, where was I? Oh yes, I had just started a load of washing," she said, slowly getting to her feet, "and I saw your arrival in the suds." She crooked a finger at Ben. "Come here and take a look, young man."

He got to his feet and joined her by the tub. She examined the soapy water for a moment before dipping the tip of her pink, sausage-like finger into the suds and tracing a pattern on the surface.

"There," she said, "do you see?"

Ben stared down into the water. Arrowbright and Penthesilean peered over his shoulder, seeing nothing but a soapy residue.

"Don't try to focus," said the washerwoman softly. "Just allow your mind to drift . . ."

The suds swirled slowly about, patterns shifting and reforming on the surface of the water. Ben allowed his mind to relax and gradually a picture began to take shape. Three shadowy figures were coming towards him, their movements slow and dreamlike. They entered a doorway which appeared amongst the soapy bubbles. The suds continued to swirl around the tub, reforming this time into four figures, one considerably larger than the others. Slowly they merged into one and the doorway disappeared just as two other figures took shape. In the back of his mind, Ben realised that he was seeing a re-enactment of the washerwoman rescuing them from the soldiers.

The image dissolved but the water was still moving and the suds reformed once more. This time he identified the image immediately. Flames leapt in slow motion to fill the surface of the washtub, then slowly they drifted to the sides, forming a ring of fire. In the centre, the remaining soapsuds clustered together to become a four-legged beast. The bubbles then separated into two smaller beasts and then again and again until there were four . . . eight . . . sixteen figures. Eventually, the image dissolved as the suds finally evaporated.

Ben slid to the ground and wrapped his arms around his knees. The washerwoman leaned down and took his chin gently in her warm, damp hand. She raised his face until his eyes met hers. "You've seen this before, haven't you Ben? The Book of Prophecies has revealed it to you."

He nodded slowly.

"May I see it?"

He hesitated. "I don't have the Book, just a single page."

He reached into his pocket and drew it out. After wiping her hands carefully on her apron, Gertie took the sheet of parchment from him. Arrowbright and Penthesilean looked at each other but remained silent, reluctant to break the look of concentration on Gertie's face.

After a long moment she looked up at him. "The markings on this sheet, do you know what they signify?"

Ben looked shocked. To everyone else, the parchment had appeared blank. Gertie noticed his surprise.

172

"I see shadows," she said, "just a faint imprint of what you see. I have a gift, but it is not as strong as yours."

"What does it all mean?" asked Ben, relieved to find someone else who could see the markings.

"This page wants to be part of the whole – you must read the signs and deliver it to its greater self."

"And the fire?"

"It is up to you to save those who are trapped," she said gently. "It is all tied up with the Book. There is one who would stop you, but you have been given the means, you have the will and now it is time for you to go and fulfil the prophecy."

The others listened to this exchange in silence. They hadn't seen anything in the tub but soapsuds, but they both sensed something momentous in the washerwoman's solemn words.

"What about us?" asked Arrowbright, laying a hand on Ben's shoulder.

"You will go with him, young man," replied Gertie, looking him in the eye, "to protect him and to help him."

She bustled through into the other room, returning with some clothes for Ben. While he changed quickly out of the school uniform and into the more nondescript trousers and shirt, she disappeared again and re-emerged a few minutes later with a large loaf of bread and a slab of yellow cheese which she packed carefully into a small canvas satchel and handed to Ben, "For your journey."

Then she fished a bottle of beer from the pocket of her apron and handed it to Arrowbright. He tucked it carefully into his jacket pocket.

"Anything for me?" asked Penthesilean with amusement, but she would not meet his eyes. Instead she glanced back towards the suds and her brow furrowed.

"You must go now," she said, her voice suddenly urgent. "You must leave Quadrivium. The soldiers have finished searching the other houses and are making their way back here."

Arrowbright ran to the door and opened it. The passageway was deserted. Beckoning the other two through, he paused for a second and looked back at the washerwoman. She nodded to him one last time.

"Take care of him," she said and closed the door firmly behind them.

* * *

As they left the washerwoman's house, Ben took the lead once more. He kept to the narrow backstreets, threading his way through the labyrinth of winding lanes, heading unerringly towards the city wall. Arrowbright followed with Penthesilean bringing up the rear, constantly looking over his shoulder. It didn't take them long to reach the grain warehouses at the very outer edge of the city.

Making their way down a narrow alleyway between

two large, windowless buildings, they caught their first glimpse of the wall up ahead. As they came to the end of the alleyway, Arrowbright pulled Ben back and peered cautiously round the corner.

"Penthesilean," he whispered, "take a look at this."

He moved back to allow the old soldier to take his place. Penthesilean gave a long, low whistle. Their route had brought them out next to the principal Southern gate and the surrounding battlements were teeming with soldiers.

"They've tripled the number of sentries on duty," he said. "It's going to be tricky getting over the wall without being seen."

He stood back to allow Ben to take a look.

"What do we do?" asked Ben. He had never seen so many soldiers in one place before. "We can't go back, the guards will be everywhere by now, looking for us."

"Give me a minute," said Penthesilean.

Before they could stop him, he had stepped out of the shadows of the warehouse and was striding towards the gate, pulling his medals out of his pocket as he went and attaching them to the front of his uniform.

It wasn't long before he was challenged by a couple of officers. They caught snatches of Penthesilean's booming voice: "Do you know who I am? . . . appalling lack of discipline . . . sent by the king himself . . . inspection of the troops…"

Ben and Arrowbright watched in disbelief as the officers

saluted him and scurried away, shouting out orders. The soldiers on the battlements began to drift towards the gate, leaving a sizeable gap unmanned.

They seized their opportunity and raced across the exposed stretch of cobblestones which separated the warehouse from the city wall, heading towards a flight of steps which led up to the battlements. They had almost made it when a carriage appeared unexpectedly and rolled to a stop in front of the gate. A liveried footman jumped down and opened the carriage door. A few seconds later, a familiar figure appeared.

Ben recognised Mayor Ponsonby immediately and froze. Arrowbright had already reached the steps up to the battlements. The soldiers were still milling around for the impromptu inspection and hadn't yet noticed Ben stuck out in the open. Acting on instinct, he dived towards an old stone water trough which stood just a few feet away. He broke his fall with a practiced roll, landing close enough to the carriage to hear every word that was spoken.

"You fools!" cried the mayor. "He's an imposter, seize him! He's one of the two mercenaries accompanying the boy, the ones you were supposed to be on the lookout for!"

As the soldiers converged on Penthesilean, Ben leapt to his feet and sprinted towards the wall. The sudden movement must have caught Ponsonby's eye, as at that moment he glanced up and looked straight at Ben. His mouth fell open, but before he had a chance to speak a dark streak hurtled from the sky, knocking him off his feet. Ben didn't wait to see what it was. He joined Arrowbright and together they raced up the stone steps, ignored by the guards who were rushing in all directions, spooked by the unexpected airborne attack on the mayor. Seconds later, they were over the wall and climbing down the other side to freedom.

* * *

Princess Madeleine set up her easel on the balcony of the great golden dome and took her sketchbook and paints from her bag. Bella crouched out of sight of anyone who might look up from the square below, and listened to the girl talk.

"There's a rumour going round the palace that you and Penthesilean left the city together last night," said Madeleine excitedly, as she began to squeeze a selection of paints onto her palette. "I thought it was so romantic – I always knew he had a soft spot for you – but here you are instead, hiding in the dome!"

"Who told you that?" asked Bella. "Who told you I had left Quadrivium?"

Madeleine put her head on one side. "I'm not sure. It couldn't have been Mother, she hasn't got out of bed yet. It might have been cook, or . . . No, wait, I remember! I thought it was strange as the mayor's household guards aren't usually in the palace this early, but I just assumed they were helping the king's men search for Prince Alexander – he's still missing you know, isn't it dreadful? Anyway, there was a handful of them in the dining hall when I went in for breakfast and I overheard them talking about it. Now that I think of it, they were talking very loudly, almost as if they wanted everyone to hear."

"Do you remember exactly what they said?"

The girl's pretty face scrunched up into a frown. "Not exactly, no. Just that one of them had seen you together, riding on horseback through the city gates in the moonlight."

Bella looked at her sharply and she blushed. "I might have added that last bit myself," she admitted. "I could just imagine the two of you galloping off into the moonlight together."

Bella sighed and wondered whether her plan would work. She reminded herself that no one was likely to pay much attention to where the princess went or what she said. She would be able to go almost anywhere in the palace without her appearance being remarked upon and, more importantly, she always seemed to hear the latest gossip.

"Great Aunt Bella," said Madeleine suddenly, "there's something going on by the Southern Gate!"

"What is it?"

Bella desperately wanted to jump up and look herself, but she couldn't risk being spotted by Ponsonby's men.

"I'm not sure," said Madeleine, moving around the dome to get a better view. "The soldiers on the battlements all seem to be leaving their posts and heading towards the gate . . . I wonder if they've found Prince Alexander? Oh, Mayor Ponsonby's carriage has just appeared. He's getting out . . . he's pointing a lot, it looks like he's giving orders. The soldiers have grabbed one of the other soldiers, a big man. He looks a bit like . . . No, it can't be."

"Who?" cried Bella in frustration.

Madeleine raised her hand to block out the sun. "Yes, it is him! Oh, my word, it looks as though they're arresting him!"

"Who?" cried Bella, clutching at Madeleine's leg. "Who is it?"

"It's Penthesilean," said the girl. "Great Aunt Bella, are you and he in some sort of trouble?"

13

They ran until Ben thought his lungs would burst. Each time he looked back, the city seemed no further away. Arrowbright insisted they keep going.

"Penthesilean gave himself up so we could escape," he said between breaths. "We can't let his sacrifice be in vain."

They passed clusters of derelict buildings, the remains reminding Ben of the abandoned inn which he had called home. He supposed it too must have once been a thriving business before the wall around Quadrivium had gone up, but it was well outside the perimeter and nowhere near any of the four main gates into the city, so the owner had simply abandoned it, leaving it to Ben and his friends.

He was glad when they left the ghostly dwellings behind them and reached the open countryside. A clear blue sky arched above as they made their way down grassy avenues through fields of golden wheat rippling in the afternoon breeze. The only sounds were the occasional burst of birdsong and the wind rustling through the wheat. Eventually they slowed to a walk and, as there was no sign of pursuit, Arrowbright finally decided it was safe to stop.

They collapsed onto the grass, each absorbed by their own thoughts.

"What will they do to him?" asked Ben, finally. Arrowbright didn't need to ask who he meant.

"I don't know," he admitted with a furrowed brow. "Hopefully the king will intervene." He paused and chewed on a stalk of grass. "None of it makes any sense," he said suddenly.

"Why was Penthesilean arrested in the first place? It must have been to get him out of the way. I don't believe for a moment that he was involved in the kidnapping of Prince Alexander, after all, he's a close friend of the Dowager Bella, the queen's own mother..."

Ben stared at Arrowbright. "Is that why you came to rescue me from the school? Did Bella ask you to? How did she know I was there?"

Arrowbright laughed ruefully at the barrage of questions. "I don't have all the answers, Ben, I wish I did. But I will tell you what little I do know."

Lying back on the grass, he began by telling Ben how he had helped Penthesilean escape from the interrogation room in the dungeons. It seemed like a lifetime ago now, rather than just that morning. The plan had been for the old soldier to leave the city as soon as possible, and

Arrowbright had little choice but to accompany him, since it was only a matter of time before someone discovered Manson trussed up in the dungeon and learnt of his involvement.

Their plan had gone awry almost immediately. They had been crossing the main square beneath the golden dome when Penthesilean had been stopped by an officer. Arrowbright had hung back, thinking at first that the old soldier had been recognised: he was an unmistakeable giant of a man and once met was not easily forgotten. But the officer had simply wanted him to deliver a message to Mayor Ponsonby.

"Make sure you put this note directly into his hands," the soldier had said. "It's a matter of the upmost urgency. Go now and be quick!"

Penthesilean had hurried away with the note, but instead of delivering it, he had broken the military seal and read it himself.

Your worship, read the note, *a boy matching the description of the thief has been admitted to the school. I am sending my best men to escort you there for the interrogation. They will be with you imminently.*

"Penthesilean insisted we rescue you from the school before Mayor Ponsonby got there," said Arrowbright. "He had heard all about you from the Dowager Bella. She told him about your attempt to steal the mayor's chain – it sounded like you made quite a fool of him – but she also said that she had sent you to retrieve something from the monks, something which didn't belong to them. Penthesilean wouldn't tell me what it was, only that Ponsonby was involved in some way, but he thought you must have been successful to create such a fuss."

He looked down at Ben. "So, were you?"

Ben shifted uncomfortably. "Not exactly," he said. He was saved from further explanation by a shadow passing close overhead. They both glanced up warily, and then Ben gave a shout. "Murgatroyd!"

The great eagle circled once more and came to settle on the grass beside them. Arrowbright looked uncertainly from the bird to Ben, then his eyes widened as Murgatroyd began to speak.

"You can't stay here – the soldiers have sent trackers after you. You have to keep moving."

"How did you know where to find me?" asked Ben. "I was supposed to meet you at the inn."

"It's a long story," said Murgatroyd. "But I've been keeping an eye on you ever since Penthesilean and this young man broke you out of the school. It was I who provided the necessary diversion to allow you to get over the wall."

"You dive-bombed the soldiers!" cried Arrowbright, recovering from the shock of hearing the eagle speak. "What happened to Penthesilean?"

"I'm afraid he was arrested, there was nothing more I

could do for him . . ."

"And Bella?" asked Ben, remembering Murgatroyd's original purpose for returning to Quadrivium.

"She refuses to leave, but she's safe for now – unlike you. Ponsonby thinks you have the Book, Ben, and he will stop at nothing to find you! We must find the Book of Prophecies before he finds us."

Ben gazed back in the direction from which they'd come. They had covered a fair amount of distance in their initial headlong dash, but he could still make out the turrets and dome of the palace, hazy in the summer afternoon. He drew the parchment from his pocket and unrolled it slowly. Murgatroyd could barely contain his curiosity as he watched Ben's eyes flicker between the city and the page from the Book.

"What do you see?"

"Let him think," cautioned Arrowbright, his brow furrowed as he looked over Ben's shoulder at the blank parchment.

Ben stood up and rotated slowly until his back was towards the city, the parchment held out in front of him. He took a few steps and then suddenly swung back round and stared intently back the way they had come.

Arrowbright turned to see what he was looking at. He noticed that the afternoon haze had become unusually thick and grey. Murgatroyd had also noticed the change and quickly took to the sky for a better view. He returned almost immediately.

"They're burning the crops!" he cried.

They watched in dismay, the parchment forgotten, as thick columns of smoke spiralled up from the fields. The scent of burning wheat soon reached their nostrils, carried on the breeze which had suddenly sprung up. Before long, they could see an orange glow beneath the smoke and feel the heat from the flames. The fire was moving rapidly in their direction.

Ben jumped as a huge rat appeared from the field of wheat, twice the size of a cat and with a thick tail as long as its body. It ignored them and raced past, squeaking hysterically. The wheat started to rustle and shake as a procession of small animals began to emerge, flowing around them like water before disappearing into the field beyond.

"You need to get moving," shouted Murgatroyd, taking to the sky. "The fire will soon be upon you!"

Arrowbright turned to run, following the animals.

"No!"

He turned back to see Ben facing the rapidly approaching fire with his arms raised up to the sky, the parchment clenched in his fist. His eyes were unfocussed as though his mind was in another time and place.

"Come on, Ben! We can't risk getting caught by the fire after all we've been through."

Ben ignored him. Instead, he shouted out a single word

which reverberated with sheer fury, "Stop!"

A streak of lightning ripped across the sky. The light turned an ominous shade of greenish grey as a storm cloud gathered overhead, more lightning flickering in the midst of its dense darkness. The cloud billowed out across the sky, heading for the blaze, the wind whipping Ben's hair across his face.

A moment later, the wind dropped and they stood once more in bright sunshine. In the direction of the city, a thick, grey curtain of rain descended from the cloud to the horizon. A faint smell of sulphur reached their nostrils, wafted in on the fresh, post-storm breeze.

Arrowbright examined Ben out of the corner of his eye. The boy was gazing after the cloud with a look of complete calm on his face. Before he could question him, Murgatroyd came in to land in a rush.

"The scouts started the fire," he called, "trying to smoke you out! They must be really desperate to find you, Ben, to burn the city's food supply so recklessly."

Ben seemed to wake as if from a trance. He looked at Murgatroyd and then at Arrowbright.

"The animals," he said quietly, "are they safe?"

Arrowbright took his arm gently. "Yes, the fire is out and the animals are safe."

"Good," said Ben, shaking his arm free and walking away. "We need to go this way."

* * *

They set off at a slower pace than before. After the sudden storm, it was once more a perfect, warm afternoon. The occasional gentle gust of wind rippled through the wheat and cooled their faces. Murgatroyd circled overhead, keeping watch. There were a few false alarms, the eagle swooping down on them suddenly, hissing at them to take cover, but each time he returned to give the all clear.

Arrowbright walked in silence, a question forming in his head.

"Ben," he began eventually, "what did you see on the parchment?"

Ben looked at him. "It's hard to explain." He thought for a few moments. "First I saw the city – just a simple outline with no colour or detail – but when I turned to face the other way, the picture changed completely. It became lifelike, only even more real than real, if you can understand that. It was like a mirror image of what I saw around me, but better, as though it was coaxing me in that direction. But then a shadow appeared where the city had been and – well, you know what happened next."

Arrowbright nodded and they continued in silence, each deep in their own thoughts.

Gradually, the heat of the afternoon began to take its toll. Ben yawned as he walked, wiping beads of sweat from his upper lip with the back of his hand. They began to relax. The occasional rustlings in the wheat had yielded no hostile scouts, only a couple of field mice which provided Murgatroyd with a tasty snack, and so finally they decided to stop for a break. Arrowbright and Ben sank thankfully to the ground.

"We'll take ten minutes," said Murgatroyd, "and then another couple of hours' march before nightfall."

Ben rolled his eyes. He and Arrowbright flopped backwards where they sat, ignoring the prickly wheat against their backs. Murgatroyd paced round in circles, patting the stalks flat before settling himself. Within seconds, all three were sound asleep.

* * *

Ben woke to find his mouth full of feathers. He tried to sit up before he realised it was Murgatroyd's massive wing covering his mouth. The bird's other wing was over Arrowbright's face and they were both staring at the wall of wheat before them. The long shadows of early evening were draped all around them.

"What is it?" whispered Ben, spitting feathers out of his mouth.

Without moving his wings, the bird thrust his head towards the wheat. Ben strained his eyes, but couldn't see anything out of the ordinary. Minutes passed. As he stared in the direction of Murgatroyd's gaze, faint shapes began to float at the edges of his vision. He blinked to clear his sight, and then drew in his breath. Directly in front of him, perhaps no more than a foot away, was a pair of eyes staring straight at him. He had only noticed them because they had just closed and reopened in a blink which had mirrored his own.

A moment later, he felt his nose begin to itch. He twitched it furiously, trying to wriggle away the tickle, and then sniffed, once and then once more. But the pressure was building up inside him, and all at once the sneeze came rushing out, shattering the silence.

He looked up slowly through his fringe which had fallen across his eyes. Neither Murgatroyd nor Arrowbright had moved. They stared back at the eyes. A second later, all three of them jumped as the wheat parted and the eyes entered the clearing, accompanied by a pair of silky ears and a wet black nose. Following after was a body covered in fur which was almost exactly the same golden shade as the wheat.

"It's a dog," observed Ben with relief. He reached down to pat the animal's head as a furiously wagging tail thrashed the wheat.

"What's that round his neck?" asked Murgatroyd from a safe distance.

Ben bent down, laughing as the dog tried to lick his face.

"It's a disc," he said, pushing the animal's chin up so

that he could read the inscription. "Tobias," he read out loud. "I suppose that's his name."

"Does it say anything else?" asked Arrowbright.

Ben turned the disc over. On the other side were some symbols that he couldn't interpret.

"Just some weird squiggles," he said. "Maybe it's his name in dog language."

He laughed and stood up. Murgatroyd approached cautiously.

"Dog language?" he repeated. Edging closer to Tobias, yet keeping out of range of his long, pink tongue, he looked into the dog's eyes.

"Can you talk?" he asked, pronouncing each word slowly and clearly.

Tobias put his head on one side as though giving the question his careful consideration. The three of them waited. Suddenly the dog's ears pricked up and he look around, his nose twitching. Then, leaping towards Ben, he grabbed hold of one of his trouser legs in his teeth and began to tug.

"Whoa, boy!" laughed Ben, almost falling over.

"Shhhh!" Murgatroyd stood motionless, listening. Suddenly they could all hear what Tobias had picked up first: the sound of wheat rustling as someone or something made its way towards them.

"Run," hissed Murgatroyd, launching himself into the air.

Tobias released his grip on Ben's trousers and dashed into the wheat. Without thinking, Ben rushed after him with Arrowbright close behind.

The wheat field ended suddenly and they stumbled out onto a riverbank bordered by tall reeds. Tobias launched himself into the river, disappearing for a moment before bobbing back to the surface, kicking with all four paws. After a brief hesitation, the others leapt in after him. The water closed over Ben's head before Arrowbright grabbed his arm and dragged him back into the shallows, amongst the reeds.

A moment later, the first of their pursuers appeared. He was a small, lean man dressed from head to toe in green. A peaked cap cast a long shadow over his face as he surveyed the riverbank. He had a bow and a quiver of arrows strapped onto his back and a badge on his breast pocket identified him as a member of the King's Tracker Scouts, the letters 'KTS' embroidered in gold.

He was soon joined by three similarly dressed men who proceeded to scurry around picking up bits of grass and wheat before discarding them. The lead scout had fallen to his knees and was peering intently at the ground. He moved slowly towards the reeds by the river, where he examined the broken stems.

Ben was close enough to see the sweat on the man's brow as he moved steadily towards their hiding place. Very slowly, he looked towards where Arrowbright was crouching next to him. Without turning his head, the young soldier held up two fingers and a thumb, before closing his hand into a fist. Ben nodded his head fractionally, shifting his weight so that he would be ready to leap out of the water on Arrowbright's signal.

The scout crept closer. Arrowbright's thumb slowly uncurled from his fist. Ben took a deep breath, readying himself. Arrowbright's index finger went up. Still the scout came closer. Just as Ben was about to spring, the scout suddenly jumped to his feet and stood to attention.

Ben raised himself up slightly and risked a peek over the top of the riverbank. The scouts had been joined by a large, red-faced man with gold epaulettes on the shoulders of his jacket.

"Report, Scouts!" he ordered, returning their salute.

"They went this way, sir!" cried the lead scout triumphantly, pointing into the river before snapping back to attention. "I believe they may still be in the vicinity."

The Scout Sergeant glanced towards the river, stroking his dark moustache nervously. He pulled an enormous, red spotted handkerchief out of his pocket and pressed it to his brow.

"Permission to continue the search, sir!" cried the lead scout eagerly.

"Caution, private!" replied the scout sergeant. "We don't know how many of them there are or if they are armed."

"I can report that there is a man and a youth, plus at least one other, maybe two – species undefined at this present time."

The scout sergeant shook open his handkerchief and blew his nose noisily into it. He examined the contents carefully, before folding it and putting it back in his pocket. He thought back to the extraordinary briefing given earlier that day by the unnaturally pale man in civilian clothing who had accompanied Mayor Ponsonby. The news had been quite unexpected: there were mermen loose in the waterways surrounding the city. Mermen! If any of the officers had been tempted to take the briefing as a joke, just one hard look from this stranger had silenced the lot of them. The sergeant was still finding it difficult to take in. As a boy, he had been taught that the mer-people were extinct; later he had been told they had never even existed. Even more recently, a rumour had circulated that a tribe of them had appeared and were terrorising the city. The civilian had not clarified the situation and none of the men had been brave enough to question him. Mayor Ponsonby had ordered them to keep this information highly confidential; there was no need to scare the citizens of Quadrivium, but in the event of an encounter to take no chances and shoot to kill.

The sergeant cleared his throat, about to give the order to continue their pursuit with bows at the ready, when a large shape exploded out of the water in front of him.

Hideous snarls erupted from a wide mouth open to reveal terrifying white fangs.

The sergeant threw up his arms and shrieked out loud. "Run! Run for your lives!"

In an instant, the scouts were stampeding their way back through the wheat field, hot on the heels of their sergeant. Only the lead scout stood his ground, staring in bewilderment at the rapidly departing backs of his fellow scouts.

"But sir," he said weakly, "it's only a dog . . ."

Tobias shook himself thoroughly, drenching the lone scout and bringing the man to his senses. He stared at the dog for a long moment, thoughts flying through his head. He knew that his career would suffer if he came up with a different story from the rest of his colleagues, particularly his sergeant. Making up his mind, he turned on his heel and raced after the other scouts.

* * *

Ben heaved a sigh of relief. Pressed into the mud beneath the reeds, just inches from the scout's feet, he had been certain they would be discovered.

"That was close," he whispered to Arrowbright.

Arrowbright nodded grimly, hauling himself out of the water and onto the riverbank. Ben followed, water streaming from his clothes, and Tobias immediately trotted over to him, his tail spraying drops of water in every direction as he wagged vigorously.

"If it wasn't for this fellow here," said Arrowbright, "those scouts would have found us."

Tobias looked very pleased with himself, as though he had understood every word, then he slid back down the muddy bank and lapped thirstily at the water.

Murgatroyd landed next to the others.

"So you hid in the river," he said, eyeing their wet clothes. "Good thinking."

Tobias chose that moment to scramble back up onto the riverbank. He stood panting next to Murgatroyd, tongue lolling, and then proceeded to shake himself. The eagle gave a loud exclamation and glared at Tobias with his large yellow eyes.

"Get that animal away from me," he said through gritted beak.

Ben turned to Tobias and rested a hand on the dog's head. "But he's our very own early warning system, Murgatroyd."

Tobias panted loudly as if in agreement, then jumped down into the river and bounded a little way along, splashing through the water in the shallows. He paused at a bend and gave a soft woof.

"It looks like he also wants to be our guide," laughed Ben.

Murgatroyd spread his wings, trying to dry his damp

feathers. "We have no idea where he's from. For all we know, he could be working for the enemy."

"No way," said Ben. "Those tracker scouts would have found us if it hadn't been for him. He scared them off. You should have seen him!"

"All I'm saying is that we should keep an eye on him."

"Murgatroyd's right, Ben," said Arrowbright, trying to keep the peace. "We don't know where the dog's come from, or who he belongs to. And I'm sure that Murgatroyd would have heard the scouts coming in time for us to escape. But for now, Murgatroyd, it looks like Tobias has the right idea. If we walk in the water, the scouts will find it more difficult to pick up our trail if they return."

Murgatroyd was slightly mollified by Arrowbright's intervention and he couldn't fault his logic. He was unable to fly while his feathers were still wet and reluctantly accepted the young soldier's offer to let him ride on his shoulder. But he refused to join in the banter about their narrow escape from the scouts and the terror in the men's eyes when they had seen Tobias leap out of the water. His suspicions remained intact as the large, golden-haired dog led them along the riverbed.

* * *

The party of scouts made it back to Quadrivium in record time. As soon as they passed through the gate into the city, the sergeant and the lead scout were separated from the rest of the scouts and escorted by armed guards down a steep flight of stairs and into a small, windowless room.

The lead scout stood smartly to attention in the centre of the room. His sergeant stood beside him, trembling slightly as he tried not to catch the eye of the pale man who had given the briefing about the mermen. Mayor Ponsonby observed the proceedings in silence, seated in front of a plain white table, while the pale man stalked round the room. He examined the pair from every angle before speaking directly to the lead scout.

"And you say the beast had a tail like a fish?"

"Yes, sir," said the scout, his eyes fixed on a corner of the ceiling which was unusually devoid of cobwebs. "It was exactly as the scout sergeant said, sir."

The pale man sighed. "Dismissed," he said, finally.

"Wait!" he snapped, as they both turned to leave. "You! Stay," he ordered, staring at the lead scout with his inscrutable gaze as the scout sergeant scuttled gratefully from the room.

"Now," said the pale man, "why don't you tell me what really happened?"

It took the ambitious scout less than a second to weigh up his options: he could either stick to the story agreed with his sergeant or he could tell this civilian, who appeared to have authority even over Mayor Ponsonby, exactly what had happened and reap the reward, perhaps even a promotion.

When he had finished, Mayor Ponsonby rose from his chair. "It is as you suspected, master."

"It is," agreed the pale man. "Fools! How could they ever think to outsmart me! Send your best men in pursuit, Ponsonby."

"What about me, sir?" asked the ambitious scout hopefully.

"You?" said the pale man vaguely, as though he had already forgotten the man's existence. "Ah yes. Guards!"

The two guards who had been outside the door entered immediately.

"Take this man to the dungeon! He is to be charged with perjury and insubordination. Get him out of my sight!"

The scout was dragged away, protesting loudly.

"Useful little man," said the pale man, looking thoughtfully at Ponsonby. "But I do hate ambitious tell tales . . ."

14

After Princess Madeleine had witnessed Penthesilean's arrest, Bella felt she owed the girl an explanation, and she had been honest up to a point. She told her great niece about Mayor Ponsonby holding her captive in one of the palace turrets after throwing Penthesilean into the dungeons, and that he had confessed to being behind baby Alexander's disappearance, but she left out the mayor's reason for kidnapping the prince and any mention of the Book of Prophecies.

"And you think he's hiding Prince Alexander somewhere in the city?" said Madeleine with wide eyes. "Then we must try and find him! Please, Aunt Bella, please let me help. I've never liked that man. I caught him staring at you and Penthesilean at the banquet last night, but I thought he was just jealous. He must have started the rumour about you leaving the city together so that no one would think to look for you."

"This could be very dangerous," warned Bella, remembering how Ponsonby had threatened Penthesilean with a knife.

"I don't care!" cried Madeleine. "I really want to do something to help!"

After extracting promises from the young princess that she would be very careful, Bella sent her to see what she could find out about Penthesilean's arrest.

While she was gone, Bella retreated back into her secret room and used the girl's sketchbook to draw a rough diagram of the palace and its surrounds. She then marked the areas which she thought might be of importance with a large 'X', starting with Ponsonby's villa and the monk's rooms beneath the palace, where she had first sent Ben. She reasoned that if the monks had collaborated with the mayor to hide the Book of Prophecies, they may also be prepared to conceal the young prince.

She had almost finished when she heard Princess Madeleine's light footsteps running up the stone staircase. She opened the trapdoor.

"Did you find him?"

"Yes," gasped the girl, trying to catch her breath, "he's being held by the palace guards in the barracks, and Mayor Ponsonby has told everyone that he's responsible for your disappearance!"

"What?"

Bella quickly released the ladder and Madeleine climbed

up.

"And he's also being accused of kidnapping baby Alexander," she said as she squeezed into the secret attic room beside her great aunt. "Only no one believes that because he was at the banquet when Alexander went missing . . ."

"How did you find all this out?" asked Bella curiously, noticing that her great niece was still a bit breathless and her eyes were bright with excitement.

Madeleine blushed. "Nimrod was on duty. He's a friend of Marcus's and a favourite of Mama's. He often visits us at home."

Bella managed a smile. Marcus was Madeleine's older brother who, as the king's favourite nephew, had received a much sought after post in the Royal Household Guards, providing Madeleine with introductions to many handsome young men.

"So tell me more of what Nimrod said."

"Well," began Madeleine, "Penthesilean is something of a hero in the barracks, and none of the men believe that he had anything to do with Prince Alexander's disappearance. And if the mayor is lying about that, Nimrod and his friends think he's probably lying about Penthesilean kidnapping you too, which, of course, I know he didn't because you're here."

"You didn't tell anyone, did you?"

"No, of course not," replied Madeleine indignantly.

"Does the king know what Penthesilean is accused of?"

"The king doesn't even know he's been arrested. Ponsonby has forbidden anyone to speak to him of it, saying that it will upset the king too much if he knows that one of his oldest friends is responsible for the disappearance of both his son and his mother-in-law!"

"Is Penthesilean being well treated?" asked Bella.

"Very!" said Madeleine. "I even went to the kitchens and brought him back some freshly baked raisin loaf, which is when I bumped into the scouts returning from beyond the wall."

"The king's scouts?"

"Yes, and they were in such a state, Aunt Bella. They were telling anyone who would listen that they'd seen a monster!"

"A monster?" repeated Bella. "What kind of a monster?"

"Well, they couldn't quite agree, but whatever it was had leapt out of the river and attacked them while they were searching for some fugitives. Some of them said it was big and hairy, with fangs, but then I heard the scout sergeant use the word 'mermen' . . ." She glanced up at Bella sheepishly as she said this. Mermen belonged in fairytales and she was worried that Bella would think she was too young to help after all, if she repeated such nonsense. But her great aunt merely appeared thoughtful.

"It's late, you'll be missed," she said finally, without commenting on what Madeleine had told her. "And I have work to do. If you still want to help, return first thing tomorrow – by then I should have a plan."

* * *

Ben walked in the shallows of the river in the soft golden light of the early evening, watching tiny fish dart round his ankles as the sandy bottom gently massaged his tired feet. Tobias dashed back and forth around him, splashing joyfully through the water with his tail constantly wagging. Arrowbright was relaxed but keeping his eyes and ears open, while Murgatroyd was fully alert. Once his feathers were dry he took to the skies, determined to be the first to spot the next source of danger.

Gradually the temperature started to fall as the sun dropped towards the horizon. The fields of wheat on the far side of the river had been replaced by trees and Arrowbright suggested that they make camp on the wide, grassy clearing at the edge of the wood. Murgatroyd checked out the spot and gave his approval, although Tobias seemed reluctant at first to leave the safety of the water. Eventually Ben coaxed him up onto the bank.

Arrowbright began to gather firewood and Ben went to help him. Tobias thought this was a great game laid on for his benefit, and as fast as they could gather sticks, he would pick them up in his mouth and redistribute them around the clearing. After a few stern words from Murgatroyd, he abandoned the game and flopped down with his head on his paws, panting noisily.

Once Arrowbright reckoned they had enough wood for a fire, he got down to the serious business of building it. Ben watched for a while but soon realised his help wasn't needed and looked around for something else to do. Tobias had fallen asleep and Murgatroyd had disappeared into the trees to hunt, which gave Ben an idea. He had noticed earlier that Arrowbright carried a hunting knife, and they needed food so, without distracting the soldier from his task, he quietly slipped the knife from the sheath on his belt and wandered into the woods.

It was very quiet amongst the trees. By now, the sun had disappeared beyond the horizon and the light was fading fast. Ben placed each foot carefully on the ground as he walked deeper into the forest, avoiding the twigs which would snap loudly underfoot. Every few paces, he used the knife to carve a cross into a tree trunk.

One by one, the night creatures began calling to each other.

Now and then he would catch movement out of the corner of his eye and spin around, knife at the ready, but he was never quick enough to catch even a glimpse of the forest creatures before they disappeared into the dark undergrowth.

The shadows around him deepened as twilight set in, until the trees were mere shapes against the darkening sky.

Gradually he became aware of a light up ahead. As the last of the daylight faded into night it became brighter, throwing shadows against the surrounding trees and bushes. It was like a welcoming beacon shining out from the now complete darkness of the forest.

Intrigued, Ben moved towards it. A clump of bushes blocked his path but he forced his way through, ignoring the sharp twigs which scratched his bare arms. The urge to be near the light, to bathe in its glow, to touch it, if possible, was growing ever more powerful. He broke into a stumbling run, pushing through bracken and colliding with tree trunks in his haste. Everything else was forgotten in his desire to reach the light.

Then he put his foot in a burrow hidden amongst the sprawling roots of an ancient tree, and his ankle twisted as he slid into the hole. The sharp pain broke his concentration and he looked up, away from the light.

He realised immediately that he was lost. He had wandered off the path and thick undergrowth surrounded him on all sides. He heaved desperately at his foot, but it was caught fast and the pain made him weak and nauseous. He rested his head against the gnarled tree root and found himself gazing at the light once more. From this low vantage point, he could see directly into the clearing where the light was coming from.

As he watched, a pair of feet danced into view, bathed in a golden glow. They were almost close enough to touch as they pirouetted past. Entranced, he reached out his hand and pushed up the low ferns so he could see more clearly. He recoiled at the sight which greeted him.

The figure was made entirely of leaves. An unworldly breeze tossed them here and there, grouping them roughly into the head, torso, arms and legs of a person. It danced a crude jig, dipping and swaying, the leaves drifting apart and then regrouping, bound by the light which shone from within its torso. Despite his fear, Ben once again felt drawn to it.

The spell was broken by a sudden loud bark behind him. The figure jumped as if shot and instantly disintegrated into hundreds of leaves which fluttered down to join the rest of the woodland debris on the forest floor. As the leaves settled, the light faded until Ben was left in pitch darkness.

* * *

Arrowbright was coaxing the fire into life when Murgatroyd returned from hunting his supper.

"Where's Ben?" asked the bird, looking around the clearing.

Arrowbright raised his head. "He must be with Tobias. Perhaps they went into the forest."

Murgatroyd looked up at the sky which was already a deep indigo. His feathers twitched nervously.

"I don't like it," he said. "We don't know where that

dog came from or where its loyalties lie. Who knows what trouble it's got Ben into?"

Arrowbright got to his feet. "Let's not jump to conclusions, Murgatroyd. I don't think we should assume the worst of Tobias, after all, he did save us from those scouts earlier . . ." He sighed as he saw the expression on Murgatroyd's face, then continued. "Look, Murgatroyd, no one's blaming you for not spotting the scouts – I could just as easily blame myself. All I'm saying is let's give Tobias the benefit of the doubt. The important thing now is to find Ben."

They both looked towards the forest which seemed to have grown even darker in the few minutes they had spent talking. Arrowbright put his hand to the sheath on his belt, then paused and looked down.

"What's the matter?" asked Murgatroyd.

"My hunting knife . . . it's gone."

They looked at each other. "Ben!" they cried simultaneously.

Arrowbright selected a piece of wood from the pile next to the fire and thrust one end into the flames.

"Leave it," said Murgatroyd, "it will only spoil our night vision. Stay close to me, your eyes will soon adjust to the dark."

They entered the wood, moving slowly at first until Arrowbright found that he could easily follow the narrow path through the trees.

"Look at this," said Murgatroyd, pointing to a cross freshly cut into one of the tree trunks.

"It must have been Ben. If we follow them, they should lead us to him," said Arrowbright, relieved. "Ben! BEN!"

They moved noisily through the undergrowth, shouting Ben's name and whistling for Tobias. When the marks on the trees suddenly came to an abrupt end with still no sign of Ben, Arrowbright started to worry.

"Come on, Ben!" he shouted. "Where are you?"

"Look!" Murgatroyd held up a wingtip. "Do you see that?"

Arrowbright strained his eyes in the direction the bird was pointing. He was just about to ask what Murgatroyd was talking about, when he saw a dim light flickering through a thicket of bracken up ahead.

"Is it a campfire?" he asked Murgatroyd softly. "Perhaps Ben has found some fellow travellers."

Suddenly there was a short, sharp bark and the light went out. A second later, a dark shape streaked out of the bushes and raced past them.

"Tobias!" cried Arrowbright.

The dog stopped dead and turned his head in their direction. His ears were pinned back and they could see the whites of his eyes. He gave a low whine and then shuffled towards them, his belly pressed low to the forest floor, and pushed his wet nose into the soldier's hand.

"What's the matter, boy?" The dog's eyes gleamed out

of the darkness as Arrowbright knelt down in front of him. "Tobias, where is Ben? Find Ben!"

Tobias pricked up his ears and whined gently. He took a few steps forward, towards where the light had been, and then stopped, standing motionless with his ears pricked and his nose twitching. He turned to look back at Arrowbright. It was obvious to the soldier that he was reluctant to proceed.

"Where is he?" said Arrowbright. "Good dog! Find Ben!"

Tobias gave another low whine and pushed his way into the bracken. The others followed close behind him. Every few seconds, the dog paused to make sure they were still following him.

They hadn't gone far when they reached a clearing. Tobias ran back and forth across the open space, his nose pressed to the ground. He burrowed his snout amongst a pile of fallen leaves, sneezed and moved quickly on. Finally he seemed to catch a scent and raced into the bushes on the far side of the clearing, reappearing with a scrap of material in his mouth which he dropped at Arrowbright's feet.

He stooped and picked it up, lifting it close to his eyes.

"It looks like it could be from Ben's shirt," he said, "but I can't tell in this light."

"Give it to me," said Murgatroyd. He examined it briefly. "Yes, that's definitely his," he agreed. "So where is he?"

Tobias had trotted back to the place where he had found the scrap of fabric and was once again weaving from side to side, searching for Ben's scent. Finally he gave up and lay down with his head between his paws.

"He can't have just vanished into thin air," said Murgatroyd in exasperation.

Arrowbright suddenly felt a chill run down his spine. He thought back to the flickering light they had seen through the trees.

"This reminds me of a story the village shaman used to tell when I was a boy," he began slowly, "to scare us into not going into the woods at night. I always thought it was just a tale . . ."

Murgatroyd looked at him sharply. "Well?" he said, finally.

Arrowbright's eyes were distant as he immersed himself in his childhood memories. He had grown up far from the royal city with its processions and protocols. Instead, he had enjoyed the freedom of the forests surrounding his village, learning the traditions and folklore of his people which were passed down through generations. He tried to recall when he had first heard the story of the will-o'-the-wisp, but it seemed to him that he had always known it.

"They say the light is the one thing that remains constant," he said, gathering his thoughts, "a friendly, beckoning light that calls out to lone travellers – usually just after sunset, before one's eyes fully adjust to the dark.

But at the centre of the light lies a malevolent spirit. In some stories it's a misshapen dwarf carrying a glowing ember, in others it appears as a beautiful woman with the legs of a donkey."

"Sounds like a fairy tale to me," said Murgatroyd. "Why is the spirit said to be so bad?"

Arrowbright hesitated before answering, recalling the beliefs of his youth. "The stories were always told by the shaman, who claimed she witnessed the events in her visits to the spirit world. It is said that no one who has seen the will-o'-the-wisp has lived to tell the tale."

Murgatroyd snorted dismissively, and Arrowbright held up a hand to silence him. "I know what you're thinking, but there is often a grain of truth in the old tales. Look at you, for instance: not many people believe an eagle can talk, yet here you are."

Once he was sure he had Murgatroyd's attention, he continued. "The story I remember most clearly concerned the village priest, who was married with a young son. One day, the priest's son went out at dusk to collect firewood. Shortly after, his mother noticed what she thought was a storm approaching and went out to call him back, but it was too late. He had already gone. Lights flickered in the forest like lightening, but there was no thunder or rain. When the boy had still not returned by nightfall, the priest and his wife decided to go into the forest together to look for him. Only the priest came back. He was found lying unconscious in the village square, his hair bleached white."

"I thought you said that no one who sees the will-o'-the-wisp lives to tell the tale?" said Murgatroyd, always looking to pick holes in a story.

"That's right," confirmed Arrowbright, "but it wasn't the priest who told the villagers what had happened. He'd been struck dumb and never spoke another word for the rest of his life. That same night the shaman went into a trance and entered the spirit world. It was she who told of the horror that had taken place . . . The next day the boy was found at the bottom of a ravine with a broken neck. His mother was discovered nearby, felled by a tree that was rotten to its core, her hair turned white like her husband's – exactly as the shaman had said."

"A tragic accident?" suggested Murgatroyd.

Arrowbright looked at him. "Not an accident. The shaman witnessed both mother and son being lured to their deaths by lights which vanished at the crucial moment. The boy was enticed by a beautiful young woman – he was at the age when he was starting to notice girls – but this beauty had the hind legs of a donkey, hidden by the undergrowth. When she finally revealed herself to him, the shock made him stumble over the side of the ravine and he plunged to his death. Hoof prints were found near the edge."

"And the mother?" asked Murgatroyd, interested in spite of himself.

"It was the image of her own son which led to her death," answered Arrowbright softly. "By this time he was already dead, and what she witnessed was the evil spirit taking her son's form. The priest managed to escape the falling tree which killed his wife, but he never escaped the horror of what he had seen . . ."

The soldier's voice trailed off and the silence seemed to envelop them. Tobias whined, pawing at the leaves which covered the forest floor.

"There's nothing more we can do tonight," said Murgatroyd abruptly. "Perhaps Ben's found his way back to camp and is waiting for us there?"

"Perhaps," agreed Arrowbright, wishing that he'd kept a closer eye on the boy. With heavy hearts, they slowly made their way back to the camp.

* * *

Ben woke suddenly, straining his ears to hear past the thud of his heartbeat. The last thing he remembered was the dancing figure of leaves collapsing to the ground. He had no idea how long he had been asleep, but sensed from the darkness that there were still many hours until dawn. He wondered what had caused him to wake.

Rolling onto his side, he drew in his breath. Crouched by the remains of a fire, close enough for him to feel its warmth, was a beautiful young woman, prodding the dying embers with a stick. She was half turned away from him, her profile outlined by the dull orange glow. Gradually, she coaxed a tiny flame from the burnt logs. Then she turned towards him, and he realised he had been mistaken: she was not a girl but a haggard old woman; the shadows cast by the flickering flames danced in the gaunt hollows of her cheeks. She lifted a pipe to her wrinkled lips and sucked deeply on its stem, then blew a long stream of smoke towards him. Its sweet, cloying scent made him feel lightheaded.

As she watched him, words began to fill his mind. They told him to seek her and all would become clear. The message spiralled round and round in his head as his eyelids gently closed. He was asleep again before his head even hit the ground.

15

Although it was early in the morning when Bella woke up, she found Madeleine already waiting for her below the entrance to the secret room. Bella let down the ladder and drew out the map of Quadrivium. She had stayed up most of the night completing it from memory and was eager to show it to her great niece.

Taking one look at the map, Madeleine tried unsuccessfully to suppress a snort of laughter.

"What's wrong with it?" asked Bella.

"Nothing," smirked the girl, "except that the palace is much too big compared to the surrounding buildings and you've missed out the monastery, as well as the barracks and the new school."

Bella turned the map back towards herself and eyed her handiwork. Madeleine was right: the scale was all wrong for a start. She handed her the pencil.

"You're the artist, you do it."

With a grin, Madeleine accepted the pencil and, with a few swift strokes, reduced the size of the palace and added in the missing buildings. Bella looked over her shoulder as she worked.

"Now mark the monastery with an 'X'," she instructed, "like Ponsonby's villa. This is where we'll begin our search for Prince Alexander."

Madeleine did as she asked.

"But surely the guards will already have searched everywhere?" she commented. "They haven't stopped looking for Alexander since he disappeared."

"And Ponsonby's men have been helping them," pointed out Bella. "Think about it: we already know that Ponsonby is the one behind the prince's kidnapping, so all we need to do now is find out which areas of the palace were searched by his men and –"

"– that's where the prince will be!" finished Madeleine. "We must tell the king straight away!"

Bella raised her head from the map. "No!"

Madeleine looked at her, shocked. "But why not?"

"Ponsonby has spies everywhere," replied Bella. "One of his men is bound to overhear if we tell the king, and Ponsonby will have the prince moved to a place he'll never be found, perhaps even out of the city. Remember: we have no proof that the mayor kidnapped the prince, it would be my word against his. Our best chance is to find Alexander ourselves."

"But what if someone sees you?" cried Madeleine. "You know too much! I bet Ponsonby has told his men to keep searching for you while they pretend to be looking for Alexander!"

"Then I'll have to wear a disguise," said Bella.

* * *

"You'll never take me alive! Be off, foul beast!" Arrowbright sat bolt upright, his arms flailing against his attacker. Tobias released the soldier's sleeve and pawed at his chest.

"Be off, I tell you . . . what? Tobias?"

The events of the previous night came flooding back as he became fully awake. It was a dull, grey morning. The fire had gone out sometime during the night and was now just a pile of damp, grey ash. In the cold light of the new day, it was difficult to believe that Ben had vanished, but a quick glance around the clearing showed him that the boy was still missing. Murgatroyd was also nowhere to be seen.

He stood up and looked around, ignoring Tobias who stared imploringly up at him. On the far side of the river, the wheat fields stretched in both directions, rippling in the early morning breeze. On the near side, where they had camped for the night, he noticed just how steeply the land sloped upwards into the forest; the only level bit was the clearing where he had slept. He didn't recall the incline being so extreme. The thought also crossed his mind that the trees had been further back. He was sure they had set up camp in the centre of the clearing, but their gutted campfire was now right on the edge of the forest. It was almost as though the trees had slid down the hill towards them during the night.

Tobias grabbed hold of his sleeve and began to tug insistently. it was at that moment that Arrowbright noticed the wind. What had been a gentle morning breeze was rapidly working up into a gale. Dark clouds, which had been gathering unnoticed on the horizon, now rolled out across the sky, quickly blotting out the sun. Leaves swirled down from the trees to be whipped into a frenzy along with the cold ash of the long dead fire.

Tobias was making anxious, low growls. He ran back and forth, his tail wagging half-heartedly between his legs.

"What's going on, boy?" cried Arrowbright against the rising howl of the wind. "You want me to follow you?"

The dog bounded into the trees and turned to stare intently back at him. Arrowbright looked towards the campfire, undecided. As he did, he suddenly noticed three or four saplings standing between the river and the dead fire, their thin branches flailing like arms in the strong wind. He knew for certain that the trees hadn't been there before. He began to feel increasingly uneasy as leaves surged around his feet like water.

At that moment, Murgatroyd fell out of the sky and

landed in a heap at his feet. The instant the bird stood up the wind took him again. He was bowled over, tumbling like a farmyard chicken towards the forest, squawking indignantly. Arrowbright raced after him.

The wind dropped the instant they were amongst the trees. Arrowbright gazed out at the storm raging just an arm's length away. There was an almost visible division between the forest and the clearing, as though a huge window was keeping the storm out. The hairs on the back of his neck prickled: he had a strong sensation that some supernatural force had just herded them deliberately into the trees.

He knelt before Tobias and looked into the dog's deep brown eyes. "Tobias, it's really important that we find Ben. Do you understand? Find Ben!"

Tobias nosed at the scrap of cloth from Ben's shirt, while Murgatroyd picked himself up and tried to straighten his ruffled feathers.

"Strangest weather I've ever seen," he muttered to himself. "One minute it's fine, the next I'm in the middle of a tornado . . ."

Once Murgatroyd had rearranged his feathers, Tobias led the way deeper into the forest, pushing his nose into every bush and round every tree before leading them onwards. Arrowbright noticed that the large dog wasn't his usual boisterous self. His tail drooped and his ears were pulled back, alert to the slightest sound. The only time he showed any animation was when the occasional leaf fluttered down from above. Leaping up, he would grab it between bared teeth before it could touch any of them, shaking it violently before spitting out the shredded remains.

Murgatroyd no longer complained about Tobias taking the lead, aware that the dog's sense of smell was their best chance of finding Ben. Now and then, he launched himself into the air, always taking care to stay below the lowest branches. Otherwise, he perched on Arrowbright's shoulder, uncharacteristically quiet.

Suddenly, Tobias stopped. He raised his head, nostrils twitching, then trotted forward a few paces and stopped again, his nose held high to sniff the air. Abruptly he took off at a sprint, leaping over tangled thickets of bracken and heading deeper into the forest. He quickly vanished from view, but they could still hear him crashing through the undergrowth.

At first they tried to follow, but the bushes grew too close together for Arrowbright to push his way through. Murgatroyd chose not to fly in case they were separated even further, and the two of them continued together along a narrow path which seemed to head in the general direction taken by the dog. Eventually they heard a bark up ahead and Arrowbright broke into a run.

"Tobias! Where are you?"

"Arrowbright! Murgatroyd!"

In a small clearing beyond a group of trees, they found Ben trying to sit up. This was made next to impossible by Tobias, who was excitedly trying to climb into his lap. Ben finally managed to push the dog away and stood up.

"What in Tritan's name were you thinking?" demanded Murgatroyd, worry sharpening his tone. "How could you wander off alone? Who knows what's lurking in these woods!"

"I'm sorry," said Ben. "I thought I'd be able to find my way back, but I got distracted, lost my way and . . ." He wondered whether he should tell them about the strange, dancing figure of leaves and the young woman who had turned into an old hag before his eyes, but decided that Murgatroyd would just think he had been dreaming, so he finished lamely, "And then I fell asleep."

"Well, we're all back together now," said Arrowbright brightly, "but I for one would like to get out of this forest."

* * *

The day dragged on as they made their way through the forest, staying where possible on the narrow trails left by the woodland creatures. A subdued light penetrated the thick canopy of leaves overhead, making it impossible to tell whether it was still morning or afternoon, and they soon lost track of time. Every now and then, the path they were following would peter out and they would have to retrace their steps, or beat their way through the undergrowth until they found another. All around them were the massive trunks of ancient trees, stretching into the distance until they seemed to merge into a solid barrier.

After a while, Ben started to notice a change. The fresh scent of pine resin replaced the slightly damp, mouldy smell of rotting vegetation, and an occasional burst of birdsong pierced the silence. The others had noticed too. Tobias lifted his nose from the ground and pricked up his ears. Murgatroyd lost his concentration and flew into a branch, shaking leaves onto the group below. But for the first time since they had entered the forest, the leaves didn't seem to bother Tobias.

The overhead canopy thinned out to let in more light, and a starburst of sunlight glinted through the leaves up ahead. Their pace quickened. Soon they could see breaks in the trees and the bare ground was replaced by a carpet of grass and small wildflowers. Then suddenly the trees were behind them and they were out in the open at last.

Ahead of them was a grassy meadow dotted with small white flowers. They could see no further as the ground sloped gently upwards until it met the blue of the sky. To reach the meadow they had to clamber over a pile of rocks that appeared to be the remains of a stone wall which still stood in places, as though to hold back the encroaching forest.

Tobias was the first one over. He flung himself joyfully

onto his back and rolled luxuriously in the long green grass. Ben quickly joined him, enjoying the lush springiness of the meadow beneath his body and his unobstructed view of the wide open sky. He saw a black dot circling high above and realised it was Murgatroyd. Watching the great eagle soar, Ben felt an overwhelming sense of freedom and light after the oppressive atmosphere of the forest. Then Tobias's head appeared in his line of vision and he laughed out loud as the dog tried to lick his face. Pushing him away, he sat up feeling slightly giddy.

Arrowbright was the last one over the wall and stood quietly to one side, one hand raised to shield his eyes from the bright sunlight.

"What's wrong?" asked Ben.

Arrowbright didn't answer. Instead, he strode off up the meadow.

"Hey, Arrowbright!" cried Ben, jumping up and running after him.

"I know this place," muttered the soldier under his breath. His face suddenly lit up and he broke into a trot, and then into a full sprint, shouting out loud, "I know this place!"

Ben raced after him, finally catching up with him as he came to an abrupt halt just before the top of the rise.

"Ben! Stay back!"

The sudden note of urgency in his voice brought Ben up short. Arrowbright was only a couple of strides away and he could tell immediately that something was wrong. He was standing with his legs hip distance apart with his arms outstretched as if for balance. And he was sinking.

Ben watched in horror as Arrowbright's feet, calves and then knees disappeared beneath the grass. This was like no quicksand that he had ever seen: the ground looked no different to that on which he himself stood. He took a couple of involuntary steps back.

"Ben, where's Murgatroyd?" cried Arrowbright, urgently.

"I don't know!" replied Ben, helplessly scanning the sky. "He took off as soon as we came out of the woods. I can't see him!"

Arrowbright tried to keep the panic out of his voice as he felt the ground encompass his waist. He placed his palms on the grass and tried to lever himself up without success. "And Tobias?"

Ben turned to see the dog crouched at a distance, his ears flattened against his head. He wagged his tail sheepishly when Ben called to him, but refused to come any closer.

"Ben, listen carefully to me," said Arrowbright, taking quick, shallow breaths as the earth squeezed his chest. It had now reached his armpits. "Over that rise is a village . . . No, listen!" he snapped, as he saw that Ben was about to interrupt. "Find help and hurry!"

Ben didn't hesitate. Carefully skirting the ground around Arrowbright, he ran as though his life depended on it, expecting at any moment for the earth to give way beneath his feet. As he topped the rise, he saw the village spread out before him, just as the soldier had said. It was no more than a hamlet, just a handful of small houses and a couple of barns clustered around a larger, round hut.

It was only when he reached the first house that he noticed how quiet it was. There were no animals or people anywhere to be seen.

"Hello?" he called out. "Is anyone there?"

He ran to the nearest house and banged his fist on the closed door. It swung open at his touch, but a quick glance inside told him it was empty. The second house was the same, and the third. Ben stood in the centre of the village almost crying with frustration. It was then that he saw the smoke drifting from a chimney in the central hut. He ran all the way round it looking for the door, but all he found was a solid wall of hard, red mud.

"Help!" he cried. "Someone! Please, help!"

"Are you looking for me?"

A soft voice behind him made him spin round. He drew in a sharp breath: it was the young woman from the forest. She stood with her head proudly raised and her arms held loosely at her sides. Her thin, pale grey dress billowed around her legs, buffeted by some wind that Ben could not feel.

Gathering his wits, he spoke quickly. "I need help. My friend is trapped, he's sinking . . ."

He saw something flicker in her eyes.

"Arrowbright." She rolled the name round in her mouth as though tasting it. "I will come."

And suddenly she was gone.

* * *

Ben raced back through the deserted village. A growing sense of panic gave him speed he hadn't known he possessed. He reached the grassy slope and pounded up it, his legs burning and his breath rasping in his throat.

Cresting the hill, he stopped in horror. Crouched over the spot where Arrowbright had been was a huge, black crow. It covered the ground with its wings, its head thrust down towards the earth. Ben rushed forward, looking for a stick with which to beat the creature away, but, before he could reach it, a familiar dark shape appeared from the sky like a speeding arrow and knocked the crow onto its back.

"Stay back, witch!" shrieked Murgatroyd.

Ben stared at the figure lying on the ground in astonishment. It was the old hag with a long black cloak draped around her shoulders.

"Help!" came a muffled cry.

They both looked down. Just visible between the blades of grass was a face. The eyes flicked from Ben to Murgatroyd as the mouth struggled to form the words. "Where is she?"

"I'm here," sighed the hag, standing up and brushing herself down. "Your friends are a little on the zealous side,

Arrowbright."

Ignoring Murgatroyd's protests, she bent once more over Arrowbright and spoke softly. "It has been a long time . . ."

"Gretilda," Arrowbright formed her name with difficulty, "can you get me out of here?"

"Of course I can!" she cackled. "The question is whether I choose to."

"Stop playing games!" cried Ben. "Get him out, you old hag!"

Gretilda straightened up slowly. "Tut, tut, Ben, you really should show more respect for your elders!" She turned to face him full on. "Or is it that you see more to me?" she continued coyly, twirling a lock of her lank grey hair around a long, crooked finger. "You do have the gift, after all."

He gasped as she threw off her black cloak to reveal the slender figure of the young woman.

"Do I have your full attention now?" she asked sweetly, as her grey hair melted into gold before his eyes. "Yes, I think perhaps I do, so listen carefully: before I help Arrowbright, you must promise me something."

"Yes, anything," cried Ben. "I promise!"

"That's not good enough," said the young woman. She stretched out a hand and pulled Ben's locket from under his shirt, then flicked it open and ran a finger over the miniature portrait inside. "Ah, the beautiful Teah!"

He flinched and made as if to draw back, but she clenched her fist around the locket. "Do you swear on your mother's life that you will help me if I release your friend?"

"My mother is dead," said Ben in a low voice, "but I will swear on her memory to do all that I can to help you if you release Arrowbright."

Tobias crept closer, his tail tucked between his legs. He appeared to be listening closely to the exchange.

"I need you to recover something which was stolen from me. Once this is returned I will release Arrowbright from his earthen prison and send you on your way."

"Release Arrowbright first!" cried Ben. "I have made you the oath you wanted!"

"No!" hissed Gretilda, her beautiful young face suddenly dissolving into the wrinkles of the old woman. "Those are my conditions! Accept them or say farewell to your friend!"

Murgatroyd drew Ben to one side.

"The Book is our priority," he murmured, glancing over his shoulder at Gretilda, then held up a wing as Ben started to object, "but the least we can do for Arrowbright is find out what has been stolen and see if it's in our power to recover it and return it to her."

Tobias skirted around Gretilda and trotted over to where they stood. He thrust his wet nose into Ben's hand.

"Why are you so scared of her, Tobias?" asked Ben as he

stroked the dog's velvety ears.

"She is a Shaman: she possesses the old magic," replied Murgatroyd, looking over to where Gretilda paced up and down on the grass. She had reverted back to her younger form and moved gracefully, almost skipping across the grass. "He senses her power, as do I."

A groan from Arrowbright drew their attention. They moved slowly over to where he was trapped, careful not to stand on his face.

"Leave me," said the soldier softly, forming the words with great difficulty as the earth pushed against his cheeks. "She won't hurt me, I'm sure of it . . ."

"Things have changed, Arrowbright."

Gretilda stood behind them. Tobias slunk away as Ben and Murgatroyd turned slowly to face her.

"Although I hate to admit it, I need help and this is the only way I can be sure of getting it. You followed your father into the king's army and you weren't the last young man to do so. When the rebels came, the village was defenceless. The only people left were women and children and they were taken as slaves."

"Why didn't they take you?" asked Ben, imagining that she must have taken on the appearance of the old woman and been ignored by the rebels.

"They didn't want me!" she cried. "They wanted the Sacred Stone!"

Murgatroyd understood immediately.

"They wanted your magic!" he exclaimed. "Someone must have known that holding you captive close to the Stone would allow you to use its power – which is why you were left behind. But I don't understand how they got you far enough away from the Stone to steal it?"

"They tricked me!" said Gretilda, her eyes flashing with anger. "There were reports of lights in the forest and I suspected a rogue will-o'-the-wisp, but it was just a distraction to get me out of the way so the rebels could take the Stone."

Ben thought back to the figure of leaves in the forest. "What I saw in the forest last night," he began slowly, "was that . . . ?"

"Yes, that was a will-o'-the-wisp," said Gretilda, "but it was completely under my control, you were in no real danger. I used it to draw you in."

Ben thought about her strange powers for a moment before something occurred to him. "Why can't you get the Stone back yourself?"

Murgatroyd answered for her. "A Shaman is tied to the land, Ben. Their magic is drawn from a powerful source of raw, natural energy like a large river, a mountain or a forest. Once they leave the source of their magic, they are just ordinary mortals, unless they possess a Sacred Stone."

"My Sacred Stone encapsulates the ancient power of the forest," confirmed Gretilda. "With it, I can roam wherever I want and remain as powerful as I am now. But if I leave the forest without it, I am powerless."

"Release me, Gretilda, and I will return your Stone to you."

They all looked down at Arrowbright who was staring back up at them through the blades of grass.

"No!" cried Gretilda, stamping her small foot on the ground. Ben felt the earth tremble. "How can I trust you, Arrowbright, when you've already deserted the village once, and have returned only through chance? No, it's him I want." She pointed at Ben. "He will return my Stone, and the dog and the bird will go with him. When they return, you will be released."

With these words she turned, her dark cloak swirling out behind her, and made her way back to the village.

16

"Aunt Bella! Great Aunt Bella!" Madeleine raced up the stairs to the top of the dome, calling out.

"What is it?" asked Bella, hurriedly pulling up the trapdoor to her secret room. "Is it Ponsonby? Are his men after you?"

She cursed herself for allowing her great niece to become involved; Ponsonby had already proved himself to be a dangerous man.

"No, I mean yes!" gabbled Madeleine, staring up at Bella but making no move to climb the ladder. "Yes, it's Ponsonby, but no, his men aren't after me! Quickly, Aunt Bella, come and see."

Confused, Bella climbed down the ladder and followed Madeleine through the small wooden door and out onto the wide balcony of the great dome. It was the hour when most people were in their homes eating their evening meal with their families, and the square below was deserted.

"What is it, Madeleine?"

Her great niece was staring intently at the labyrinth of lanes that ran down to the city wall. She remained silent for a long moment and then, "There! Do you see?"

"What am I looking for?"

Madeleine came and stood behind Bella. Although she was barely sixteen, she was at least a head taller than her great aunt. She leant over Bella's shoulder and pointed.

"On the other side of that group of warehouses is the south eastern gate – you can just about see a section of the wall through the gap between them. Keep your eyes on that gap."

Bella watched and waited. She tried not to blink as her eyes began to water. Then she felt Madeleine tense beside her.

"There," said the girl. "There he is."

A figure had detached itself from the shadows and was cautiously making its way across the exposed space between the grain warehouse and the wall, leading a pony which appeared to be heavily laden. Bella couldn't make out the man's features from this distance, but she identified him immediately from his size.

"It's Ponsonby! Where's he going?"

"He's leaving Quadrivium!" cried Madeleine. "I bumped into him as he was coming out of the stables. I think he was more shocked than me – he obviously didn't want to be seen! He tried to pretend that he was going for a ride around the city, but his saddlebags were fully loaded."

"But where could he be going?" mused Bella, possibilities running through her head. Madeleine had said that the king's scouts had been tracking fugitives – could that have been Ben? Perhaps Ponsonby was leaving to go and arrest him and bring him back to Quadrivium, but why would he travel alone?

"Does it matter?" said Madeleine impatiently. "Aunt Bella, he's gone and he definitely didn't have Alexander with him! Now that he's out of the way, we have a good chance of finding the prince!"

"We still have to be careful," said Bella, trying to quell her excitement, "but you're right – with Ponsonby out of the way, our task will be a lot simpler!"

Late for her evening meal, Madeleine hurried off, promising to return the next morning. Bella continued to stare at the wall long after the mayor had disappeared in the direction of the gate. Twilight settled in and lights began to appear in the buildings below her, but she remained on the balcony, gazing out at the deepening shadows beyond the wall.

Finally, she saw what she had been waiting for: a bright wink of light, so quick that she would have missed it had she blinked. It was followed by two more quick flashes and then a long pause before the sequence was repeated. Although the light was fading rapidly, Bella knew what she was looking for, and it wasn't long before Ponsonby's figure appeared, still leading the pony, and made its way towards the signaller.

She felt a brief thrill of satisfaction. She had suspected he wouldn't leave the safety of Quadrivium's walls alone, but who could he be meeting?

* * *

Arrowbright could hear the others arguing in whispers a few feet from where he was trapped. The occasional fierce squeak of frustration from the eagle gave him some idea of how the conversation was going. Despite the bond they had formed, Murgatroyd's priority was to find the Book of Prophecies; he did not want Ben to be distracted from this quest and would be in favour of abandoning the soldier to his fate. Arrowbright had to admit that he would probably do the same in his position, but the boy was young and idealistic. He would not want to leave him after all they had been through together.

He tried to stretch his neck. His face was pointing up at the sky, a position he had been forced into to get what he had expected to be his last breath. Earlier, Tobias had attempted to dig him out, but Arrowbright had quickly asked Ben to stop him after he had felt himself start to sink even further.

Patiently, he watched orange streaks appear in the sky as the others talked on into the evening. Despite his awkward position, he wasn't in any great discomfort. His head and body were supported by the earth around him and although the night air was cool, the soil was warm and dry. But it was still disconcerting to be held utterly motionless for so long.

With no agreement reached, Ben and Murgatroyd broke off their whispered discussion. Ben had loyally decided to camp in the meadow beside the buried soldier rather than sleep in a bed in the deserted village. He began to erect a rough shelter over the bit of Arrowbright's face which was still visible above ground.

"You'll need a sturdier branch than that to support the roof," commented Murgatroyd, watching him work.

"There isn't going to be a roof," snapped Ben, his arms aching from the effort of dragging fallen branches up from the forest. "I'm going to pack some dry grass over the top instead."

"It'll blow away," said Murgatroyd, reaching out a claw to test the stability of the rough frame. The structure wobbled.

Ben turned on him. "Stop it! I'm not finished yet!"

"Do you think you two can try and get on?" Arrowbright's voice cut through their bickering. "Murgatroyd, why don't you gather some moss for the roof? Ben, you'll need to dig the two main struts into the ground for extra stability – Tobias can help you."

Under the soldier's supervision, the makeshift shelter

was soon finished and shortly after, Gretilda reappeared. She brought with her a basket of food and a bundle of sticks which burned with an iridescent glow, these she stuck into the ground around them like candles. She was still in the guise of the young woman and Ben found himself starting to warm to her. But Arrowbright refused her offer of food and Tobias watched her unblinkingly from a safe distance, while Murgatroyd remained aloof.

Over supper, the shaman told them everything she knew. The Stone had been taken two nights ago, on one of the darkest nights of the year. She had been searching the forest for signs of the will-o'-the-wisp when the rebels had struck.

"I heard the Sacred Stone's scream echo through the forest as they tore it from its resting place." She spoke with her eyes closed, reliving the pain she had felt – as though the stone were a physical part of her. "I hurried back to the village immediately, but it was too late. The rebels had already gone, taking the villagers with them."

"Where were the men?" asked Arrowbright, his disembodied voice floating up from amongst the grass.

"Haven't you been paying attention?" cried Gretilda, opening her eyes and wavering between her young and old forms. "There were no men. They had all followed your example and left to join the king's army . . . although it wasn't always voluntarily."

"What do you mean?" asked Murgatroyd sharply.

"As soon as the boys came of age, they would be taken by the Conscriptors," said Gretilda bitterly. "They always seemed to know. The day after the boy's eighteenth birthday, a group of men would arrive and cart him off to be trained as a soldier. There was nothing we could do."

"I didn't know," said Arrowbright in a small voice. "Why didn't you send word?"

"We needed every available pair of hands to keep the farms going," said Gretilda. "Anyway, we thought you must have known – you're a soldier, aren't you?"

Arrowbright was silent. It didn't make sense to him. He hadn't noticed an influx of trainees and there was always a shortage of troops to fight the rebels. He wondered where the new conscripts had been taken.

"So there was no one to stop the rebels when they came to steal the Stone?" asked Ben, drawing Gretilda back to the story.

"Exactly. I suspect rumours of the will-o'-the-wisp were planted by the rebels to ensure I would be out of the village when they attacked. A few of the villagers may even have been involved. It would have been impossible for someone to have taken the Sacred Stone if I'd been within the radius of its power."

She moved closer to Arrowbright.

"So you see, I can't trust anyone anymore," she said softly, looking down at what could still be seen of his face. "I didn't want to do this to you, my friend, but I need to be sure that the boy will return with my stone." She looked up at the others who were still listening intently. "They went north towards the foothills of the Outer Reaches. If they manage to cross the Mountains of the Outer Boundaries, the Stone will be lost to me forever."

She glanced down once more into Arrowbright's face. When she lifted her eyes, Ben saw that they were the wrinkled, bloodshot eyes of the old hag.

"And your friend will be lost to you also."

With that, she turned and made her way back down to the village, her shoulders stooped and her footsteps slow and heavy.

The shaman's parting words left behind a sombre atmosphere and it was a moment before anyone spoke.

"You should get some rest," said Arrowbright finally. "I doubt I'll be able to sleep, but there's no reason for us all to stay awake."

Not even Murgatroyd objected. With a muttered promise to keep watch, he withdrew to a tree at the edge of the forest. Ben lay on his back beside Arrowbright, glad of the warmth radiating from Tobias as the dog stretched out next to him. But he was unable to sleep, his head spinning with questions. Finally he gave up trying and propped himself up on his elbow.

"Arrowbright," he began. But to his surprise, the soldier's eyes were closed and his breathing was deep and even.

Tobias's tail thumped on the ground as Ben pulled himself up into a sitting position. He gave the dog a reassuring pat and then wrapped his arms around his legs, resting his chin on his knees. He stared into the darkness, his mind filled with images of frightened villagers being herded by the rebels into the mountains. He had no idea how he was supposed to rescue them from the rebels, not to mention the shaman's Stone, particularly without Arrowbright's help.

Out of habit, he reached up to touch his mother's locket on its chain around his neck. His mind drifted back to his meeting with the mermen in the underground lake and how Prince Trestan had created the silver chain from a single strand of hair. It all seemed so long ago now. He suddenly felt the urge to examine the chain more closely and pulled it over his head. He marvelled at how fine and yet deceptively strong it was, able to take the weight of both his locket and Bella's key. He let the chain run through his fingers, enjoying the fluid coolness of the fine links against his skin.

He gasped and leapt to his feet, staring at his hand in shock. Drops of moisture glistened on his fingers. Tobias jumped up too and tried to lick his hand.

"What's the matter?" Murgatroyd appeared out of the darkness and perched on top of the makeshift shelter.

"My chain, it's just vanished!" said Ben, looking at the ground around him in bewilderment. He stooped and picked up his locket and Bella's key from where they had fallen, put them in his pocket and turned to face Murgatroyd. "One minute I was holding it in my hand, the next . . ."

He broke off, interrupted by a loud coughing and spluttering from the ground behind him. He turned to find Arrowbright's face half covered by water welling up from the ground and dribbling into his nose and mouth.

"What's happening?" Arrowbright whispered, his eyes wide with panic.

Ben dropped to his knees and began to scoop the water away from Arrowbright's face. The moisture had softened the sun-baked ground and he found that the wet earth came away in handfuls. Soon he had freed Arrowbright's chin, but the spring was flowing more quickly.

"Hold on, I'm going to get you out," cried Ben, digging frantically. He paused to push his hair off his forehead, and in that brief moment water immediately filled the ditch he had created. Arrowbright thrashed his head from side to side, coughing and choking.

"We need to siphon it off somehow," said Murgatroyd, pacing up and down. "Or perhaps . . ."

Instead of finishing his sentence, he spread his wings and took off into the night sky. Ben resumed his digging, too absorbed in his task to wonder where the bird had gone. Each time he paused, Arrowbright's face was submerged once more. Tobias began to dig alongside him, gouging out the earth with his front paws and flinging soil and water in an arc behind him. But they had only reached as far as Arrowbright's shoulders and as fast as they could dig, the hole refilled with water.

"Quick, put this in his mouth."

Murgatroyd had silently reappeared and dropped a reed onto the ground next to Ben. Without pausing to question him, Ben picked it up and inserted it between Arrowbright's lips. He immediately stopped writhing and a soft whistling sound could be heard as he drew in lungfuls of air through the hollow reed.

As they watched, a trickle of water escaped the trough around Arrowbright's face and snaked through the grass towards the meadow. Soon it had grown into a small stream as more and more water was diverted into the channel. Ben stopped digging and watched it flow downhill into the meadow. When he looked back, the water level had subsided enough for the young soldier to breathe normally.

He spat out the reed. "I think I can move my legs, but my feet are still caught fast."

Ben and Tobias immediately resumed their efforts, reaching beneath the gushing water to scoop away the loosening soil from around Arrowbright's body. As the stream gathered momentum, the earth around him collapsed outward and the water level fell rapidly to his waist. Soon it was only thigh deep.

The spring continued to bubble up out of the ground,

but more gently now. After a while, Arrowbright found that he could pull his feet from the earth and he clambered gratefully out of the hole, water streaming from his clothes.

He stood up and stretched his arms above his head. "Ah, that feels good!"

Tobias trotted over and bent his head to lap thirstily from the stream, but as he did so, the water began to soak rapidly back into the ground. The channel which the stream had carved into the hill was soon no more than a dry furrow. Ben stepped forwards and looked down into the hole which Arrowbright had vacated only moments before, now no more than a hollow in the ground. It was empty but for a trace of water at the bottom, shimmering in the starlight. On a whim, he jumped in and felt around.

"Ben! What are you doing?" exclaimed Arrowbright. He grabbed him by the arm and hauled him out. But Ben had a smile on his face, and in his hand he clasped Prince Trestan's silver chain.

"We should get a move on before Gretilda wakes up and finds you gone," he said, slipping the chain over his head. "She won't be pleased to find her enchantment broken."

Arrowbright shook the dirt from his clothes which had dried almost immediately once the spring had disappeared, while Ben plucked the shaman's glow sticks from the ground and stuffed them into his satchel. As soon as their light was extinguished, they all noticed the glimmer of the approaching dawn.

"Which way now, Ben?" asked Murgatroyd, impatient to leave.

Ben drew out the page from the Book of Prophecies. He unrolled it and glanced at it only briefly before looking up at the sky.

"We head east," he said, "towards the rising sun."

Arrowbright looked around.

"We'll have to head west back into the forest first," he said, "and then re-set our course eastwards once we're clear of the village."

"No," said Murgatroyd firmly. "The shaman may wake while we're still in the forest. It's her domain; she'd know exactly where we were immediately. We'll take the most direct route through the village and hope she's not an early riser."

As quickly and as quietly as they could, they made their way down into the deserted village, skirting the huts until they reached the wide expanse of dusty open ground which separated them from the safety of the cornfield on the other side. They paused in the shadows of a dry stone wall, their breathing loud in the eerie quiet of the pre-dawn. Overhead, the stars were already beginning to fade.

Arrowbright set off first, running stiffly, with Murgatroyd flying close overhead. Ben watched their silhouettes disappear into the field of corn. The eagle reappeared briefly and, at his signal, Ben left the safety of the stone wall, Tobias running at his heels. He had almost reached the cornfield when he felt something drop out of his pocket. He realised immediately what it was: he had forgotten to replace his locket and key on Prince Trestan's silver chain! Tobias bounded ahead, but Ben stopped and ran back. He found the key almost immediately by its dull, phosphorescent glow, but his locket was nowhere to be seen.

"Ben!" he heard Murgatroyd whisper loudly. "Come on!"

Desperately Ben scrabbled in the dust, searching for his locket. The night sky was growing lighter with each minute that passed. The promise of the approaching dawn created faint shadows in the dirt, offering false clues. Finally he spied his locket lying near the wall. As he sprinted back towards it, the silence was suddenly shattered by the piercing crow of a cockerel.

Ben was paralysed for a split-second, caught out in the open. In that moment he saw the shaman's slim, youthful figure detach itself from the dark mound of the central mud hut. He glanced back towards the cornfield where he knew the others would be watching, then, quickly making up his mind, he dived towards the ground, landing in a roll which brought him up against the stone wall. He scooped up the locket and clenched it tightly in his fist.

Raising his head, he cautiously peered over the wall. The village was full of shadows, but no movement. He took a deep breath and started to run back across the exposed stretch of land. The moment he left the shelter of the wall, a clear voice spoke out behind him, making his blood run cold.

"She's not dead, you know – your mother."

He stopped dead. Very slowly, he turned around to see Gretilda sitting on top of the stone wall. She jumped down and moved slowly towards him until he could make out her youthful features.

"You should know that I am allowing you to leave – go and fulfil your quest. But if you want to know the fate of your mother, return with my Stone before the year is out."

As the cockerel crowed a second time, she vanished back into the shadows, leaving Ben standing alone.

17

It was much colder away from the shelter of the village. They soon left the cultivated fields behind them and turned their feet to the east, lowering their heads against the relentless wind which blew dust into their eyes. In the dull light of dawn the stony land seemed to stretch on forever, flat and featureless.

Ben felt hollow inside. He knew he should feel pleased that his mother was alive, but it was hard for him to comprehend. He had believed for too long that she was dead. And now, with each step he took, he was heading further away from the one person who claimed to know what had happened to her.

Arrowbright sensed that Ben didn't want to talk and plodded along in silence beside him. He had his own demons to confront: he was consumed by guilt over what had taken place in his village. Gretilda seemed to think that he had started the exodus, but he couldn't believe that.

When he had first left to join the army, there had been plenty of young men who had chosen to remain behind and farm the land. And he had never before heard of the Conscriptors.

"Ben," he said suddenly, "have you noticed more soldiers in Quadrivium lately, particularly younger recruits?"

Ben looked up. "Not really," he said, "but I always tried to steer clear of the soldiers. Why?"

"It doesn't make any sense. My regiment was ordered back to the city even though there was a shortage of troops in the borderlands. And I don't recall seeing any new recruits either in Quadrivium or outside of it, so where are all these conscripts that Gretilda was talking about?"

"Conscripts," repeated Ben, thoughtfully. He was suddenly transported back to the little boat on the river, listening to Prince Trestan's voice. "I knew that word was familiar!" he said finally. "Prince Trestan told me his people were once almost captured by the Conscriptors who would travel the kingdom kidnapping "conscripts" to sell to the king's army."

"But even if that were true," said Arrowbright, "where are these conscripts now?"

Murgatroyd spoke suddenly from above. "What if someone is deliberately removing all the king's citizens of fighting age, pretending to recruit conscripts for the king's army while actually removing those who would fight for the king in his hour of need?"

"You make it sound as though someone is planning to

overthrow the king," said Arrowbright.

"It's a possibility," replied the bird grimly. "Only the Book of Prophecies can tell us for certain – we have to find it as soon as possible!"

Ben kept quiet. He hadn't told them what the shaman had said to him about his mother as he had left the village. He was the only one who could lead them to the Book of Prophecies by interpreting the signs on the parchment, and he had given the others the impression that it was still guiding him east, towards the foothills of the Outer Reaches – the same direction which Gretilda had said the rebels had taken. But in reality, he had barely looked at the parchment. He had been afraid that it would lead them in a different direction, and of the choice he would have to make if the paths diverged. All he knew was that he had to find the Sacred Stone and return it to the shaman in order to find out what she knew of his mother. The Book of Prophecies would have to wait.

* * *

As dawn broke, their spirits lifted. Tobias raced ahead, chasing tumbleweed and pouncing on imaginary victims on the dusty ground. He was back to his normal, boisterous self now that they were out of range of the shaman and her magic. Murgatroyd too seemed to be enjoying himself, soaring high above their heads with the wind in his feathers.

Daylight came quickly once the sun had risen above the

horizon. Eventually Tobias tired of his tumbleweed game and trotted next to Ben. With the dog beside him, Ben no longer felt quite so miserable. He picked up his pace and began to take notice of his surroundings. The barren landscape was broken only by the occasional misshapen thorn bush which managed to cling, against the odds, to the windswept and sandy ground. Behind them, the village and its surrounding fields had already faded into the distance. Ahead of them, a dark smudge had appeared on the horizon. Ben wasn't sure whether it was a cloud or their first glimpse of the foothills.

The rising sun had taken the chill off the early morning and the wind had dropped. Ben rolled up his sleeves, enjoying the warmth of the sun on his bare arms.

"Come on, Tobias," he said. "I'll race you to that bush!"

The big dog wagged his tail, his tongue lolling from the corner of his mouth. Ben took off at a sprint, his satchel bumping against his back as he ran. Tobias raced ahead of him and waited for the boy to catch up, his head on his front paws and his wagging tail in the air. He leapt up as Ben passedand danced around him, trying to jump. Finally reaching the thorn bush, they threw themselves to the groung, Ben laughing as the dog tried to climb on top of him.

"Off!" he laughed, pushing him away. As he did so, something caught his eye. An object was nestled deep amongst the bush's gnarled, woody branches, the bright colours noticeable against its greeny-grey leaves. He got to his knees and stretched his arm into the heart of the bush, carefully avoiding its sharp thorns.

"Got it!" he cried, sitting back on his heels. He stared down at the object in his hands. It was a child's doll, stitched together from scraps of mismatched fabric. Its face had been roughly sewn on: two crosses of blue twine represented its eyes, two smaller crosses in plain undyed string for the nose and a curved line of uneven running stitches in a faded shade of red for the mouth. A few strips of sack cloth which passed for hair hung limply from the top of its head. Yet despite its crudeness, there was a warmth about the doll which made Ben sense that this had been a much loved toy.

Tobias thrust his head over Ben's shoulder and sniffed at the doll. As he made to take it in his mouth, Ben pushed his head away.

"No, Tobias," he said, feeling strangely protective of the toy.

"What's that?" said Murgatroyd, suddenly appearing out of nowhere to land beside them.

Ben showed him the doll. "Maybe it's a sign. Maybe it was left here by the villagers for us to find."

"Well, you can forget about any rescue attempt," said Murgatroyd immediately. "The rebels will have them well guarded. Our aim is to find the Book of Prophecies, and avoid the rebels at all costs."

Ben muttered under his breath as he stuffed the doll into his satchel. His aim was to retrieve the shaman's stone from the rebels so he could find out what had happened to his mother.

"Come on, then," he said, grumpily. "No point in hanging around."

"My sentiments exactly!" agreed Murgatroyd as he launched himself back into the open sky.

"That's the wrong way!" called Ben. "East is this way."

Tobias trotted a few paces in a completely different direction, looking back over his shoulder as if he expected them all to follow him. Ben and Murgatroyd looked at each other, then at Tobias.

"Are you sure that's the right way, Tobias?" said Arrowbright as he joined them. He had been aware that their easterly route was leading directly towards the foothills of the Outer Reaches, and he looked for the telltale shadow on the horizon which he had noticed earlier. The glare made it difficult to see and he brushed a trickle of sweat from his forehead as he shielded his eyes from the sun. He turned slowly to peer in all directions. There was no sign of the foothills.

"The parchment," said Murgatroyd to Ben, "what does it say?"

Reluctantly, Ben drew the page from the Book of Prophecies from his satchel.

"Well?" asked Murgatroyd expectantly.

Ben blinked in shock. He had unrolled the parchment to find that it was completely and utterly blank.

* * *

Bella pulled the thick, brown hood of her habit further down over her head and slipped into a back pew of Quadrivium's grand cathedral. The monks were saying prayers for the young prince's safe recovery. They had kept an ongoing vigil for the prince ever since his disappearance, and there was a steady stream of figures in brown robes, just like Bella's, entering and leaving the cathedral, ensuring that her appearance went unnoticed.

Princess Madeleine had returned first thing that morning with a monk's habit which she had found in her old dressing up box. It had fitted Bella's tiny frame perfectly, having already been altered for a child.

"But surely your size will draw attention to you?" Madeleine had worried.

"Everyone will just assume that I'm a novice," replied Bella as she had tied the rope belt around her waist, "I noticed that they had an intake of boys only last month."

"But novices don't wear the cowl," Madeleine had pointed out, finding things to worry about now that they were actually putting their plan into effect.

"Stop fussing," Bella had said to her great niece as she hoisted up her robes to descend the ladder from her secret room in the dome. "I'll blend into the background, you'll see. Didn't you have a call to make on Mayor Ponsonby's charming daughter?"

Bella briefly wondered how Madeleine was getting

on as she surreptitiously looked around the cathedral. A group of monks were shuffling slowly down the aisle towards her. Joining her palms together in front of her face, she risked a glance at them, then hurriedly ducked her head as she recognised the one in front. It was the monk who had entered the ballroom the night of Prince Alexander's disappearance, the one who had been speaking so animatedly to Ponsonby, the same monk who had been with Ponsonby when he had taken her hostage. She waited until they had passed and then quietly rose and followed them out.

The monks headed directly for the monastery which was built on the outer boundary of the palace grounds, not far from the cathedral. Keeping her head down, Bella shuffled after them. She caught up as they entered the monastery and slipped in after them, nodding to the novice who held open the heavy door without raising her head.

As soon as the door closed behind them, the monk Bella had recognised turned to his companion, clearly agitated. "He hasn't been seen since yesterday afternoon."

The other monk laid a hand on his sleeve. "Brother Bernard, we have our instructions. All will be well."

But Brother Bernard would not be pacified.

"What if someone finds out?" he cried. "What then, Brother William? With Ponsonby gone, we are the ones who will carry the blame!"

Bella edged closer, caught up in the exchange. Suddenly the monk called Brother William turned and spoke directly to her. "You, boy! Run to the kitchens and fetch a jug of ale for Brother Bernard."

She froze, hoping that her face was sufficiently hidden by her hood, but Brother William had already turned back to Brother Bernard.

"Calm yourself, Brother," he said. "It won't be for very much longer, you'll see. Once the mayor returns with the Book, everything will go back to normal and the king will be none the wiser."

He turned to see Bella still standing behind them, listening.

"What are you still doing here?" he cried. "I told you to fetch some ale! Better make it two jugs and bring them straight to my study. Run along!"

Bella dipped her head in a quick nod and turned to go.

"Where do you think you're going?" roared Brother William. "The kitchens are that way! Honestly, novices!"

Her heart pounding, she turned and shuffled off in the direction of his raised arm, wondering what he would say if he knew who he was speaking to.

* * *

The desert sun shone directly overhead, beaming down like a giant spotlight on the little party of travellers. After some bickering, they set out in the direction chosen by Tobias, preferring to trust the dog's instincts rather than each others'. None of them, however, were convinced this was the right direction, and tempers were not improved by the rising temperature which had rapidly changed from being pleasantly warm to unbearably hot.

"I don't understand why you can't read the parchment," complained Murgatroyd, "just when we need it the most. Has it been damaged in some way?"

Ben sighed irritably. "No, I've told you before: it doesn't seem to get damaged! It's been dunked in water countless times, I've had it stuffed into my pocket and under my shirt, and this is the first time anything like this has happened."

But deep inside, he felt guilty. He had contemplated leading them away from the Book of Prophecies and he was tormented by the thought that perhaps this was the reason the parchment had remained blank. He wondered if he had jeopardised their entire quest in order to find his mother.

Tobias dashed from one tiny patch of shade to the next as the ground scorched the pads of his feet. Arrowbright tore strips from his shirt and wrapped them round the dog's paws to offer some protection against the searing heat. Once he had finished, Tobias sniffed suspiciously at each paw in turn before trying them out. After a few uncoordinated steps, he got the hang of his new cloth shoes and plodded along next to Ben, his long, red tongue hanging out of the side of his mouth and his tail drooping.

They trudged onwards. Walking became more arduous as soft sand replaced the rocky soil. Ben felt as though the moisture had been sucked from every part of his body. His nostrils burned when he inhaled, and when he blinked he could almost hear his eyelids scraping against his eyeballs. They had long since drained Arrowbright's water bottle.

"What's that?" croaked Arrowbright, looking back in the direction from which they'd come.

Ben dragged his eyes from the ground, squinting against the glaring white light. He couldn't see anything but desert.

"There," said Arrowbright, pointing.

Ben blinked, feeling the crusted sand crack in the corners of his eyes. The horizon appeared to ripple as the heat rose off it in waves. Then Ben saw what Arrowbright was pointing at: an entire section of the horizon was billowing upwards and outwards. Tobias lowered his belly to the hot sand and placed his head between his paws, showing the whites of his eyes as he stared up at Ben.

"Where's Murgatroyd?" said Arrowbright.

A black dot appeared from the direction of the growing mass, moving swiftly towards them. As it got closer, they recognised the eagle. He was calling out to them, but his words were drowned out by a low, thunderous growl which seemed to follow him. It was only when he was directly above that they could hear his voice.

"Sandstorm! Find shelter, quick!"

He didn't stop, but flew on and was soon a speck in the distance.

Ben looked at Arrowbright in horror, and then back at the roiling mass coming closer by the second. He could now clearly see the wall of sand moving rapidly in their direction. A hot wind had whipped up and was hurling stinging gusts of sand into their faces.

Tobias bounded forward a couple of steps, and then stopped. He lowered his head and ripped the cloth off his paws with his teeth. Then he raised his head and gave a couple of short, sharp barks, jolting the others out of their shock. They stumbled after him, glancing backwards every few seconds to see the sandstorm coming ever closer.

It went suddenly dark as the swirling mass blotted out the sun. The wind shrieked and howled, driving sand and grit into their eyes and ears and against any patch of bare skin.

Arrowbright grabbed hold of Ben's arm. "We mustn't get separated," he shouted into his ear.

Ben looked round for Tobias, but he had already vanished behind the curtain of sand. "Tobias," he yelled, but the wind whipped the words from his mouth as soon as he had uttered them, shrieking back at him like a living thing. He thought he heard a bark, but had no way of knowing from which direction it had come.

They stumbled to a halt, unsure of which way to turn. The sand swirled around them, creating shifting shapes and images which the wind gathered up and flung into their faces. Sinking to the ground, they huddled against each other, drawing their knees up to their faces and clasping their arms over their heads.

A moment later, Ben felt something bump against his side and raised his head a fraction to see Tobias crouched beside him. The dog backed up a few paces, wriggling against the ground, his ears pressed flat against his head, then stopped, waiting for Ben to follow him. Ben tugged Arrowbright's arm and together they crawled on hands and knees after Tobias.

Not wanting to lose each other, Ben held loosely onto the dog's tail and Arrowbright held Ben's ankle as they slowly battled their way through the storm. After what seemed like hours, Tobias suddenly disappeared into a hole in the ground. Still holding onto his tail, Ben followed him down and found himself at the entrance to a tunnel. He hastily crawled further in so that Arrowbright could follow.

It was eerily quiet out of the storm. They could still hear the wind whistling above them and a few grains of sand blew into the tunnel, but it was infinitely peaceful compared to the full fury of the sandstorm. They spent a few moments spitting sand out of their mouths and shaking it out of their ears and hair while Tobias waited patiently. When they had finished, he trotted a little way into the tunnel and looked back at them, his eyes glowing in the darkness.

"I think he wants us to follow," said Ben, hesitantly.

"He hasn't put a paw wrong yet," said Arrowbright. "What are we waiting for?"

The tunnel was too low even for Ben to walk upright, so they followed Tobias on their hands and knees. It quickly became too dark to see their hands in front of their faces as they moved away from the entrance.

Ben took off his satchel and pushed it ahead of him. Tobias's tail wafted across his face every now and then and he could hear Arrowbright close behind. He was wondering just how far the tunnel went when he felt a wet nose in his face and realised that the large dog had been able to turn around. Tentatively reaching out, he discovered he could no longer feel the earthen walls or ceiling. He stood up slowly. Only when he had stretched himself up to his full height did the top of his head scrape the roof of the tunnel. He opened his satchel and felt around for the shaman's glow sticks, then, holding one up in front of him, he examined his surroundings.

The tunnel had opened into a small chamber. The roof wasn't quite high enough for Arrowbright to stand fully upright, but even to the tall soldier it felt spacious after the confines of the tunnel. The spindly root system of some dry desert plant grew down from the ceiling like an organic chandelier. Ben wedged his glow stick in amongst the roots and its shadows stretched like fingers across the earthen walls.

The chamber was bare except for a small pile of smooth, white stones piled in a pyramid on the far side. Tobias sat beside them wagging his tail proudly as though he had just created a fine work of art. Ben walked over to take a closer look. Each stone was about the size of his fist. He plucked one from the top of the pyramid and weighed it in his palm. It was lighter than he had expected, firm but not solid, with the texture of leather and slightly warm to the touch. He turned it over, half expecting to see some stitching like the balls he used to kick around back in Quadrivium, but it was completely smooth and blemish free. He felt something shift inside as he turned it over in his hands.

"There's something in the tunnel." Arrowbright spoke softly into his ear. Ben looked up to see Tobias facing the tunnel through which they had just come, the hackles on the back of his neck bristling. He strained his ears but couldn't hear anything over the loud thumping beat of his heart. Tobias took a small step backwards. Ben could hear it now: a soft, slithering sound like something heavy being dragged over dry leaves. The large dog took another step back, his haunches pressing up against Ben's legs. A low growl started deep in his throat as the sound came steadily closer.

A gust of foul air rushed into the chamber. Tobias tried to back up further, pushing Ben towards the wall. Ben took an involuntary step back and his foot knocked against the pyramid of stones. He felt it shift. For a split second, he clung to the hope that it would stay upright, but slowly, inexorably, it collapsed, the small, leathery objects rolling in all directions.

At that moment, the creature entered the chamber.

* * *

Standing in the shadowy corridors of the monastery, Bella had no intention of fetching ale for the two monks. Instead of making her way to the kitchens, she had doubled back and followed Brother Bernard and Brother William at a safe distance until they disappeared through a door into what she assumed to be Brother William's study. The conversation she had overheard convinced her that she had been right: the monks had collaborated with Mayor Ponsonby in hiding Prince Alexander until the Book of Prophecies was returned.

She was wondering whether she'd be able to ease open the door to eavesdrop further when a third monk came running past her and wrenched it open.

"Brother William! Brother Bernard! Come quickly!"

He didn't enter the room but remained on the threshold, clinging to the doorframe. Bella edged closer.

"I don't know!" he cried in response to a query from within the room. "I'm not a nursemaid or a doctor. He could be sick or just missing his mother – I don't know why he won't stop crying!"

He took a step back as Brother William appeared in the doorway.

"Did you try picking him up?" he asked irritably.

"No," said the monk, wringing his hands, "I was scared of dropping him – he is the heir to the throne, after all. Will you come and take a look?"

With a sigh, Brother William turned back into the room and instructed Brother Bernard to: "stay here until you've calmed yourself down, and don't speak to anyone else," before closing the door to his study firmly behind him and following the other monk down the passageway.

They passed Bella without a second glance. She was about to follow them when Brother William stopped and turned back.

"Just take the ale straight into the study, boy, and stop loitering!" he snapped, not appearing to notice that she wasn't holding any jugs.

"Yes, Brother," she muttered, turning away. But as soon as their footsteps had receded, she hurried after them, keeping out of sight in the shadows.

At first she thought they were making their way back towards the front door, but, instead, they turned abruptly into a narrow passageway. It was so unobtrusive that she could easily have missed it had she not been paying attention. She hitched up her robes and trotted over, but when she peered round the corner she found that it was no more than a shallow alcove, and there was no sign of either of the monks. She looked both ways along the corridor, wondering if she had made a mistake.

Suddenly she had an idea. Stepping into the alcove, she began running her hands over the stones in the wall. It only took a moment before she found what she had been looking for: one of the stones protruded slightly from the others. Once she had worked it loose, she wasn't at all surprised to find a lever hidden behind it. And once she had put her ear up against the wall, she wasn't at all surprised when she heard a baby's piercing wail.

* * *

"Keep. Perfectly. Still," said Arrowbright in a low voice.

It seemed to Ben as though all the air had been sucked out of the chamber the moment the creature appeared. He stared up into the two huge nostrils which twitched independently at the end of the long snout, and then he flinched as a forked tongue shot out, flickering as it tasted the air. A reptilian foot appeared, followed by another which narrowly missed the scattered white stones.

Slowly, the creature dragged itself into the chamber. It was so close that Ben could see a glistening membrane flicker across its amber eye. He caught a glimpse of its other eye as its head swayed in their direction before twisting up towards the glow stick fixed just above its head. It appeared mesmerised by the light, weaving from side to side to view it from different angles. It took another step into the chamber and then paused briefly to shrug free part of its upper torso which had caught on the roof of the tunnel. At first, Ben thought it had prominent shoulder blades but, as the rest of its body entered the chamber, he saw that it was a pair of wings which were tightly folded against its scaly back.

"There's another way out," said Arrowbright softly, "just behind you. Wait for my signal . . ."

Ben watched in horrified fascination as the creature's

head bobbed and dipped around the glow stick. Suddenly, it lunged, hitting the stick and knocking it to the ground. The light faded and the chamber was plunged into darkness.

"Now!" hissed Arrowbright, grabbing Ben's arm and pushing him towards their escape route. Ben threw himself into the darkness. A second later he hit the ground with a jolt, hard enough to knock the wind out of him. He lay stunned for a second before Tobias landed heavily on his back and leapt off. Ben managed to roll out of the way just in time to hear Arrowbright hit the ground behind him. He scrambled to his hands and knees, realising as he did so that he still held one of the stones from the chamber.

A blast of scorching heat followed them, accompanied by a strong smell of bonfires. A moment later, there was a long, piercing scream, louder than anything Ben had heard in his life. He felt the stone-like object stir in his hands and realised with dawning horror that it was an egg.

He was brought to his senses by Arrowbright fumbling around for him in the darkness.

"Come on, Ben!" he whispered, grabbing hold of his arm. "This way! Quickly!"

Another scream reverberated from the chamber overhead. Without thinking, Ben slipped the egg into his pocket and jumped to his feet. His only thought was to get as far away from the creature as possible.

They ran for what seemed an eternity, pursued by the high-pitched screams. Ben stumbled in the darkness. It was so dark that it made no difference whether his eyes were open or shut. He half-expected the ground beneath his feet to give way at any moment and plunge him into a bottomless hole.

The creature's cries echoed after them and the smell of brimstone was strong in the air. The shrill noise created a throbbing pain in Ben's temples. It was as though the sound was inside his head, echoing against the walls of his skull. He staggered to a halt and put his fists against his ears, trying in vain to block out the noise. Something moved in his pocket and he flinched, remembering the egg. He stared wildly into the darkness. He realised that he had no idea which way the others had gone. He couldn't hear anything above the screams.

The egg moved again. He reached gingerly into his pocket. If he left it on the tunnel floor, perhaps the creature would leave them alone. He felt a sudden, agonising pain in the fleshy part of his palm, as though it had been pierced by a dozen needles. He yelped and yanked his hand out of his pocket, cradling it with his other hand. His palm felt wet and sticky. At that moment he realised that the screaming had stopped.

His short, panicky breaths were loud in the watchful silence. The thing in his pocket scratched his leg through the fabric of his trousers, making his skin crawl. Then he heard movement in the darkness. He backed away slowly, his hands reaching out for the tunnel walls. The scrabbling against his leg was becoming more urgent. He jumped as a high-pitched chirrup came from the vicinity of his trouser pocket. The response was immediate and closer than he had expected; his hair streamed backwards from the force of the blast and he screwed up his eyes against the burning heat.

No longer caring which way he was headed, Ben turned on his heel and broke into a flat out sprint. He darted to one side to avoid an outcrop of rock, then turned a sharp corner and pounded up a steep incline. It took him a moment before he realised he could actually see where he was going. There was light at the end of the tunnel. He raced towards it gratefully, turned another corner and was suddenly in full daylight.

He staggered into the cave, momentarily blinded by the sunlight which flooded in through the wide entrance no more than a few paces away. As his vision cleared, he spotted Arrowbright and Tobias standing at the entrance to the cave with their backs to him. He started towards them with a cry, partly of relief but mainly of warning. Then his words died in his mouth as he saw what they were staring at. Arrayed before the mouth of the cave, like an audience watching a performance on a stage, were hundreds of men on horseback.

18

Ben stood motionless. It was as though his feet were glued to the floor of the cave. The only sound as he looked out over the horde of men was the occasional jingle of a bridle or the soft thud of a horse's hoof as it shifted impatiently on the soft sand. Some of the men were dressed in mismatched items of uniform belonging to various regiments of the king's army, others wore simple leather jerkins over dirty brown leggings. All were heavily armed with longbows and swords.

Ben glanced at Arrowbright who shrugged back at him with an air of resignation. Even Tobias seemed subdued, his tail hanging low between his legs. Thoughts ran through Ben's head: these men must be rebels, perhaps the same ones who had stolen the shaman's stone. He might be able to work this to his advantage.

His hopes were dashed as he caught sight of the corpulent figure of Mayor Ponsonby seated astride a tired looking pony. The mayor tipped his feathered riding hat sardonically at Ben, then grabbed quickly at his pony's mane as the beast shifted uncomfortably under his weight.

Suddenly the shrill scream of the creature in the tunnel echoed around the cave, reverberating off the walls – but to Ben's astonishment the grim expressions on the faces of the armed men did not falter. He could tell from Arrowbright's expression of alarm and the raised hackles on Tobias's back that they had heard the sound, although neither moved a muscle, but the rebels didn't appear to have heard a thing.

Ponsonby kicked his pony forward a few paces. He ceremoniously withdrew a roll of parchment from his saddle bag and unfurled it with as much of a flourish as he could manage while grasping the front of his pony's saddle with his other hand. He cleared his throat.

Ben heard a clattering of stones from the tunnel behind him. He glanced quickly at Arrowbright then flicked his eyes towards a large rock near the entrance. The soldier nodded imperceptibly then turned his attention back to Ponsonby who was about to speak.

"I have in my hand a warrant for your arr . . . aaaaaahhhhh!" The smug expression on Ponsonby's face changed in a split second to one of sheer terror. He flung the document into the air, scrabbling desperately for his pony's reins.

Ben dived behind the rock, narrowly avoiding being crushed by the creature's dark green body as it rushed past, its clawed feet scrabbling against the rocky ground. It was briefly airborne, its short stubby wings beating the air frantically, before landing amongst the rebels.

Its screams competed with those of men and horses. Ben, Arrowbright and Tobias watched from behind the rock as the rebels scattered in blind panic. Long tongues of flame spurted from the creature's nostrils, scorching the backs of the fleeing men. It thrashed its tail on the ground, narrowly missing Mayor Ponsonby who had collapsed in a dead faint, having been thrown by his pony which had bolted the instant the creature appeared.

Arrowbright leapt out from behind the rock and vaulted the creature's tail. Taking hold of Ponsonby's shoulders, he tried to drag him to safety. Ben went to help him, realising that the fat mayor was too heavy for Arrowbright to lift on his own. He didn't notice the frantic scratching in his trouser pocket until it was too late. A plaintive chirrup pierced through the terrified shouts of the rebels. The creature turned, its head poised on one side, listening.

The shrill cheep sounded again. Ben took a few paces backwards, deliberately drawing the creature's attention away from Arrowbright and the unconscious mayor. It took an unsteady step towards him, ignoring the rebels who scattered in panic. Its head moved from side to side and its tongue flicked in and out, tasting the air for the scent of its offspring as it moved slowly and relentlessly towards Ben. Arrowbright watched helplessly.

Very, very slowly, Ben reached inside his pocket. He cupped his hand around the pieces of broken egg, feeling something shift on his palm as he carefully drew it out. The creature appeared to be watching his every move, its head moving slowly down and then back up as Ben placed the gooey mess of broken egg and the tiny wriggling object gingerly on the floor of the cave. The creature hovered, opening and closing its wings in agitation until the tiny figure raised its head and gave a loud chirrup. Finally the creature moved. Dipping its head, it took its offspring gently in its mouth, then, without a backwards glance, it headed back to its tunnel.

"Mama, mama," mumbled Ponsonby, dazedly looking up at Arrowbright.

"You'll need your mother by the time I've finished with you," said Arrowbright harshly, pulling the mayor to his feet. "But first, you're going to answer some questions."

* * *

Arrowbright bound Ponsonby securely, using the mayor's own bootlaces to tie his hands and feet together, even though there was nowhere for him to run. Around them the landscape was deserted. The rebels had fled, taking their injured with them and leaving Mayor Ponsonby to his fate. Ben sat quietly to one side as Arrowbright began the interrogation.

"What were you doing with the rebels?"

"Give me the boy and I will show some mercy," said Ponsonby pompously. His arrogance had returned once he was sure the monstrous creature had gone.

"You're in no position to be making demands," said Arrowbright. "Now, tell us why you were with the rebels."

"I can offer you anything you want," said the mayor, again ignoring Arrowbright's question, "a promotion, an honourable discharge, extreme wealth – you name it and it's yours. Just hand over the boy."

Arrowbright tried for a third time. "What business did you have with the rebels?"

"Perhaps it's a place on the king's council you want?" continued Ponsonby. "That is easily within my reach. A young man like you will go far in the new order."

"I am not interested in your bribes!" said Arrowbright, suddenly raising his voice. Tobias added a warning growl, his hackles raised.

"Then you're a fool!" cried Ponsonby, covering his velvet riding habit in flecks of spittle as he spat out the words. "We control both the king's army and the rebel forces. There is no escape for you! My men will return, and when they do you will rue the day you crossed Mayor Ponsonby!"

"Do you really think they are going to come back and risk the wrath of the dragon?" said Arrowbright, as he paced up and down. "Or perhaps you didn't notice the dragon summoned by the boy to attack your rebel troops. Perhaps Ben should get it back to finish the job?"

The mayor turned white. "That's impossible," he blustered. "No one commands the wild beasts of the desert . . ."

At that moment, Murgatroyd appeared silently from above, descending swiftly to land at Ben's feet.

"At last, I've found you!" he cried. "I've just seen a large group of rebels on horseback galloping across the desert as though Tritan's hounds were at their heels . . ."

Ponsonby's mouth dropped open as he heard the eagle speak, and he started to whimper, his bravado suddenly gone. Murgatroyd whipped his head round. He was almost as surprised at seeing the mayor as Ponsonby was on hearing him talk, but before he could speak again, Arrowbright stepped forward.

"The child commands the birds from the sky and the creatures from the earth. I think you should tell him everything he wants to know."

Ben pushed out his chest, doing his best to look powerful and dangerous. Murgatroyd quickly got the gist of what was happening. He raised a claw and examined his razor sharp talons.

"If you refuse," he said, "I'll be tearing strips off you to feed to my friends the vultures . . ."

"All right, I'll talk!" cried Ponsonby, cowering against the rock. "The rebels are under my master's control, just like the army. I had orders to lead them into the desert to this exact spot."

"Then what?" asked Arrowbright.

"He was only interested in the boy. The rest of you were to be, er, disposed of. The child was to be taken back to Quadrivium – alive."

"How did you know exactly where I'd be?" asked Ben. "The desert's a big place."

A cloud passed over Ponsonby's face. "The master directed me here," he said, refusing to meet their eyes. "I don't know how he knew. I was just following orders . . ."

"You are an appalling liar," said Arrowbright. "I have half a mind to throw you into that tunnel and leave you there."

"No!" cried Ponsonby, his chins wobbling in fear. He glanced briefly at the dark entrance to the tunnel and then back at Arrowbright. "Occasionally it suits my master's purpose to make use of the ancient arts," he said, reluctantly. "In this instance, I believe he used a Sacred Stone to track down the boy."

"So your master is a thief," said Arrowbright contemptuously. "He stole the Stone from my village and took the defenceless villagers from their homes!"

"This is all his fault," said Ponsonby, staring at Ben with loathing. "If he hadn't stolen the Book of Prophecies, none of this would have been necessary."

They stared at him in astonishment. Before Ben could speak, Murgatroyd drew him and Arrowbright to one side, out of the mayor's earshot. "He obviously thinks we have the Book. Let's not tell him the truth, at least not yet. I want to find out more."

Ponsonby was gazing out into the desert when they turned back to him.

"Why kidnap the king's son?" asked Murgatroyd. "And

why kidnap the Dowager Bella and Penthesilean?"

Ponsonby refused to look at him, pretending not to have heard. He didn't believe that animals could talk, he told himself. If he ignored the giant bird, perhaps it would disappear. Tobias edged closer, lifting his lips in a snarl to show his white teeth.

"Answer the question," said Arrowbright in a threatening tone.

"The queen's mother had information I required," said Ponsonby quickly. "She was undoubtedly involved in the theft of the Book and Penthesilean was just in the wrong place at the wrong time."

"And the king's son?" asked Murgatroyd. "The heir to the kingdom?"

"He was a useful hostage, that's all. I was forced to use extreme measures to get back the Book of Prophecies. I expected to be able to exchange the prince in return for the boy."

"But I don't have the Book!" burst out Ben. "I never did!"

"Liar!" cried Ponsonby. "It was secure in the depths of the underground lake before you came along – and I have a witness who places you at the scene – after which the Book disappeared, along with the mermen and every drop of water!"

Murgatroyd stared at the mayor thoughtfully for a while. Finally he turned back to the others.

"This explains why they've gone to such lengths to find

you, Ben," he said in a low voice, "but it still doesn't explain why the Mayor of Quadrivium is in league with the rebels."

Arrowbright interrupted. "Speaking of rebels, we should leave soon in case they do return with reinforcements. We're sitting ducks in this cave, so to speak. I say we make for the mountains."

Ben nodded in agreement, reluctant to refer to the parchment in case he found it blank again.

"If we start now we should reach the foothills by dawn," continued Arrowbright. "We have a better chance of not being seen if we cross the desert by night."

"What about him?" asked Ben, gesturing towards Ponsonby. "We can't just leave him here."

Ponsonby looked up, sensing that they were getting ready to leave.

"Don't leave me," he cried, piteously. "Please don't leave me! The monster might return!"

"Ben's right," said Murgatroyd. "Anyway, I want to question him further. Tobias can keep an eye on him."

Hearing his name, Tobias pricked up his ears and gave a low woof to show that he understood. He stood close to the mayor as the others gathered up their few possessions before setting out into the cool of the night, leaving the dragon and its lair behind them.

* * *

They travelled due east in the direction of the foothills.

By the time the first rays of sun beamed over the horizon, Ben was surprised to see how much ground they had covered. The Mountains of the Outer Boundaries were now clearly visible beyond the gently rolling foothills, the peaks sharply defined against the clear sky. They soon left the desert behind and the sand was replaced by a sparse, rock-strewn soil in which hardy grass grew in fat clumps with the occasional flash of colour from flowering cacti. The vegetation grew thicker as they journeyed deeper into the foothills of the Outer Reaches, providing cover from anyone who might be following.

Tobias bounded on ahead to investigate the undergrowth for rabbits, while Arrowbright paused to dig up some fleshy roots which they split open to find a refreshing liquid. Ponsonby refused to try it. He had started to complain as soon as they had travelled too far from the cave to turn back. They had untied his wrists to allow him to walk more freely, but that hadn't stopped him complaining. Then he developed a limp. Arrowbright examined him and found nothing wrong, but it slowed them all down considerably. Finally, the mayor slumped down and refused to go any further.

"I need to rest," he moaned. "My feet are covered in blisters!"

The others conferred. Lack of sleep was beginning to take its toll on each of them. The day was getting warmer as the morning wore on and they decided it would make sense to rest now and travel in the cool of the late afternoon.

They would take it in turns to keep a lookout for the rebels whilst the others slept. Murgatroyd volunteered to take the first shift. Ponsonby flopped down in the coolest spot beneath an overhanging rock, while Arrowbright and Ben sank down in the dappled shade of some thorn trees. In minutes they were asleep.

* * *

The sun had moved a long way across the sky by the time Ben was woken by Arrowbright for his shift. It was early afternoon and Ponsonby was still fast asleep, his large belly moving up and down in time with his loud snores. Tobias lay at the mayor's feet with his eyes half open. Murgatroyd muttered to himself as he clung to his perch in the thorn tree, his head under his wing.

"Nothing to report," said Arrowbright. "No sign at all of any pursuit."

He threw himself down into the patch of shade vacated by Ben and closed his eyes. Ben took his place on top of the overhanging rock, resting his back against a boulder which was warm from the sun. He gazed out over the shimmering desert, turning his head every now and then to scan the surrounding hillside.

A host of unseen insects struck up in the bushes around him, chirping loudly in the still, hot afternoon. Ben wished he had some water to splash on his face. He closed his eyes for a few seconds against the glare.

"It can't be easy for a boy like you growing up without a mother."

Ben sat up suddenly, jolted awake by the voice. It was Ponsonby. Somehow he had managed to sidle over to Ben without waking Tobias, who was now lying on his side in the shade, fast asleep.

"He could help you find her, you know – my master."

Ben couldn't help himself. "What do you mean?"

Now that he had Ben's full attention, Ponsonby sat down next to him.

"He has ways and means," he said, making himself comfortable. "Not that I always approve, of course, but in your case I would make an exception. After all, a boy your age shouldn't be without his mother."

"Why should I trust you, or your master?" scoffed Ben. "Who is he, anyway?"

"Ahh," said Ponsonby, leaning conspiratorially towards Ben, "he's a very clever man. You should meet him; I know he'd like very much to meet you."

Ben suddenly remembered what the mayor had said earlier about his master, under interrogation: "He was only interested in the boy. The rest of you were to be . . . disposed of."

He stood up and backed away from Ponsonby.

"No," he said with quiet determination, "it won't work! Don't you dare even speak of my mother . . ." He stopped suddenly as he noticed Ponsonby's eyes focus on something over his shoulder. He spun round, squinting against the bright sunlight. In the distance, a cloud of dust had appeared and seemed to be getting closer as he watched.

"Murgatroyd! Arrowbright!" he shouted. "Wake up!"

In moments, the others were standing beside him, staring at the dust cloud.

"Another sandstorm?" asked Arrowbright.

"I don't think so – he didn't want me to see it," said Ben, gesturing at Ponsonby who had a smug expression on his face.

Murgatroyd was silent. After a moment, he spoke. "I see horses. The rebels must have found our tracks."

"I told you they'd come back for me!" cried Ponsonby, triumphantly. Ben turned on the mayor, suddenly noticing that all his buttons had been ripped from his coat and tunic.

"You laid a trail for them," he said, his anger growing as the truth dawned on him. "While you were constantly complaining and holding us up, you were dropping buttons for them to find!"

"Leave him, Ben," said Arrowbright, laying a hand on his arm, "there's no time for this. Those men can move much quicker on horseback than we can on foot. Our only chance is to make it into the mountains."

Reluctantly, Ben allowed himself to be pulled away. But as they turned to go, he glanced over his shoulder at the mayor who was steadfastly gazing at the approaching dust cloud.

"I wouldn't be so smug if I were you," he said. "You've let me slip through your fingers once again. I doubt your master is going to be pleased."

With that, he raced after the others, leaving Ponsonby staring uncertainly after him.

* * *

"Where have you been?" hissed Princess Madeleine as Bella's head appeared through the trapdoor of the dome's secret room. "I've got so much to tell you!"

Bella closed the trapdoor, then pushed back her cowl and grinned at her great niece. "I've found Alexander!" she cried triumphantly.

Madeleine's reaction was not what she had expected. "What? No, you couldn't have!"

Bella picked up the map and pointed to the X over the monastery. "He's right here. As I suspected, the monks are hiding him until the mayor returns, although some of them don't seem best pleased by the situation."

Madeleine was shaking her head as Bella spoke.

"That's impossible," she said as soon as Bella paused for breath, "he's in the mayor's villa; I heard him crying!"

She proceeded to tell Bella about her visit to Mayor Ponsonby's daughter, who was the same age as Madeleine herself. "She's the most dreadful show-off. She jumped at the chance to model her new gowns for me. Luckily that gave me the opportunity to explore the rest of the villa while her maids were lacing her into some hideous concoction of satin and lace!"

"And?" asked Bella, impatient to discuss her own find.

"And there's a secret room in the mayor's cellar," said Madeleine. "I could hear the sound of a baby crying coming from behind what looked like a solid stone wall, but I found a hidden lever behind the brickwork – just like the one to release the ladder for this room. Then Phoebe called for me and I had to go and pretend to admire her outfit. I made my excuses as soon as I could and came back here . . ."

Her words petered out as she realised that Bella was no longer listening.

"The map is still wrong," said her great aunt, opening the trapdoor. "Come on!"

Confused, Madeleine followed her down the ladder and through the wooden door out onto the wide balcony of the dome.

"Now," said Bella, "where is Ponsonby's villa?"

Her great niece quickly pointed to the red-tiled roof of the mayor's home which was built just outside the palace grounds.

"And where is the monastery?"

She watched the girl's face light up as her eyes traced the short path from Ponsonby's villa to the monastery, which was tucked neatly up against the wall – just inside the palace grounds.

"So if we correct the map so that the monastery is a little further east and the mayor's house is a little further west –" began Madeleine.

"– the two buildings back directly onto one another," finished Bella. "The secret room which each of us found is one and the same: it links the monastery to the mayor's villa! Even if the king's guards had searched either property, all Ponsonby's men would have had to do is smuggle Alexander out through the other building before they got too close."

"So all we need to do now is go back to the secret room and rescue Prince Alexander!"

"And then we can tell the king everything that has been going on!" said Bella triumphantly.

19

As they climbed the foothills of the Outer Reaches, Ben couldn't help turning every few minutes to look back. Mayor Ponsonby's rotund figure had disappeared from view, but the dust cloud thrown up by the approaching rebels was still visible out in the desert.

Murgatroyd called a halt as soon as they had put some distance between themselves and the mayor.

"Ben, I think it's time you took another look at the parchment," he said. "We're almost at the foot of the mountains. Where do we go from here?"

Reluctantly, Ben drew the page from the Book of Prophecies out of his satchel. He was worried that the signs wouldn't be visible and that he would see only what everyone else saw: nothing. With his heart in his mouth, he slowly unfurled the piece of yellowed parchment. At first he thought it was blank, and then he spied the cluster of symbols on one side of the page. He let out a sigh of relief, recognising the signs which would lead them to the Book of Prophecies. He looked up into the anxious faces of the others.

"It's all right," he said, "the signs are there."

Tobias sat down and nonchalantly scratched his ear with a back paw, as if he had known all along that Ben would have no trouble reading the page.

Ben selected a few small rocks and used them to weigh down the edges of the parchment, which had a tendency to curl inwards. Then he relaxed his mind and looked down at the symbols, waiting for the path to reveal itself.

A warm, dry breeze suddenly sprang up. It blew his hair into his eyes and he absentmindedly pushed back his fringe, all his attention focussed on the page before him. The breeze became a gusty wind which threatened to dislodge the page from the rocks holding it down. A bright spark appeared out of the sky and landed inches away from Ben. He brushed it away quickly; the parchment was so dry that the tiniest of sparks could cause it to burn to cinders within seconds. He glanced up, wondering why the others had chosen this moment to light a fire so close to the precious document.

But the others had vanished, and Ben found himself suddenly alone on the hillside. The sky had turned dark, the sun hidden behind a veil of thick black cloud which hung over the mountaintops. A gust of wind brought another shower of sparks which fell all around him. He hurriedly rolled up the parchment and thrust it into his satchel, then stood up, all his senses alert. The wind was blowing from the direction of the mountains, bringing with it a strong smell of smoke. In the distance, he could hear a muted noise: almost, but not quite, like torrential rain on a tin roof.

In a dreamlike state, Ben half walked, half climbed up the hillside, the hot wind blowing full in his face. None of the sparks had yet managed to ignite the dry vegetation, but they were drifting down with increasing frequency and Ben knew that it was only a matter of time.

Eventually he reached the crest of the hill and climbed up onto a small plateau, a natural platform from which he had a clear view across a shallow wooded valley to the mountains on the other side. A fierce red glow could now be seen in the gap between the two highest peaks, reminding him suddenly of the tapestry he had seen in the throne room back in Quadrivium. He realised he had located the source of the fire. Thoughts of the screaming animals from his trance flashed through his mind and he knew that it was up to him to save those who were trapped, as the old washerwoman in Quadrivium had predicted. Somehow he had to find a way over the mountains until he reached the heart of the inferno.

* * *

A rough, wet tongue licked Ben's ear. He jumped, and then his eyes focused on Tobias's wide mouth which hung open in a panting grin, just inches from his face. The late afternoon sun glinted like gold on his fur.

Arrowbright was looking at Ben. "Are you alright?" he asked anxiously.

Ben didn't reply immediately. He stood up slowly and walked a few paces, sniffing the air and listening intently to the silence which was broken only by the clack of Tobias's claws against the rock as the dog followed him. Finally, he turned and looked over his shoulder into the expectant faces of the others.

"This way," he said, before setting off up the rocky hillside.

The plateau was just as he had seen in his trance. He looked across the valley to the mountains beyond.

"Do you see the mountain with the double peak?" he said, pointing unnecessarily. They all gazed at the highest, most forbidding mountain. "We need to aim for the area between," he concluded decisively.

They were all silent for a while, contemplating the mountain. Murgatroyd spoke first. "As the eagle flies, it will take me less than an hour to reach those peaks, but you will all have to go the long way, so I suggest we split up. I'll go on ahead to try and find a pass through the mountains."

Arrowbright looked back to where the sun was beginning to set over the desert. The dust cloud had vanished and he had a fleeting hope that the rebels had stopped and made camp for the night. But he knew it was more likely they had already reached the foothills. "We'll make our way down to the valley floor and take cover beneath the trees. How will you find us?"

"Don't worry about me," said Murgatroyd as he took off. "Just make sure the rebels don't find you before I return!"

* * *

Below them, the valley was already deep in shadow. After watching Murgatroyd fly off into the distance, Ben and Arrowbright started to make their way down the path which zigzagged down the steep hillside towards the valley floor.

A soft woof made them pause and look back. Tobias was still standing on the plateau. Once he had their attention, he trotted away from the path and began to scramble through a patch of loose stones and bushes, starting a small landslide as he slid down on his haunches.

"Where are you going, Tobias?" called Ben. "The path's over here!"

"No, he's right," said Arrowbright, as it dawned on him what Tobias was up to. "If we take the path we'll be in plain view of anyone who reaches the plateau. If we take his route we'll be hidden by that big rock."

With difficulty, they made their way across to where

Tobias was waiting. They used the hardy shrubs which were anchored to the steep, rocky slope as handholds, and slid and crawled their way slowly down to the shelter of the wooded valley.

Finally the gradient became gentler as they approached the valley floor and they were able to walk normally. The trees were not far ahead when Tobias stopped abruptly and lifted his nose to sniff the air.

"Snow on the way," said Ben, matter-of-factly.

Arrowbright looked at him in astonishment. "Impossible," he said, "it's the middle of summer!"

But Ben was facing down the valley. "Look," he said, pointing.

Arrowbright followed the direction of Ben's finger. Where previously had been the haze of early evening there now hung an ominous, deep purple cloud, joined to the earth by a gossamer curtain of pale grey. In moments, the sky overhead turned from the pale blue of a summer evening to a sombre, dirty white. Arrowbright shivered as a sudden chill wind gusted towards them, then something caught his eye and he looked up. A large snowflake appeared out of the white-grey sky and landed on his upturned face. It was quickly followed by another, and then another. Tobias shook himself violently, as though he already felt himself covered in snow.

"Come on, Ben," Arrowbright said urgently, "we need to get under cover, fast."

He bounded down the slope, closely followed by Ben and Tobias. The snow was falling thick and fast by the time they reached the shelter of the trees. Arrowbright paused and looked back, catching a glimpse of movement in the distance. The swirling snowflakes made it difficult to tell for certain, but he thought he could see figures on the plateau. Ben stumbled to a halt beside him.

"What is it?" he asked, following the direction of the soldier's gaze.

"I think the rebels have found the plateau."

Ben's keen eyes quickly located the movement. A line of figures had begun the descent down the winding path from the plateau to the valley. They were lost from view as a gust of wind blew the snow horizontally towards them. The storm seemed to be getting worse. Tobias had taken shelter behind the thick, gnarled trunk of a tree and Ben and Arrowbright joined him. During a brief lull they peered out, trying to catch sight of their pursuers.

"They couldn't have got far," said Ben, straining his eyes to see through the falling snow and the rapidly failing light, "not in this weather."

"Well, I can't see them," answered Arrowbright. "Can you?"

They both scanned the hillside. Already, there were large patches of white where the snow had been blown in drifts against the bushes and rocks.

"There!" said Ben, suddenly spotting movement. "They

look like they've turned around!"

With relief, Arrowbright saw that Ben was right. The figures were slowly retreating to the plateau, defeated by the harsh conditions. A second later, they were hidden from view as the storm picked up once more.

*   *   *

The trees sheltered them from the worst of the storm as they moved deeper into the wood. Occasionally, the howling wind would dislodge snow from the branches above them, sending it tumbling to the ground with a muffled thump. The first time this happened, Tobias, who had been trotting on ahead, raced back to them with his tail between his legs.

"It's only snow," calmed Ben, fondling his silky ears. "Come on, Tobias, we've been through worse than this!"

They decided to keep moving, even though the light was fading fast. They knew that as soon as the snowstorm had blown over, the rebels would be on the move.

"I just hope that Murgatroyd's managed to find a pass through the mountains," said Arrowbright.

He used the woodcraft he had learnt as a child to keep them on an easterly course. He taught Ben how to use the moss growing on the tree trunks as a compass. In this region it grew on the north side of the trees where there was less sunlight and more moisture. This worked well until

Ben came to a tree where the moss grew in patchy clumps all the way around the trunk. They had been walking for some time in near darkness, using their sense of touch to feel for the moss.

"We must be in the thickest part of the wood," said Arrowbright. "There's not much sunlight here so the moss tends to grow pretty evenly." He dropped his pack. "Maybe we should stop here and get some rest. We can carry on at first light."

They gathered fallen branches from the forest floor and propped them against the broad trunk of an ancient tree, then packed moss into the gaps between the branches. When they had finished, the makeshift shelter was just large enough for the three of them to squeeze into. Ben and Arrowbright sat upright with their backs against the tree trunk, huddled together for warmth, while Tobias laid himself across their feet with his tail curled up over his nose. Although the occasional snowflake found its way between the branches, it didn't take long until all three were fast asleep.

* * *

Ben opened his eyes. The crack of thunder which had woken him dissolved into a low rumble. Careful not to wake Arrowbright, he wriggled round until he could push his head out of the shelter. The dull, grey light of dawn illuminated a sea of endless trees. Behind him, Arrowbright slid down onto his side and drew his knees up to his chest. Tobias lay across the entrance with his legs stuck straight out in front of him. As Ben watched, he gave a soft yelp and his paws twitched gently as he chased rabbits through his dreams. He edged round the sleeping dog and out of the shelter.

Stretching his arms over his head, he gave a big yawn and turned slowly to look at his surroundings. Halfway round he stopped and caught his breath. Not more than a stone's throw away was a wall of rock.

He moved slowly out of the shelter of the trees towards it. The snow had stopped and a fine drizzle hung in the air like mist. He craned his neck to look upwards as he approached the cliff, squinting against the persistent rain. The rock was featureless, with no sign of any cracks from which a hardy shrub could sprout, or even a jutting handhold of rock. He looked left and right, but it was the same in both directions. The sheer cliff wall simply disappeared into the forest without a break.

He suddenly noticed how quiet it was. Apart from the constant background rumble of thunder and the muted sound of the rain, there wasn't a single sign of life: no birdsong or buzz of insects. Shivering, he wrapped his arms around his body. The misty dampness of the morning seemed to penetrate his bones.

He jumped as he felt something brush against his leg,

then looked down and laughed in relief.

"Tobias!" he cried. "Don't sneak up on me like that!"

He glanced towards the shelter where he could see Arrowbright's feet protruding between the branches.

"Tobias, go and wake Arrowbright," he commanded, but when he looked around, the dog had disappeared. In the melting snow at his feet were several large paw prints, slowly filling up with rainwater. He followed the tracks with his eyes and exclaimed in surprise. They led straight to the foot of the cliff and stopped dead. There was no sign of Tobias.

Ben ran over to the cliff, looking up at the sheer walls. There was no way the large, ungainly dog could have climbed up: there wasn't even a toe-hold. He slapped the wall in frustration, and then stumbled as his hand slid unexpectedly across the wet rock and into a fissure well camouflaged by the subtle contours of the rock.

He stuck his head inside the crack. It was wider than he had first thought and penetrated deep into the rock face. He heard a distant bark which echoed off the sides of the narrow passage.

Cautiously, he stepped inside. Tobias was nowhere to be seen, but he could hear the scuttling of claws not far away. He ran his fingers along the sides which were completely smooth as though worn down by the passage of water. High above him, between the towering walls of rock, he could just make out a narrow sliver of sky. It had grown steadily colder since he had entered the fissure and his breath blossomed in the crisp air. The fine droplets of misty rain had changed to tiny ice crystals which drifted down to land delicately in his hair.

Tobias suddenly appeared from around a corner and bounded up to him, his tail swaying good-naturedly from side to side. A fine coating of snow ran all the way along his back, and he proceeded to shake this over Ben.

At that moment, the peace was broken by a loud thunderclap. The walls of the passageway seemed to tremble and a cascade of snow tumbled down onto Ben's shoulders. He hurried back to the entrance to find Arrowbright staring anxiously into the trees, his back to the cliff. The soldier whirled round at the sound of Ben's footsteps, startled to see him appear as if from nowhere.

"Where were you?" he began. He was interrupted by another loud crack of thunder from the direction of the trees. Tobias whined softly.

"I don't like the sound of that," said Arrowbright. "Unless I'm very much mistaken, that's the sound of gunpowder. The rebels must be blasting their way through the wood. If they manage to pin us up against this cliff, we won't stand a chance . . ."

Ben grabbed his arm. "Tobias has found a way through."

"A pass? Where?"

Ben turned to face the cliff but the rain had washed away their footprints and he found it impossible to tell where the fissure had been.

"Find it, Tobias," he commanded. "Find the passageway again!"

But Tobias was staring in the direction of the explosions which were coming with increasing frequency. He gave a loud whine and trotted towards the forest, his trot becoming a canter and then an all-out dash as he disappeared amongst the trees.

"Tobias!" shouted Ben.

He and Arrowbright looked anxiously at each other. A moment later there was a commotion in the undergrowth and Tobias reappeared, moving slowly backwards as he dragged something with him along the ground. A couple of times the dog stopped and adjusted his grip, mouthing the object gingerly as though to get a firmer yet gentle hold. As he came closer, they realised it was Murgatroyd he had in his mouth.

He dropped the bird at Ben's feet and took a few paces back.

"Murgatroyd!" said Ben, falling to his knees beside the motionless eagle.

"Is he . . . ?"

Arrowbright and Ben looked at each other in dismay. Tobias stepped forward and licked the limp bird.

Murgatroyd lifted his head. "Stop it," he said, "I'm not dead."

"What happened to you?" cried Ben.

"I decided to take a closer look at our pursuers," said Murgatroyd, struggling to stand, "but unfortunately I got a little too close. I think my wing may be broken."

There was another loud explosion. Tobias cringed and ran towards the cliff.

"I see the animal found the pass," said Murgatroyd. "I think perhaps I was wrong about him after all. Now, there's no time to lose. Arrowbright, if you'd be so kind . . ."

Arrowbright crouched down. He stifled a wince as the eagle's claws dug into his shoulder, and raised a hand to steady him as he stood up. Then he watched in astonishment as first Tobias and then Ben disappeared into the rock. To Arrowbright's eyes the cliff was as impenetrable as ever, but Murgatroyd spotted the fissure and guided him towards it.

"On Tritan's beard," breathed the soldier as he entered the passage and looked around. He staggered as Tobias suddenly brushed past him and loped back towards the entrance. The dog's hackles were standing on end from the ruff of his neck all the way down to his tail, which was held straight upright. He stopped near the entrance to the fissure, a low growl starting in his throat.

"He must sense the rebels," said Murgatroyd. "It will only be a matter of time before they find the passage. We must hurry."

They made their way deeper into the mountain, listening intently for any sign that the rebels had found the gap. But all they could hear was the click-clack of Tobias's claws on rock as he pushed past once more to bound on ahead.

The passageway was full of turns and switchbacks. Tobias doubled back constantly to hurry them on, his claws skidding and sliding around the corners. Snow was still falling. At times they couldn't see the sky due to rocky overhangs above, but the tiny flakes somehow managed to find their way into the narrow cleft. Ben looked over his shoulder, anxiously noting their footprints in the fine, white layer which covered the ground. He could only hope that the snow would continue to fall and cover their tracks.

After a while the ground started to rise and they came to a series of rough steps which had been hacked into the slippery smooth surface of the rock. Arrowbright's breathing became louder and more laboured as they climbed. Ben found himself taking each step in time with his companion's panting breath, his pace growing slower and slower until finally they both came to a complete stop.

"Just . . . need . . . a . . . minute," panted Arrowbright, shifting uncomfortably under Murgatroyd's weight.

"Put me down," said the eagle.

"No," replied Arrowbright immediately. "I'm not carrying you all this way just so you can make some noble gesture by refusing to go any further."

"That's not what I meant. Tobias can carry me the rest of the way."

Arrowbright and Ben looked at him in astonishment.

"I know we haven't been the closest of friends," said

Murgatroyd, "but he's proved his worth by rescuing me back there in the forest, so if he has no objections to carrying me, then neither do I."

Ben turned towards Tobias who was sitting on the step above, waiting patiently for them to continue. "Tobias?"

The large dog got to his feet. He stood absolutely still while Arrowbright lifted the eagle down from his shoulder and onto the dog's back. Murgatroyd shifted his position until he had a firm hold of Tobias's thick leather collar, then, without hesitation, the dog turned and continued up the steps, this time with a slow and steady gait.

With a glance at each other, Ben and Arrowbright followed. Shortly after, the tunnel widened until it was possible for them to walk side by side.

"My father used to tell me stories about the mountains," said Arrowbright nostalgically. "He used to come climbing here as a boy, but the rebels had made the area too dangerous by the time I was old enough to go with him."

"Where did they come from?" asked Ben. "The rebels, I mean?"

"There have always been rebels in this area," said Murgatroyd, looking back over his shoulder. "They are descended from different tribes who made their home in the mountains. They weren't always referred to as "rebels"; they were once a peaceful race who kept to themselves."

"What changed?" asked Ben.

"According to folklore, a fierce leader united the tribes,

teaching them warlike ways . . . What is it?"

Ben had stopped suddenly. He looked at them, puzzled. "Can't you smell it?"

"Smell what?" asked Arrowbright and Murgatroyd together. Tobias stopped too and looked back, his ears raised quizzically.

"Something's burning," said Ben. He took a step forward. "We're getting closer, I can sense it."

He climbed on, the steps becoming steeper and more irregular. Tobias, weighed down with Murgatroyd, now followed at Ben's heels while Arrowbright brought up the rear. A blast of snow suddenly hit Ben full in the face as the roof of the tunnel opened up and the walls of rock on either side dropped away to reveal the mountains to either side. A bitter wind tugged at his clothing, making his eyes water. He blinked the tears away and felt the moisture already beginning to freeze on his cheeks.

He squinted into the fierce gale, towards the twin mountain peaks looming above. The peaks were significantly closer than before and instantly recognisable, backlit by a hazy orange glow. The wind brought with it a distinct smell of smoke.

Snow had piled in drifts on the steps, but Ben ignored it, racing ahead, taking the steps two at a time. He was vaguely aware of the others struggling to keep up but, when he glanced back, they were hidden by the blizzard.

The walls of rock rose up once more and enclosed the

path. As the howl of the wind faded behind him, Ben heard another sound: a faint crackling which became louder the higher he climbed. Soon the walls of the passageway flickered with the reflection of flames that he could not yet see. He felt the heat of the fire against his skin, melting the snow in his hair and on his clothes.

Ahead of him, the steps were coming to an end. He forced himself to hurry, sweat mingling with the melted snow running down his face as he battled his way through an almost physical wall of heat. He finally reached the last step and staggered into an enormous cavern, open to the sky but encircled by a huge wall of rock.

The reflection of flames danced against the cavern walls but Ben could still see no sign of the fire. Snow swirled down to the floor of the cavern and settled despite the heat. But Ben wasn't interested in this curious phenomenon, for something much more important, something indescribably exciting, had caught his attention. In the exact centre of the cavern, on a circular stone dais, stood a bronze lectern. And on the lectern lay an open book.

His weariness forgotten, Ben rushed over to it. He slowed as he approached, feeling a sense of awe creep over him, and finally he stopped a few feet away. This close, he could see that the open page was filled with exquisite illustrations in vibrant colours bordering lines of clear, black script. Taking a deep breath, he drew from his satchel the page from the Book of Prophecies which he had carried with him from the underground lake beneath the palace. He stepped up onto the dais and moved slowly towards the Book, unrolling the parchment as he approached. Then he laid it on the open page.

The thick, yellowed parchment was identical.

He was flooded with a giddy sense of achievement: he had found the Book of Prophecies! Sensing a presence behind him, he spun round.

"We did it!" he cried. But the words died on his lips. There in front of him stood a tall, pale stranger in a perfectly white suit.

The man stepped up onto the dais. As he did so, a ring of flames sprang up behind him, blocking the rest of the cavern from view.

20

"Who are you?" Ben asked the pale man. His eyes searched the flames for his friends, but he could see nothing beyond the stone platform.

"I am the reason you are here," replied the man as though it were obvious. He stood at the very edge of the dais, his body almost engulfed by the flames. Despite the heat he looked cool and calm, and his crisp white suit bore no trace of the ash which mingled with the falling snow.

"No," corrected Ben, "I'm here for the Book of Prophecies."

He took a step backwards, putting the lectern with the open book between himself and the pale stranger.

"Ah, the Book," breathed the pale man with a smile, "its prophecies once served me well."

"What do you want?"

"That's simple: I want you."

Ben shrank back as the pale man took another step

303

towards him.

"I don't understand," he said, playing for time. He expected Arrowbright and the others to arrive at any moment. Together they would easily be able to overpower this madman.

"I didn't expect you to understand," sneered the pale man. "You're just a child, after all, even if you are the Deliverer. Allow me to explain."

The man looked upwards as if gathering his thoughts, and snow swirled down to land on his upturned face, settling on his eyelashes. With growing unease, Ben realised that he was completely impervious to the intense heat.

"Fifteen years ago," began the man, "I located the Book of Prophecies in a storage room below the palace library in Quadrivium. It had been archived by the monks who were entirely oblivious to the prize in their possession. I call it a prize because the Book contained not only a detailed and accurate history of Ballitor's past, but also – as I suspect you already know – prophecies for its future.

"It just so happened that the first prophecy concerned the Great Fire of Barbearland: a disaster which would destroy not only some of the king's finest soldiers, but also many of the rebels including their leader, a man with a fearsome reputation. I was in a position to avert the tragedy, but instead I decided to turn it into an opportunity.

"I left the city and journeyed to the rebels' encampment.

As I had anticipated, their leader greeted my prediction of his death with disbelief and anger. He had me chained up outside his tent like a dog, while children pelted me with rotten vegetables. And so I watched him ride off into battle with his best warriors, knowing that none would return.

"Before leaving Quadrivium, I had left instructions with a trusted servant to relay the prophecy to the king – but his timing was to be exact: the king was not to be forewarned until it was too late to stop the devastation. You may well shudder, but the warning – even though it came too late – led to my servant gaining the trust of the king and a place on his council. He eventually rose to become the mayor of Quadrivium – a man by the name of Ponsonby whom I believe you've already met. But I'm getting ahead of myself.

"As soon as it became clear to the rebels that their leader was not coming back, and that my prediction had come true, I was unchained and treated with the respect I deserved. A few minor prophecies later, and I was elected as their new leader. They had lost much of their fighting force in the Great Fire and my first few years were spent building a fresh army. I ensured that we weren't attacked while in this vulnerable state by entering into peace treaties with the king – remaining anonymous, of course, and refusing to negotiate with anyone but my servant, Ponsonby. As a result, Ponsonby became increasingly powerful within Quadrivium and used his growing sphere of influence to have more of my people elected to the king's council, until we had a majority. Then it was a simple matter for him to be elected mayor and pass laws which would work to my benefit: such as banning all forms of clairvoyance so that no one would pick up on my grand plan, and the Compulsory Conscription Act which ensured that most men and beasts of fighting age were recruited and removed to obscure corners of the kingdom for "training".

"Finally my rebel army was ready. It was now little more than a formality for me to stroll into Quadrivium and overthrow the king – my success was practically guaranteed! But I couldn't resist consulting the Book, and that's when it all started to go wrong."

He turned to face Ben, his eyes blazing with a fierce light. "All my carefully laid plans were threatened by a mere child!"

"I don't know what you mean," said Ben. The heat from the fire was making him dizzy. He brushed the sweat out of his eyes with the back of his hand.

The pale man suddenly took a few quick strides towards him. Before Ben had time to react, he leant over the lectern and took hold of his chin, forcing it upwards.

"Have you not wondered why they call you the Deliverer?" he hissed, looking deep into Ben's eyes. "You are my nemesis: the supposed agent of my destruction! You are the one who is prophesied to overthrow me, and deliver the kingdom from my control!"

Ben stared back at him without flinching. In disgust, the pale man released his chin and in one swift movement reached beneath Ben's shirt. Without taking his eyes from Ben's he drew out the locket, brushing his thumb across the silver oval lid before flicking it open. He stared at the portrait inside with an unfathomable expression of hate and longing.

"So the prophecy is right about this too," he said softly, "you are her son . . ." He dropped the locket suddenly, as though it had burnt his fingers, and strode to the other side of the dais, stopping just before he reached the wall of flames.

"Your mother thought she could just disappear, but I traced her to Prince Trestan and his people. They claimed that they hadn't seen her for years. Of course I didn't believe them, and as punishment had them locked away in an underground lake beneath the palace – but you know all this, don't you, Ben? After all, it was you who freed them once you had sprung my trap."

He turned back to face Ben and gave a wry laugh at the shocked expression on the boy's face.

"Yes, it was a trap! You see, I knew that the Deliverer would come looking for the Book of Prophecies: it was foretold in the Book itself. I debated long and hard about where to hide it, and finally it came to me: the underground lake! The presence of the mermen would deter intruders, but I knew that Prince Trestan would recognise you as

Teah's son and take you to the Book – and that simple act would identify you as the Deliverer.

"Do you know how close you came to fulfilling the prophecy there and then? But at the very last minute, I decided against using the precious Book as bait and smuggled it out, leaving behind only a single page. That was a stroke of genius on my part, given that you managed to escape from the underground chamber! I hadn't foreseen that you would have a key, you see, an unfortunate consequence of not having the Book on hand to consult, having removed it here to the mountains. As a consequence, I was forced to steal a Sacred Stone in order to track your movements. It's a curious thing, the Stone – would you like to see it?"

Without waiting for Ben to reply, he drew a smooth, round stone from his pocket and laid it on the palm of his hand where it glowed with a dull light.

"Once I had this in my possession, it didn't take long for me to track you down – although I will admit to being slightly puzzled when I found you in the shaman's village, the very place from which I stole the Stone. Was it mere coincidence that you came to follow me there? But I have a more pressing question for you, something which has been bothering me ever since you escaped from the underground lake: how did you know where to find the Book of Prophecies?"

Ben shot an involuntary glance at the piece of parchment lying on the open Book. The pale man followed the direction of his gaze and strode quickly over to the lectern. He picked up the parchment and examined both sides before turning back to Ben.

"Don't play games with me," he said, his voice rising slightly. "There's nothing here which could possibly have given you any idea where the Book was hidden."

Ben clenched his mouth shut, determined not to give anything away.

The pale man gazed at him for a long moment and then sighed. "I suppose it's of little consequence now. The Book is of no use to anyone any more: its prophecies are exhausted. The pages are blank, all blank, just like the one you've been carrying around with you all this time."

Ben looked back at the Book. The colours seemed to leap off the page: indigo blue, rich reds and vibrant greens. He was amazed that the pale man couldn't see them. He was about to look away when one of the illustrations caught his eye. It was a figure in a suit of armour, not the figure of a man, but the long, horizontal form of a lizard, with an armour-clad ridge running from its helmeted head all the way down to its armour plated tail. It reminded Ben of the armour he had seen in the palace, and the lizard in the book was depicted before a wall of fire exactly like that which now encircled the dais.

He looked up, and stared into the flames around them.

"I'm afraid there's really nowhere for you to run," said the pale man, following his gaze.

Ben ignored him, his eyes drawn irresistibly back to the Book. The intricately painted flames curled up each side of the page, beautifully picked out in lifelike shades of dark orange and petrol blue. The effect was almost three dimensional. Ben blinked and looked at the picture more closely. Hovering amongst the flames, he finally saw the doorway which had been hidden within the picture all along.

He heard a noise and looked up to see Arrowbright step through the flames and onto the stone platform. Relief rapidly turned to dismay as Ponsonby appeared behind him, followed closely by a rabble of heavily armed men. Like the pale man, all of them seemed oblivious to the fire.

Tobias suddenly appeared in a rush and leapt towards Ben. He was jerked back as one of the rebels yanked hard on the rope tied around his neck. The normally placid dog turned on the man, growling fiercely through a tight-fitting muzzle.

Ben searched among the rebels for Murgatroyd. It took him a moment to notice that one of them carried something slung carelessly over his shoulder. It was the great eagle, hanging upside down, his legs grasped tightly in the man's fist.

The pale man walked slowly over to the helpless bird.

"Hello, Murgatroyd," he said, "it's been a long time."

Murgatroyd stared at him with his amber eyes. "Not long enough," he spat.

Taking a small hood from his pocket, the pale man reached down and placed it over Murgatroyd's head, rendering the eagle insensible to everything around him.

He turned to Arrowbright next. "I'm surprised at you," he said, "risking your commission like this. Your own father, a decorated soldier, would be ashamed of you! I thought the army was in your blood, but you've thrown away your whole career on a myth!"

Arrowbright ignored the pale man's words and instead looked over at Ben.

"Is that it?" he asked, gesturing towards the book.

Ben nodded. Infuriated at being ignored, the pale man struck Arrowbright with the back of his hand. Tobias strained at his leash, his claws scrabbling against the floor in his effort to get at the man. A growl rose menacingly from deep in his throat and his hackles bristled.

"Silence!" cried the pale man. "You are all my prisoners now and you will be silent!" He spun round to face Ben. "Now that I have the Deliverer, the Book has fulfilled its purpose. It is time for it to be destroyed."

Ben relaxed slightly. He knew from experience that the Book would be impossible to destroy. He had carried the page from the Book with him through fire and water, and yet the parchment remained in the same dry and brittle state it had been in when he had first discovered it in the underground chamber beneath the palace.

Then the pale man opened his hand. The Sacred Stone

lay on his palm, pulsating with light.

"As I am sure you are aware," he said, looking directly at Ben as though he had read his thoughts, "the Book cannot be destroyed by normal means. Fortunately for me, one of the attributes of a Sacred Stone is the ability to spontaneously combust objects which are otherwise indestructible. Unfortunately for you, both Book and Stone will be annihilated as a result."

The light inside the stone grew brighter as he brought it closer to the Book.

"No!" cried Ben, lunging towards the stone.

"Guards!" shouted the pale man.

Two of the rebels stepped forward. As Ben looked round for a means of escape, the flames on the opposite side of the dais flickered as though fanned by a sudden gust of wind. Just like in the illustration, a doorway appeared in the midst of the fire.

Ben didn't try to resist the rebels who grabbed his arms. Instead he watched, spellbound, as a figure appeared in the doorway. It was the lizard, its body hugging the ground as it stepped onto the platform. It looked around, its dewlap swinging gently, and then ambled around the dais to stand next to Ben. He glanced quickly at the others, but no one else appeared to have noticed the lizard in their midst, despite the clink of its armour on the stone floor.

"Take the boy back down to the forest," instructed the pale man. "Make sure he's securely bound and don't let him out of your sight! The others you can dispose of as you will."

Behind his back, the flames flickered once more, and a man dressed in the uniform of the king's archers appeared. His eyes took in everyone on the stone platform, lingering for a long moment on Arrowbright, before he crossed the dais to take up position beside Ben and the lizard. The soldier was followed almost immediately by the half-man, half-horse who had appeared in Ben's first trance. The centaur's human upper half was clad in the same shiny armour as the lizard. He dipped his head towards Ben as he moved to stand beside the others.

The flames gradually began to recede as more and more figures stepped through the doorway and onto the dais, until eventually there was only a tiny flickering glow which marked the door's threshold. As the fire died down, Ben caught sight of the cavern wall directly behind where the doorway had been. A huge section of the wall had collapsed outwards, and through it he caught a glimpse of a long, shallow valley stretching into the distance, from which the animals and soldiers were emerging to take their place in the cavern. He was surprised to see men dressed like the rebels, in coarse, dark-coloured garments, climbing through the gap beside men who wore the uniform of the king's regiments. With no more room left on the dais, they began to encircle it in neat rows, staring up at Ben and the Book of Prophecies.

Still no one but Ben had noticed them. Everyone else's attention was on the pale man as he prepared to destroy the Book. Ponsonby stood at his master's elbow, watching the proceedings with a smug expression. Suddenly his eyes grew large and his mouth began to open and shut as though he was trying to force out words, but no sound came out.

Tobias stopped pulling on his chain and stared at the gap in the wall, his nose twitching as he sniffed the air. Arrowbright too sensed a change. His eyes flickered left to right as though searching for something or someone.

Then Ben noticed the eyes of one of the rebels flicker away from the pale man to the wall and then back to his master again. Almost immediately, his gaze was drawn back, and this time it lingered as he followed the progress of one of the armour-clad beasts into the cavern. Ben watched the colour drain from the man's face.

Anxious muttering spread through the rebels as more of them became aware of shadowy figures in their midst. The pale man finally noticed their restlessness.

"What is it?" he cried, impatiently. "I thought I told you to get the boy out of here."

One of the rebels stepped forward, his eyes looking past the pale man at something he could sense but not yet see.

"This is a spiritual place," he said, "a place where many men have lost their lives. It is disrespectful for us to be here."

At that moment, the last of the flames flickered out and

the pale man caught the expressions of terror on the rebels' faces. Slowly he turned.

"No," he whispered, a livid red patch appearing on each pale cheek as he stared at the men and beasts around the dais. "It can't be possible."

* * *

Bella stood in the shadows of the alcove deep inside the monastery, waiting for the bell to ring for evening prayers. She was apprehensive. It would have been far easier to have entered the secret room where Prince Alexander was being held through Ponsonby's villa, but unfortunately Mrs Ponsonby – having finally noticed her husband's absence – had filled her home with weeping relatives lamenting the disappearance of the mayor, along with that of the young prince.

So once again, Bella had entered the monastery, this time accompanied by Madeleine, the girl's tall, slim figure clad in the same brown robes as her own. No one had challenged them as they entered the large, stone hallway, cowls pulled low over their heads, and it hadn't taken long for Bella to identify the corridor which led to Brother William's study and the entrance to the secret room.

She jumped as the clanging bell suddenly rang out. Almost immediately, the monastery became a hive of activity as monks dropped whatever they were doing and began to file out of the main door towards the cathedral. She pulled Madeleine deeper into the alcove as two familiar figures passed by.

"There is nothing more noble than to serve, Brother Bernard," she heard Brother William say to his companion.

"If only the rewards were more immediate," was the grim response as the two monks continued on their way to prayers.

Within minutes, the heavy door had swung shut behind the last of the monks and they were alone. They glanced at each other and quickly began searching for the loose stone which concealed the lever that would open the hidden door.

The silence was suddenly broken by a long, drawn out cry, only partially muffled by the thick stone wall which separated the secret room from the rest of the monastery. The sound made them search faster, and they soon located the loose stone and prised it free to reveal the lever. As the false wall slowly opened, the baby's persistent cries grew in volume, audible above the loud, grating sound of stones sliding against one another.

Finally the gap was large enough for Bella to squeeze her way through. The first thing she saw, in the centre of the room, was a plain wooden cot which was where the noise was coming from. She flew over, followed closely by Madeleine, and scooped up the screaming baby in her arms.

"There, there," she cooed, bouncing him gently in her arms, "I'm here now, Alexander, don't cry." Even as she spoke, the prince's screams began to subside and he soon settled down to a contented gurgle. Madeleine reached down and offered him one of her fingers which he grasped tightly in his fist. She looked up at her great aunt and they smiled at each other.

"Can you pass me the blanket?" said Bella after a moment, turning towards the cot. "I'll wrap him in that until –"

She stopped dead. Standing directly behind the false wall – which was still wide open as they had left it – was one of the monks. She recognised him immediately as the one who had fetched Brother William from the library and who had led her to the secret room. In his outstretched hand was the baby's blanket.

"Here you are," he said, "and can I just say how grateful I am to you both for stopping him crying. This is the first quiet moment I've had in this room since he arrived!"

Bella and Madeleine stared at the monk in shock. Bella was the first to recover. Taking the blanket from him, she said, "It's our pleasure, we didn't like to think of you struggling in here by yourself."

"It's been very hard," admitted the monk, shaking his head. "I'm not sure which was worse: the nappies or the crying! And I didn't think Brother William had noticed how hard I'd been working – but he must have done, to have sent you two." He looked at them hopefully before continuing, "Everything the child needs is right here."

He shuffled short-sightedly around the room pointing to piles of grey nappies and wooden pails full of milk. Bella finally realised that he hadn't seen through their disguise.

"Don't you worry, Brother," she said, trying to make her voice deeper, "we'll take care of the boy now. The first thing he needs is some fresh air."

* * *

The pale man stared at the rows of armed men and beasts congregated around the stone dais.

"But this can't be," he muttered in a low voice which nevertheless carried around the silent cavern, "you all died in the Great Fire."

As though to prove him wrong, the armoured lizard raised itself up on its hind legs and issued a bloodcurdling war cry. It was met with a loud cacophony as the various beasts growled, yapped, howled and roared their reply.

It was a terrible, awe-inspiring sound. The rebels stared ashen-faced at an army that seemed to have emerged from thin air, but despite their fear they did not flee. Standing firm, they drew their weapons and prepared to face the onslaught.

The lizard made the first move. Spinning around suddenly, it lashed out with its tail towards the pale man.

He reacted just in time, leaping over the lethally sharp armoured ridge and landing in a crouch to duck a sword which was swung at him.

Ben grabbed the Book of Prophecies and ducked beneath the sturdy bronze lectern just as a heavily studded mace swung past his head. There was chaos all around. The clash of swords mingled with the mayor's urgent screams for reinforcements and the roars, barks and shrill cries of the fighting beasts. Ben looked in vain for Arrowbright and the others, but all he could see from beneath the lectern was a confusion of legs, some clad in armour, others hairy or covered in scales. He flinched as one of the rebels fell to the floor in front of him, a large gash across his chest spurting blood.

Suddenly, through the fighting, he spotted the implausibly clean, white suit-clad legs of the pale man dodging in and out of the mass of fighting men and beasts. He was making his way towards the edge of the cavern, in the direction of the steps down to the tunnel, with Ponsonby close on his heels.

Leaping up and uttering a war cry of his own, Ben charged through the skirmishing mass of men and beasts, shoving and pushing his way through. His only thought was to get to the pale man before he disappeared again. The surge of battle shifted abruptly away from him and, through a gap in the fighting, he caught sight of Ponsonby's bald patch. He renewed his efforts and finally broke through unscathed to find himself at the top of the stone steps. He was just in time to catch a flash of white as the pale man disappeared around a bend in the tunnel.

"Ben!"

He swung round to see Arrowbright, Murgatroyd and Tobias huddled in the shadows, abandoned by their rebel guards who had gone to join the fighting. He dashed over to them and set to work on their bonds.

"That man has Gretilda's Stone! I have to catch up with him!"

As soon as Arrowbright's hands were free he pulled the hood from Murgatroyd's head while Ben undid the muzzle around Tobias's snout. The bird looked round in confusion. "Where am I? What's all that noise?"

"I have to go!" cried Ben, turning towards the steps. He was about to head downwards when the rebels' reinforcements arrived – a fierce horde of men who filled the passageway as they raced up the steps straight towards Ben. He dived to one side and they poured past him into the fracas.

Arrowbright grabbed his arm. "Ben, where's the Book?"

"You don't understand," said Ben, trying to wrench his arm free, "I must return the Sacred Stone to Gretilda: she knows what's happened to my mother!"

At the mention of the Book, Murgatroyd suddenly came to his senses. "Ben, the Book of Prophecies will tell you all you need to know. You don't need the Stone!"

Ben stopped struggling and stared at Murgatroyd as understanding suddenly dawned. He turned slowly back to face the battle, realising with dismay that he had dropped the Book in his haste to follow the pale man. Finally he spied it beneath the feet of the combatants, its pages flapping as it was kicked around.

Murgatroyd followed Ben's eyes and raised his uninjured wing to his head in horror. "The Book!" he squawked.

But Ben had already dived back into the melee, ducking under swinging swords and leaping over fallen bodies until he reached the Book which was pinned to the ground beneath the hoof of a large, angry bull. The bull lowered its head as it prepared to charge a knife-wielding rebel, completely oblivious to the boy tugging desperately at its hoof. Suddenly it lunged forward, releasing the Book and causing Ben to stagger backwards into the man behind him. The force of the collision pushed the man forward onto his knees before his attacker who immediately stepped forward and raised his sword to deliver the coup de grâce. Without thinking, Ben shouldered the fallen man aside and took his place, holding up the Book to thwart the sword blow. He braced his arms, expecting to feel a heavy blow rain down on the hard outer cover of the Book.

When nothing happened, he slowly lowered his arms. Above him, the rebel stood with his sword raised, but, instead of delivering the blow, he was staring at the man who Ben had knocked out of the way.

"Dowid?" he said, finally lowering his sword. "Is that you? It's me: Jethrid!" He bent down and pulled the other man to his feet. They stared at each other, first in shock and then with growing joy.

"How could this be?" cried Dowid. "You were lost in the Great Fire! Are there more of our tribe who survived?"

Without waiting for an answer, he pulled a small horn from his pocket and blew a long, piercing note. Those in battle around him faltered and turned towards the two men who now stood side by side.

"Men! Stop fighting and look about you: we are fighting our brothers!"

Gradually, the cry spread through the cavern and more men laid down their arms. A few of the pale man's rebels continued to fight until they realised that they were outnumbered and fled for the tunnel.

Finally the fighting ceased altogether. On shaking legs, Ben stepped up onto the stone dais and looked around. The cavern was littered with bodies, and the walls echoed with the groans of the injured and dying. But above that there rose joyous cries of recognition.

All around him men were greeting kinsmen whom they had for years believed to be dead. A large, fierce looking man was hoisted aloft on the shoulders of the rebels. He stretched down to clasp hands with the uniformed soldiers around him and to touch the shoulders of the mighty beasts by whose side he had fought.

Ben looked around for his friends. He saw Arrowbright pushing his way towards the tall soldier who had been one of the first to emerge through the gap. The two men held each other at arms' length for a long moment, as though not trusting their eyes, before falling into a fierce embrace.

Ben averted his eyes and found himself staring at a young rebel weeping over the still body of an older man. Their reunion had come too late, and it made him think of his own longed-for reunion with a mother whom he had also believed dead. With a sinking heart he looked down at the Book in his hands. He ran his fingers over the cover with its bronze inlay and leather worn smooth from generations of hands. A warm, wet tongue rasped against his hand and he looked down to see Tobias sitting at his feet, staring up at him with his deep brown eyes.

Ben rested the Book on the lectern and slowly opened it, half expecting to see its pages torn and ruined. But instead he looked down at the perfectly preserved parchment.

The Book was indeed indestructible.

21

Once they were out of the monastery, Bella and Madeleine didn't stop running until they reached the main entrance to the palace. The towering wrought iron gates were heavily guarded by soldiers armed with long, shiny sabres who glowered at them threateningly as they approached. But as soon as Bella flung back her cowl, they snapped to attention.

"You!" she cried. "Find the queen, my daughter, and tell her I have found her son."

Six of the guards immediately raced off in different directions. The massive gates were opened and two of the remaining guards escorted Madeleine and Bella, with Alexander bundled tightly in her arms, through a pair of large double doors and into the grand reception hall of the palace.

"What if they're Ponsonby's men?" whispered Madeleine, looking nervously at the guards.

"I'm counting on most of the palace guards being loyal to the king," answered Bella in a low voice. "Even if they're not, we're inside the palace with the king's son in broad daylight – what is the worst that can happen?"

At that moment, Prince Alexander began to make loud gurgling sounds which echoed off the vaulted ceiling. On the gallery above, they heard a door open and the sound of running feet. A moment later, an answering cry came from the top of the wide staircase which led down into the hall.

"Alexander!"

In moments, the queen was standing beside them, scooping her son from Bella's arms and cradling him to her chest.

Behind them, the double doors swung open and the king appeared, followed by the palace guards and a chattering procession of courtiers.

"Is it true?" he cried. "Is my son really found safe and well?"

The hall was suddenly filled with the sound of excited voices and laughter as the king strode forward followed by his retinue who swarmed around the queen and her newly found son.

Bella, small and unnoticed in her brown robes, quickly became separated from her daughter and grandson. She stood on her tiptoes, trying to see over the tops of the heads in front of her, but she couldn't even see Madeleine. Suddenly she felt very tired and dirty and in much need of a bath. There would be plenty of time to explain, she thought, when everything had calmed down. The king would want to hear of Ponsonby's treachery, but now was not the time.

* * *

Ben gazed out through the gap in the cavern wall at the vista below him. A path led down to a narrow, grassy valley, the same path which the warriors had taken to reach the cavern just a few short hours before. The valley was bordered on both sides by snow-topped mountain ranges which stretched into the distance before disappearing in the hazy, early evening light. The scene appeared extremely peaceful with no sign that it had recently been occupied by an army of men and beasts.

He jumped as a hand touched his shoulder.

"Ben," said Arrowbright. Standing beside him was the older man Ben had seen him embrace a moment ago. The resemblance was remarkable. "This is my father: his name is Bartholomew. I think we should hear what he has to say."

Ben allowed himself to be led back towards the stone dais, Tobias following at his heels. The huge cavern was now almost completely empty except for the motionless bodies lying on the ground. Snow had begun to fall once more, the flakes coming thick and fast through the open roof and covering the fallen warriors with a clean white blanket. Ben looked back longingly towards the sun-drenched valley, but from this angle all he could see was the blue sky which began to turn white as he watched, as if a mist or a thick cloud had rolled in.

He sighed and followed the others back to the stone dais where he had left the Book of Prophecies. Murgatroyd was perched on the edge of the lectern, studying the open book. As Ben drew closer, he noticed that the book was open to an illustration of the battle which had just taken place.

An elegant, long-limbed cat, almost as tall as Ben, with dark gold spots shimmering on its flanks, followed them onto the platform and approached Bartholomew. The soldier bent his head and listened as it spoke some words into his ear and then padded off, delicately shaking the snow from each paw as it crossed the cavern and disappeared into the tunnel. Tobias watched its every step, but didn't move from Ben's side.

"The traitors have escaped," said Bartholomew, straightening up. "For the time being, at least. It appears they had horses waiting at the bottom of the mountain. The sun leopards are tracking them as we speak."

"I wonder what they plan to do now," said Arrowbright, a worried frown creasing his forehead.

"I wouldn't worry too much about them," replied his father. "They won't get far."

Ben looked around, suddenly noticing how empty the

cavern was. "Where is everyone?" he asked.

Bartholomew smiled for the first time. "Apart from the sun leopards who are pursuing the traitors, most are waiting for us at the bottom of the mountain. It's been many years since they have seen the outside world, and I'm afraid they couldn't wait."

Ben looked back over his shoulder towards the gap in the wall, towards the lush grassland which seemed safer and much more preferable to him than the cold, damp, thickly wooded valley at the bottom of the mountain. But the gap had grown noticeably smaller and continued to shrink before his eyes, until the wall sealed itself and the swirling mist disappeared behind solid rock.

"That valley has been our prison for the past fifteen years, Ben, ever since we were trapped there by the Great Fire of Barbearland."

"Father," interrupted Arrowbright, "why don't you tell us what happened, from the beginning?"

They settled down to listen to Arrowbright's father, Tobias making himself comfortable across Ben's feet.

Bartholomew began by describing the early skirmishes with the heavily armed rebels which had escalated into a full-blown war. More and more troops had been sent from Quadrivium, but the rebels were also sending more men and neither side could gain the upper hand.

"Both sides were throwing everything they had into the fighting," he explained. "The general consensus was that this was the deciding battle, and each side was willing to do whatever was necessary to win it." He paused for a moment, his eyes resting on Ben, "But then came the Great Fire."

Even Murgatroyd remained silent as Bartholomew told of the push into the mountains. The conditions had been appalling, but the king's men had managed to drive the rebels back through the heavy snow and finally over the mountains and down into the valley beyond.

"This was what we had been trained for. The valley provided plenty of room to execute our formations and attack plans – we couldn't have wished for a better arena. In contrast, the rebels appeared disorganised. They had apparently suffered heavy losses as we pushed them back over the mountain.

"Each squadron was in place and we were awaiting the order to attack when there was a commotion at our rear. It was the first sign of the trouble that was to come. Panic spread rapidly as we saw the first of the flames and smelt the smoke. The fire had cut off our retreat and was forcing us into the arms of the enemy.

"But the rebels were in the same predicament. The fire had spread through the long grass and was approaching their flanks. Slowly we were driven towards each other, but fighting was no longer on our minds, just pure survival. We were no longer fighting each other, we were fighting the fire, and we soon discovered we were enemies no longer.

The moment the truce was acknowledged the fire receded, but it quickly became apparent that there was no way out of the valley. Any attempt was met by a wall of flames. We lost a few good men that way."

"So what I saw in my dream," said Ben slowly, "when I saved the man who was half horse – that was actually happening?"

Bartholomew nodded slowly. "And the sight of you gave us hope. When you appeared, the beasts amongst us were reminded of a legend. It differed slightly between species, but the essence was the same: that a child would come to them in their greatest hour of need. They all believed that we would be saved." He looked at Ben. "And we were."

Ben looked away, embarrassed by the attention. "What happens now?" he asked gruffly.

"We return to Quadrivium with the Book of Prophecies!" cried Murgatroyd triumphantly.

"But what will happen to me?" asked Ben in a small voice. "Will I have to go back to school?"

The others looked at him in astonishment.

"Of course not," answered Murgatroyd. "You'll be needed to advise the king on future prophecies!" He reached down and turned a page of the Book. "You see, Ben, we can only see what has already taken place. The pages which show the future are blank to the rest of us."

Ben slowly relaxed. He wouldn't have to go to school or back to a life of thievery. He would return to Quadrivium a hero and, more importantly, he would be able to search the Book of Prophecies for clues to his mother's whereabouts.

He glanced down at the Book, his eyes flicking over the open page. For a moment, he wondered why this particular page was not the same thick, yellow parchment as the rest of the Book, but instead a crisp sheet of the purest white paper.

The thought was driven from his mind as Murgatroyd slammed the Book closed with his good wing. "Back to Quadrivium!" he cried.

* * *

Bella yawned and opened her eyes. She blinked for a moment, expecting to see the cracked ceiling of the dome's secret room above her, before remembering that she was back in her own bed in the palace. The thick, heavily embroidered bed-curtains had been tightly drawn to keep out the light, and she wondered how long she had been asleep. She heard the sound of her maid padding quietly about her room and poked her head through the curtains.

"What time is it, Helena?" she asked, stifling another yawn.

The girl gave a quick curtsey before answering. "It's almost noon, ma'am."

Bella frowned. It had been late afternoon when she had stumbled into bed after a hasty bath. She must have slept through. It was no wonder she felt so hungry.

"Could you bring me some breakfast? I think I will have it in bed for once."

Her maid hesitated. "Pardon me, ma'am, but their majesties the king and queen asked to see you as soon as you woke."

Bella sat up quickly as the events of the last few days came flooding back. How could she even think of breakfast? She had to inform the king of Ponsonby's betrayal!

Her maid had already laid out her clothes and Bella dressed quickly, scolding herself for sleeping late. The instant she had done up the buttons of her gown she flung open her bedroom door, desperately impatient to see the king. Then she stopped, shocked to find two heavily armed guards at her door. She stared up at their towering forms. Her first instinct was to run, but she could see more guards down the corridor. They turned towards her and she tensed her muscles, preparing to flee.

It took a moment before she realised that they were bowing their heads respectfully, and she exhaled in relief, accepting their offer to escort her to the throne room where the king and queen awaited her presence.

The sound of music and laughter filled the corridor as they made their way towards the throne room's stately doors. As they approached, the doors swung open and a flood of chattering courtiers left the room, smiling and curtseying as they passed her.

Bella entered the packed room. Immediately, the

conversation faded away and the crowds parted before her. At the far end of the room, she saw the king and her daughter, the queen, seated on their thrones with the baby Alexander between them in a beautifully carved cot. The queen saw Bella and stood, then reached down and took Alexander from his cot. As she did so, the king leapt to his feet.

"Traitor!" he cried.

Bella's heart sank. No, this was all wrong, she thought in panic. How could the king suspect her of treachery when it had been she who had found Alexander and returned him to them?

Then she noticed that everyone had turned to face the open doorway directly behind her. Slowly she turned to see what they were staring at. There before her, dressed in travel-stained clothes and looking as surprised and shocked as she felt, was Ponsonby.

Behind him stood a tall, pale-faced man dressed in a crisp, white suit, one hand laid heavily on the mayor's shoulder.

"Your majesties," cried the pale man, "I bring you he who betrayed you!"

Bella's gasp of shock was drowned out by the applause which greeted the man's words. He stepped forward to catch her as she fell into his arms with a cry of joyful recognition.

"Hello mother," he said.

Book Two

RACE the FOR heIR

Ben returns home to the royal city of Quadrivium expecting a hero's welcome. Instead, he finds the city in turmoil. The king has been found dead in suspicious circumstances, clearing the way for someone to rule the kingdom through the infant prince.

Ben immediately suspects his old enemy, the pale man. Or could it be the vainglorious Cardinal Bolt, who shows an excessive interest in the Book of Prophecies?

The race for the heir is on when the prince is discovered to be missing. Accompanied by his old friends, Murgatroyd and Tobias, Ben sets out on a perilous journey across the uncharted waters of the Sylver Sea to the Abbey of the Ancients, where he believes the prince is being held. Hindered by sea monsters and savage storms, and helped by unexpected allies, Ben battles to be the first to reach the prince - but an unexpected surprise is waiting for him at his destination.

About the Author

Kirsty Riddiford was born in Lancashire but moved
with her family to South Africa at the age of nine.
She left South Africa after university to see the world,
and finally settled in South West London where she
lives with her husband, Matt.

Most of her time is spent writing, visiting schools and
walking their two Labradors, Toby and Megan.

You can discover more about Kirsty,
her books and her school visits at:

www.kirstyriddifordbooks.com.